BOOK
of the
VAMPIRE

BOOK
of the
VAMPIRE

Nigel Suckling

Original Illustrations by Bruce Pennington

AAPPL

Dedicated to Thomas Casey Esq. of Friarstown, Co Westmeath

BOOK OF THE VAMPIRE
Nigel Suckling
Illustrations by Bruce Pennington

Published by
Facts, Figures & Fun
An imprint of
AAPPL Artists' and Photographers' Press Ltd.
Church Farm House, Wisley, Surrey GU23 6QL, UK
info@aappl.com   www.aappl.com

Sales and Distribution
UK and Export: Turnaround Publisher Services Ltd
orders@turnaround-uk.com
USA & Canada Sterling Publishing Inc. sales@sterlingpublishing.com
Australia & New Zealand: Peribo Pty Ltd michael.coffey@peribo.com.au
South Africa: Trinity Books trinity@iafrica.com

A catalogue record for this book is available from the British Library.

ISBN 9781904332824

Design (contents and cover): Malcolm Couch
mal.couch@blueyonder.co.uk

Printed in Malaysia for Imago Publishing   info@imago.co.uk

CONTENTS

INTRODUCTION

FOR, LET ME TELL YOU, the vampire is known everywhere that men have been. In old Greece, in old Rome, in Germany, France and India, even in the Chersonese; and in China, so far from us in all ways, there even he is and people fear him to this day. He has followed the wake of the berserker Icelander, the devil-begotten Hun, the Slav, the Saxon, the Magyar. The vampire lives on and cannot die by the mere passing of time; he flourishes wherever he can fatten on the blood of the living. He throws no shadow, he makes in the mirror no reflection. He has the strength of many in his hand. He can transform himself into a wolf or become as a bat. He can come in mist which he creates, or on moonlight rays as elemental dust. He can, when once he finds his way, come out from anything or into anything, no matter how close it be bound. He can see in the dark - no small power this in a world which is one half shut from the light.

Ah, but hear me through. He can do all these things, yet he is not free. Nay, he is even more prisoner than the slave of the *galley, than the madman in his cell. He cannot go where he lists; he who is not of nature has yet to obey some of nature's laws. He may not enter anywhere at the first, unless there be someone of the household who bids him come. His power ceases at the coming of the day. It is said, too, that he can only pass running water at the slack or the flood of the tide. Then there are things which so afflict him that he has no power, as the garlic and things sacred, as this symbol, my crucifix. The branch of the wild rose on his coffin keeps him that he may not move from it; a sacred bullet fired into the coffin will kill him so that he be true dead; and as for the stake through him, or the cut-off head that giveth rest, we have seen it with our eyes.*

Dr Abraham Van Helsing
in Bram Stoker's *Dracula*

Introduction

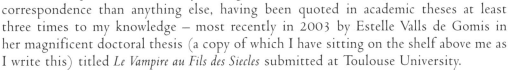

IN 1996 I HAD THE IDEA of writing a book about vampires, with half an opportunistic eye on the centenary of *Dracula's* publication the following year. My publishers at the time made vaguely enthusiastic noises and even half-commissioned an artist to illustrate it, but then everything went quiet. Then came a call from another publisher asking if I'd like to write a book about vampires for them. Well, to cut a long story short I ended up doing two – a much shorter version of this one and a drastic précis of a Montague Summers tome on vampires which we intended to publish as *An Illustrated Guide to Vampires*. So 1997 looked very promising for me on the vampire front. Then both publishers hit the rocks, as they regularly seem to do, and nothing came of either project. *C'est la vie.*

The Summers précis was at least paid for, which was some compensation. I posted it on my website as *Montague Summers' Guide to Vampires* and curiously enough it attracts more correspondence than anything else, having been quoted in academic theses at least three times to my knowledge – most recently in 2003 by Estelle Valls de Gomis in her magnificent doctoral thesis (a copy of which I have sitting on the shelf above me as I write this) titled *Le Vampire au Fils des Siecles* submitted at Toulouse University.

I've also come across my edited Summers text either complete or in part on other people's websites (usually Goth ones), which I take as a great compliment. This *Book of the Vampire* however just languished in need of a publisher until this chance finally came along, being dusted off occasionally and worked on whenever any fresh vampire news caught my interest. That's both the problem and pleasure of unpublished books – you can't leave them alone. Once they're done and dusted, published and packed neatly into pages you can't do any more. For better or worse they are as they are; but an unpublished book keeps calling for attention and while it is a pleasure being able to make improvements and look deeper into some of the questions, it's also a relief finally sending it off to the printers so it can be read by strangers.

However, there was more to the original idea of this book than just spotting a promising publishing window. That simply provided a plausible justification. Writing about vampires was something I wanted to do anyway out of simple and long-standing curiosity. Most of my books look into the bright aspects of imagination – angels, unicorns, leprechauns and so on – and I was curious to see what would happen if I just aimed for the dark side and explored the subject of vampires in the same spirit because, after all, we each have a monster side of which we are usually unconscious, and in some curious way paying attention to vampires helps bring it into focus. That could just be me, of course, though I was encouraged by a quote from Cretan writer Nikos Kazantsakis (*Zorba the Greek, Christ Recrucified* etc.) who once declared: 'What is Light? To stare into darkness with eyes wide open.'

Also, I had recently been asked to write an introduction for a reprint of Sabine Baring-Gould's classic 1865 *Book of Werewolves*, and was taken by his curiously healthy angle on an equally morbid topic. Sabine Baring-Gould was one of those dauntingly hyperactive Victorians who managed to combine a Church career with writing about thirty novels and a hundred other books. He was also a leading authority on archaeology and folklore. On the side he collected folksongs and wrote hymns, including *Onward Christian Soldiers*. So, a robust and eminently sane pillar of Victorian society, though one suspects his home life must have suffered . . .

What impressed me with his *Book of Werewolves* was the fascinated but detached angle he took on the subject. There was something so refreshingly wholesome about it that I

wondered if something similar could be done with vampires. They had always fascinated me too, but in an ambiguous way. There's a decadence about them and they're dangerous too, because the more joky, Halloween and camp sides of vampires segue off into realms of genuine evil. When I started work, in fact, I dug out an old rosary and hung it over my desk, just to be on the safe side. I resisted the garlic though, apart from eating it in the usual palatable quantities.

So, writing the preface to Sabine Baring-Gould's book probably sparked the idea of this venture. Later I learned it had also been a major inspiration for Bram Stoker's *Dracula* first time around. Such coincidences are wonderfully encouraging when working on an idea. It's often an illusion, but writers and artists tend to be superstitious that way.

Although the early draft of this book missed the centenary, Bram Stoker's *Dracula* has remained the focus because, although fiction, it is steeped in genuine vampire lore and probably did more than any other book to revive a fading tradition. Most of the novel's first readers in 1897 had long stopped taking vampires seriously and had even almost forgotten about them. In highbrow circles the lamia, the blood-drinking temptress of classical Greece and Rome, was celebrated in poetry by Keats and others. There were also a few vampires already lurking in Victorian melodramatic fiction, but they had made no wide impact. Vampires were not really part of the popular cultural furniture the way, say, ghosts or goblins were. It was *Dracula* who unleashed hordes of the undead into the twentieth century and beyond.

Critics are fond of saying that *Dracula* is not in fact particularly well written. Maybe so in a strictly literary sense, but it still rates as a masterpiece of storytelling. The language may seem a bit crusty in parts these days, but the story is as potent as ever and the idea of vampires has become universal largely because of it. Open almost any newspaper and you are likely to find a mention of Dracula or vampires somewhere, even if only as a figure of speech. Meanwhile in over 800 movies vampirism has been used as a metaphor for sensuality, drug addiction, Aids and much else, besides being simply a good tool for scaring the pants off an audience.

Which was almost certainly Bram Stoker's main conscious aim in the first place. He was a theatre man and simply wanted to create a melodramatic sensation in his novel, something to stir his readers' nightmares and possibly pave the way for a stage show. It just happened that when digging around in his subconscious for some suitably creepy monster, he unearthed a peculiarly potent and shadowy one.

Over a century later his creation still shows little sign of running out of steam. On all levels from the sublime to the ridiculous, vampires continue to be endlessly reinvented. They are taken seriously by the mad and laughed at by children – because Dracula has proved, a little surprisingly, to be a great comedian. There are endless spoofs, but unlike most scary figures that come to be laughed at he has also proved quite able to make a shocking comeback, as in Frances Ford Coppola's 1994 film *Bram Stoker's Dracula*. On the bookshelves, Anne Rice's *Vampire Chronicles* also managed to stir some discomfort, while the 1994 film by Neil Jordan of her *Interview With the Vampire* managed to break out of its genre to reach a mainstream audience at about the same time as Coppola's movie.

Across the spectrum between serious creepiness and light humour, taking in *Sesame Street, Count Duckula, The Rocky Horror Show* and *Buffy the Vampire Slayer* along the way (plus, come to think of it, Quentin Tarantino's *From Dusk Till Dawn*), vampire appreciation societies flourish, particularly in North America and Europe where it is often hard to tell just how much the members of these societies are play-acting.

Then there are the 'real' vampires that are still taken very seriously by large numbers of people, and these are not just the occasional lunatics or war-crazed cannibals who develop a taste for human flesh and blood. One of the strangest developments of the late twentieth century was the Chupacabras mania that swept Latin America. These goatsuckers may have been very different to Stoker's spectral Count, but they tapped into the same vein of superstition to show that the fear, at least, of vampires is far from dead today.

In Malaysia there were similar hysterical outbursts around the same time over the resurgence of their own local bloodsuckers, the terrifying Penanggalan, disembodied flying heads which flit thirstily through the night with their entrails dangling behind them. London's Highgate Cemetery is less lively than in the '70s, but is still worth giving a miss at night, as were the famously creepy cemeteries of New Orleans before Hurricane Katrina in 2005. For most of us vampires have been safely relegated to a genre of fiction but they still scratch at the window, trying to pick their way back into our reality, because they embody a very real and persistent aspect of the human psyche. Mockery or trivialisation is not enough to banish them because they simply return in other guises. Shape-shifting has always been one of the vampire's talents.

The aim of this book is to look into the background of vampires in fiction, legend and history, starting with the ideas that inspired Bram Stoker. We look at the literary vampires that came before and the superstitions that Stoker had access to. Historically we consider a few real life monsters that have also fed the myth, not least Elisabeth Bathory, whose famous Iron Maiden inspired one of Stoker's short stories as well as his masterpiece. Also of course we look at Vlad the Impaler, the original Dracula, whose true history is steeped in more horror and gore, plus chilling black humour, than any fiction.

In writing this I'm not setting myself up as any great authority on the subject. My starting point was simple uninformed curiosity and this book, with Bruce Pennington's atmospheric original illustrations – plus archive material – is where it led. With any subject like unicorns or vampires there is a certain necessary repetition of basic sources and facts for those readers who are fresh to the area, and that is the case here. I apologise to any reader already familiar with some of the ground I cover, but it was mostly new to me when I came to it and will be new to many other readers; but, when dealing with well-worn topics such as the Polidori-Byron confusion and the true authorship of the groundbreaking thriller *Varney the Vampyre*, I have tried to add some fresh details that even the well-informed will probably not have come across.

One of the first pleasures in tackling the subject of vampires from the viewpoint of *Dracula* was learning what a pleasant, affable and unassuming chap Bram Stoker was, the complete opposite of his famous protégé and quite unlike what I had previously imagined from the resounding syllables of his name.

Chapter I

DRACULA'S DYNASTY

IT ALL SEEMED LIKE A HORRIBLE NIGHTMARE *to me, and I expected that I should suddenly awake and find myself at home, with the dawn struggling in through the windows. But my flesh answered the pinching test, and my eyes were not to be deceived. I was indeed awake and among the Carpathians. All I could do now was to be patient, and wait the coming of the morning.*

Just as I had come to this conclusion I heard a heavy step approaching behind the great door, and saw through the chinks the gleam of a coming light. There was the sound of rattling chains and the clanking of massive bolts drawn back. A key was turned with the loud grating of long disuse, and the great door swung back.

Within stood a tall old man, clean shaven save for a long white moustache, and clad in black from head to foot without a single speck of colour about him anywhere. He held in his hand an antique silver lamp, in which the flame burned without chimney or globe of any kind, throwing long, quivering shadows as it flickered in the draught of the open door. The old man motioned me in with his right hand and with a courtly gesture, saying in excellent English, but with a strange intonation:

"Welcome to my house! Enter freely and of your own will!" He made no motion of stepping to meet me but stood like a statue, as though his gesture of welcome had fixed him into stone. The instant, however, that I had stepped over the threshold, he moved impulsively forward, and holding out his hand grasped mine with a strength which made me wince, an effect which was not lessened by the fact that it seemed as cold as ice — more like the hand of a dead than a living man.

Jonathan Harker in
Bram Stoker's *Dracula*

Dracula's Dynasty

THE LASTING TRIUMPH of Bram Stoker's *Dracula* would astonish most readers of the first 1897 edition. At the time Stoker's mother proudly declared: 'My dear, it is splendid. No book since Mrs Shelley's *Frankenstein* has come near yours in originality or terror. In its terrible excitement it should make a widespread reputation and much money for you.' Which was true enough in a way except that the book did not really take off till well after Bram Stoker's death and it was only his widow who benefited financially from it. Some London critics even shared his mother's enthusiasm but initial sales were disappointing and less than 3,000 copies of the first printing were sold. To the general reading public it seemed just one more book among many.

Which was sad because writing was Stoker's strongest passion and he had premonitions of greatness while composing *Dracula*. It was a cruel disappointment when it stirred no more than a few ripples of enthusiasm. His dream of being able to support himself entirely by his pen, if he wished, remained as distant as ever.

Years earlier in his native Dublin, Stoker had become well known as a theatre critic, journalist and editor. He had even written some promising shock-horror stories featuring the Phantom Fiend for the *Shamrock* magazine, but these were all labours of love. For his living Stoker drudged reluctantly as a clerk in Dublin Castle. Family finances had forced him straight into this job after graduating from Trinity College, where he had been both a sporting and cultural star. He had hoped for a more exciting life after university, but seemed to bear his lot quite cheerfully. He was rarely to be found in a bad mood when out on the cultural town in the evening, and his enthusiasms were infectious.

Bram Stoker

His chance to escape the castle finally came after thirteen years when his love of the theatre finally repaid him. Henry Irving, the British theatrical supremo of the day, had been won over by the passionate young Dublin critic who, besides having boundless energy and a tidy mind, happened to be Irving's greatest fan in Ireland. After a few meetings, he invited Stoker to become his personal business manager and also run the Lyceum Theatre in London, which he had just acquired. Stoker packed his bags on the spot and in no time was sailing for London with his new bride Florence, who had once been courted by Oscar Wilde.

Managing the Lyceum and Irving's tangled financial affairs were to be Stoker's main occupations for the next twenty-seven years. He grew famous in London society as the jovial giant with the flaming red beard (contrasting with the darker hair on his head) who greeted the audience on the steps of the Lyceum as they arrived. In this guise he was soon on friendly terms with everyone in high society from the Prince of Wales down, and he was often referred to as 'Irving's Treasure' for being the organisational power behind the scenes of the theatre. Francis Ford Coppola drops a passing reference to all this in his 1994 *Dracula* film. In the background of one London scene we see a sandwich board advertising Hamlet at the Lyceum, the play which launched Irving's career there and provided one of his most famous and enduring roles.

Stoker's first book was published soon after the move to London. Entitled *The Duties of Clerks of Petty Sessions in Ireland*, it proved a useful manual for former colleagues back home, but hardly set the literary world alight. In later years Stoker used to ask admirers solemnly if they had read his first book, *The Duties*, which he had been assured showed clear signs of promise . . .

Despite an enormous workload at the theatre and famously late nights (he and Irving regularly stayed up till dawn after performances to discuss the shows and life in general), Bram Stoker continued to write on the side and published several novels and short stories. They won some praise from the critics and were fairly popular, but no-one imagined he was on the way to creating one of the most vivid literary characters of all time.

Choosing the vampire as his theme was Stoker's lucky idea, his stroke of genius, but he was not writing in a vacuum. Throughout the nineteenth century there had been an undertow of interest in vampires, fuelled by rumours of vampire epidemics in Eastern Europe a hundred years before. The earliest known use of the word vampire (or 'vampyre' as it was spelled) in English was in *The Travels of three English Gentlemen, from Venice to Hamburgh* published anonymously in 1734 but probably written by John Swinton, later keeper of the Oxford University archives. In it vampires in Eastern Europe were said to be the 'bodies of deceased persons, animated by evil spirits, which come out of the grave in the night-time, suck the blood of many of the living and thereby destroy them.' Whether or not this was the original source, use of the word 'vampire' rapidly spread through the British press, as it was simultaneously doing in mainland Europe. No-one is quite sure but it is generally assumed that the word is of Slavic origin.

Quoting from one of the leading authorities on vampires, John Heinrich Zopfius (*Dissertatio de Vampyris Serviensibus* 1733) Swinton elaborated: 'They attack Men, Women and Children, sparing neither Age nor Sex. The People attacked by them complain of Suffocation, and a great Interception of Spirit; after which, they soon expire. Some of them, being asked, at the Point of Death, what is the matter with them, say they suffer in the Manner just related from People lately dead, or rather Spectres of those People upon which, their Bodies, from the Description given of them, by the sick Person, being dug out of Graves, appear in all Parts, as Nostrils, Cheeks, Breast, Mouth, &c. turgid and full of Blood. Their Countenances are fresh and ruddy; and their Nails, as well as Hair, very much grown. And, though they have been much longer dead than many other Bodies, which were perfectly putrefied, not the least Mark of Corruption is visible upon them. Those who are destroyed by them, after their Death, become Vampyres; so that, to prevent so spreading an Evil, it is found requisite to drive a Stake through the Dead Body, from whence, on this Occasion, the Blood flows as if the Person was alive. Sometimes the Body is dug out of the Grave and burnt to Ashes; upon which, all Disturbances cease.'

Several German poets took up the theme, notably Goethe who in 1797 portrayed an ancient Greek vampire in *The Bride of Corinth*, giving the subject a certain respectability and successfully blending the classical tale of Philinnion by Phlegon of Tralles with contemporary notions about vampires. The poem is about a young woman who returns from the grave to seek her lover.

> From my grave to wander I am forced,
> Still to seek the God's long sever'd link,
> Still to love the bridegroom I have lost,
> And the lifeblood of his heart to drink.

Around the same time Samuel Taylor Coleridge wrote *Christabel*, often considered the first English vampire poem and inspiration for Sheridan le Fanu's *Carmilla* in 1872. Gottfried Burger's poem *Lenore* also fired British poetry audiences through translations by Sir Walter Scott and others, including Dante Gabriel Rossetti. But considering the vogue for Gothic romance at the time – fuelled, it has often been suggested, by a reaction to the rationalism of the Enlightenment – it's amazing how slow novelists were to see the dramatic potential of vampires.

The first on record was John William Polidori, who was coincidentally uncle to Rossetti – poet, Pre Raphaelite and spiritual vampire in the making if ever there was one. With his dark good looks, piercing eyes and predatory approach to women, Rossetti had all the makings of a good Dracula. There is also the creepy story of how when his tragic wife Elizabeth Siddel died, Rossetti buried with her the only copy of some of his love poems to her. Years later he churlishly had second thoughts and opened the grave to get them back, only to find the beautiful Elizabeth seemingly but asleep in the coffin, completely untouched by decay and lying in a nest of her own flaming red hair which had continued to grow after her death. So the story goes anyway, though some say it too has grown in the telling.

POLIDORI'S VAMPYRE

John William Polidori

Polidori, translator of Walpole's Gothic classic *Castle of Otranto* into Italian, owed the inspiration for his own tale to Byron, whose companion, doctor and fellow debauchee he was for a time. Having been commissioned to write an account of the great poet's adventures in Europe, Polidori revelled in sharing them and repaid the patronage by writing out drug prescriptions along the way.

The story is famous of how Mary Shelley was moved to write *Frankenstein* by the tedium of a rain-soaked holiday she enjoyed as the poet Shelley's teenage mistress. Her own preface tells us: 'In the summer of 1816 we visited Switzerland and became the neighbours of Lord Byron. At first we spent our pleasant hours on the lake or wandering on its shores. But it proved a wet, ungenial summer, and incessant rain often confined us for days to the house. Some volumes of ghost stories . . . fell into our hands.' One of these books was *Tales of the Dead* (1813) translated by Sarah Utterson from French and German originals, which Mary Shelley recalled with vivid fondness many years later. During one of the recitals the excitable Percy Shelley famously rushed from the room and when he finally calmed down, confessed to having been seized by a sudden nightmarish vision of Mary with eyes in place of her nipples.

After entertaining themselves like this for a while, on Byron's suggestion they then each decided to write their own flesh-creeper, of which hers was the only one to reach print – the poets, as Mary described it, having soon been 'annoyed by the platitudes of prose'.

Less well known is that the same holiday at the Villa Diodati near Geneva effectively gave birth to the vampire in fiction. Polidori was also present and borrowed Byron's germ of an idea for the basis of his own novella. Titled *The Vampyre*, it appeared three years later, first in instalments in *Colburn's New Monthly Magazine* and later as a complete volume on its own. It was an immediate and roaring success, largely because everyone thought Byron had written it. Even the great Goethe declared it to be Byron's finest piece of writing to date, which proves something about the nature of celebrity that hasn't changed much since.

When the truth came out, Polidori's book sadly plummeted out of favour, in Britain at least, leading to his suicide; or at least the reckless drug abuse that killed him at the age of twenty-six. *The Vampyre* did however inspire several popular stage productions in Paris that were booked out for years and thus possibly inspired the Paris scenes in Anne Rice's *Interview with the Vampire*. One of the most popular Paris plays was by Charles Nodier, who elsewhere (*De Quelques Phenomenes du Sommeil* 1831) drew this verbal portrait of vampires in Morlacco (Croatia), introducing the idea of the unwilling vampire: 'There is no village in which a good number of vampires cannot be counted, and there exist places in which there is a vampire in each family, like the "saint" or "idiot" indispensable to any Alpine family. But, in the case of the Morlacco vampire there is not that complication of degrading infirmity which saps the very basis of reason. The vampire is conscious and aware of all the horror of his situation, is disgusted by it, and detests it. He tries to combat his tendencies in all possible ways, has recourse to remedies prescribed by medicine, to religious prayers, to the removing by himself of a muscle, and even the amputation of the legs. In certain cases he even decides to commit suicide. He demands that after his death his sons will drive a stake through his heart and nail him to the coffin, in order to bring peace to his body in the instant of death and free it from criminal instincts. The vampire is usually a well-behaved man, often an example and guidance to his tribe: not infrequently he discharges the public functions of a judge and he is often a poet.

> 'Through the dark sorrow arising from his consciousness of his condition through the memories and presentiments of a sinister, nocturnal life, there still shines a tender, generous and hospitable soul who asks for nothing better than to love his fellows. But the sun has only to set, and the night to lay its leaden seals on the eyelids of the poor vampire, for him to begin again to scratch at the grave of a dead man with his fingernails or to disturb some little girl removed from the shelter of her cradle. For the vampire can be nothing else but a vampire, and neither the efforts of science nor the exorcism of priests can dispel his evil.
>
> 'Death does not cure him, for even in his coffin he will keep some traces of life, and because his conscience is soothed by the illusion that his crimes are involuntary, we should not be surprised that he is often found fresh and smiling in his coffin.'

Nodier's play is believed to have prompted Alexandre Dumas to write his own vampire play some thirty years later in 1851. Dumas's plot was closely based on Polidori but with certain dramatic improvements, such as having the vampire satisfyingly impaled at the end rather than escaping to continue his depredations. In European translations the myth of Byron's authorship was perpetuated for several years because, as one German publisher said, more or less: 'who's heard of Polidori?' Thanks to this ruse the novella survived much longer than at home, particularly in Germany where it sparked many imitations and sequels.

For a synopsis of Polidori's *The Vampyre* see Appendix 1 (page 216).

THE VAMPYRE ON STAGE

Polidori's antihero, Lord Ruthven, established the aristocracy of vampires that has persisted in fiction ever since (not least perhaps because of the growing perception in the nineteenth century that many of the aristocracy weren't doing much more than leeching off the rest of society, often also preying on them sexually in a very vampire-like way). The general tone of the story also slots it straight into place as the start of the vampire genre in fiction. There were other ghoulish tales around that could loosely be termed vampirish, but Polidori and Byron between them produced Count Dracula's direct literary forebear.

One of the more colourful stagings of Polidori's tale was *The Bride of the Isles* by the prolific dramatist James Robinson Planche, who would have thrived a century or so later in Hollywood. For this production Planche invented a trapdoor allowing for dramatic appearances and disappearances of the vampire on stage. It became standard theatre equipment and was called the Vampire Trap long after the play itself had been forgotten. The production was billed as being 'Founded on the popular Legend of the Vampire by Lord Byron' while owing almost nothing to the original story, let alone mentioning Polidori. The action is transposed to the Western Isles of Scotland, using Fingal's Cave on Staffa as the scene for some of the more supernatural episodes. Lord Ruthven, the Earl of Marsden, is an innocent hero who dies in battle and is re-animated as a vampire.

The anonymous novelisation of the play on sale to the audience explains what follows by describing a popular Scottish tradition that: 'the souls of persons, whose actions in the mortal state were so wickedly atrocious as to deny all possibility of happiness in that of the next; were doomed to everlasting perdition, but had the power given them by infernal spirits to be for awhile the scourge of the living. This was done by allowing the wicked spirit to enter the body of another person at the moment their own soul had winged its flight from earth; the corpse was thus reanimated . . . and in this state they were called Vampires. This second existence is held on a tenure of the most horrid and diabolical nature. Every All-Hallow E'en, he must wed a lovely virgin, and slay her, which done, he is to catch her warm blood and drink it, and from this draught he is renovated for another year, and free to take another shape, and pursue his Satanic course.'

Sadly this was pure invention as there is little evidence of any great belief in vampires as we think of them in Scotland, certainly not at the time of the story's setting. There is a whole raft of bloodthirsty sprites in Celtic folklore, but they are distant cousins. However, in the play this is what happens to the heroic Ruthven. After dying in battle abroad his body is taken over by the evil spirit of one Oscar Montcalm. This villain had once been rejected as a suitor by Ruthven's fiancée, and much of the play's action revolves around uncovering the impersonation in time to save the fair Lady Margaret, daughter of the Lord of the Isles.

In a curious anticipation of Hollywood, stage versions of *The Vampyre* were often paired in a double bill with equally loose adaptations of Mary Shelley's *Frankenstein*, though no playwright went so far as to try and combine them into a single play, as has been done on film. Byron, on whom the character of Polidori's original Lord Ruthven was obviously and not very flatteringly modelled, distanced himself completely from Polidori's tale, though he had already memorably tackled the theme himself in this curse from his poem *Giaour* written in 1813:

But first on earth, as Vampyre sent,
Thy corpse shall from its tomb be rent;
Then ghastly haunt thy native place,
And suck the blood of all thy race;
There from thy daughter, sister, wife,
At midnight drain the stream of life;
Yet loathe the banquet which perforce
Must feed thy livid living corpse,
Thy victims, ere they yet expire,
Shall know the demon for their sire;
As cursing thee, thou cursing them,
Thy flowers are withered on the stem.
Then stalking to thy sullen grave
Go – and with Ghouls and Afrits rave,
Till these in horror shrink away
From spectre more accursed than they.

Polidori's choice of Ruthven for the name of his antihero was prompted by Lady Caroline Lamb's character Ruthven Glenarvon in her first novel *Glenarvon* published in 1816, which was a thinly disguised attempt to win Byron's affections back after their brief, tempestuous affair. As such it failed miserably and in fact led her husband, the future Prime Minister Lord Melbourne, finally to divorce her because of the scandal caused not only by her dark, thinly disguised portrait of Byron but of other figures in high society. Much licentiousness was tolerated in that social circle, but only as long as it was discreet. It was Caroline Lamb who labelled the poet 'mad, bad and dangerous to know.'

So even though Lord Byron did not write *The Vampyre* he was very largely responsible for the image of the vampire as a gifted, glamorous, charming but dangerous aristocrat who leaves a trail of broken lives in his wake. He was the original Goth favouring black clothes, drinking vinegar to make his skin pale, using human skulls as goblets and living in the romantic ruin of Newstead Abbey in Nottinghamshire which he described in a long poem that begins:

> To Norman Abbey whirled the noble pair,
> An old, old monastery once, and now
> Still older mansion - of a rich and rare
> Mixed Gothic, such as artists all allow,
> Few specimens yet left us can compare
> Withal: it lies perhaps a little low
> Because the monks preferred a hill behind
> To shelter their devotion from the wind.

In crashing through the social mores of his time (including that of incest as one of his great loves was his half-sister Augusta Leigh) Byron seemed bent on his own destruction as much as anything else, and his early death at the age of thirty-six while preparing to fight against the Turks for Greek independence seemed in keeping with his death-wish. But all was not quite as it seemed because an autopsy apparently revealed 'the brain of a very old man' and the onset of 'ossification' of the heart. Perhaps he was so reckless in life because some instinct warned him that he was going to die young anyway. He may even have been half conscious of this, given the sentiments of this poem written when he was barely thirty:

> So we'll go no more a-roving
> So late into the night,
> Though the heart be still as loving,
> And the moon be still as bright.

For the sword outwears its sheath,
And the soul outwears the breast,
And the heart must pause to breathe,
And love itself have rest.

Though the night was made for loving,
And the day returns too soon,
Yet we'll go no more a-roving
By the light of the moon.

VARNEY THE VAMPYRE

The next landmark in British vampire literature is *Varney the Vampire: Or the Feast of Blood* by (possibly) Thomas Preskett Prest, a manically prolific author of penny dreadfuls and shilling shockers now best remembered for his evergreen *Sweeny Todd, the Demon Barber of Fleet Street*. He was also famous in his day for a highly coloured version of the true tale of Sawney Bean and his tribe of Scottish cannibals which numbered over forty, including eight sons, six daughters and various incestuously conceived grandchildren. In the sixteenth century this unsavoury family lived in Bennane Cave in south Ayrshire, supposed to run for a mile underground and whose entrance was covered by the sea at high tide. They terrorised the Galloway coast for a quarter of a century, robbing and eating passing travellers until a search party led by King James VI himself happened to pass the cave entrance at low tide and the hounds sniffed out the terrible lair.

There have been suggestions that *Varney* may in fact have been written by another popular author, Malcolm James Rymer, or possibly several different hands, but whoever actually wrote it, the story proved so popular that it was spun out for over a hundred episodes.

Varney was first published in weekly instalments, then as a complete volume in 1847, the year Bram Stoker was born. At over 800 pages it is long and, as even enthusiasts admit, rambling to the point of often completely losing the thread of its own plot. It's much like trying to read the collected scripts of a soap opera and personally I gave up after a hundred or so pages, but the beginning is great and in places throughout it is

THE VAMPIRE
Lord Lytton, 1858

I found a corpse, with glittering hair,
Of a woman whose face, tho' dead,
The white death in it had left still fair,
Too fair for an earthly bed!
So I loosened each fold of her bright curls roll'd
From forehead to foot in a rush of red gold,
And kissed her lips till her lips were red,
And warm and light on her eyelids white
I breath'd, and pressed unto mine her breast,
Till the blue eyes oped and the breast grew warm,
And this woman, behold! arose up bold,
And lifelike lifting a wilful arm,
With steady feet from the winding sheet
Stepp'd forth to a mutter'd charm.

And now beside me, whatever betide me,
This woman is, night and day.
For she cleaves to me so, that, wherever I go
She is with me the whole of the way.
And her eyes are so bright in the dead of the night,
That they keep me awake with dread;
While my life blood pales in my veins and fails,
Because her red lips are so red
That I fear 'tis my heart she must eat for her food;
And it makes my whole flesh creep
To think she is drinking and draining my blood,
Unawares, if I chance to sleep.

It were better for me, ere I came nigh her, -
This corpse, - ere I looked upon her, -
Had they burn'd my body with penal fire
With a sorcerer's dishonour.
For when the devil has made his lair
In the living eyes of a dear dead woman,
(To bind a man's strength by her golden hair,

The Vampire Philip Burne-Jones 1897

And break his heart, if his heart be human),
Is there any penance, or any prayer,
That may save the sinner whose soul he tries
To catch in the curse of the constant stare
Of those heartbreaking bewildering eyes, -
Comfortless, cavernous glow-worms that glare
From the gaping grave where a dead hope lies?
It is more than the soul of a man may bear.
For the misery worst of all miseries
Is Desire eternally feeding Despair
On the flesh, or the blood, that forever supplies
Life more than enough to keep fresh in repair
The death ever dying, which yet never dies.

gripping stuff. For a decade or two the book was enormously popular and extracts have appeared in vampire anthologies ever since, as have intermittent reprints of the whole book. Originals have mostly disintegrated because of their cheap paper but electronic copies can now be found quite easily on the internet.

Prest's vampire was nowhere nearly as well researched as Stoker's. The Introduction blithely states that Scandinavia is the original home of vampires and it is a book of Scandinavian lore that provides the characters with crucial information about their enemy such as:

> 'With regard to these vampyres, it is believed by those who are inclined to give credence to so dreadful a superstition, that they always endeavour to make their feast of blood, for the revival of their bodily powers, on some evening immediately preceding a full moon, because if any accident befall them, such as being shot, or otherwise killed or wounded, they can recover by lying down somewhere where the full moon's rays will fall on them.'

There is, it's true, a lively Scandinavian tradition of the marauding undead, people rising from their graves to molest the living (and Scandinavia is also home to a thriving tradition of werewolves), but as with the Scottish bloodsuckers they don't much resemble what we think of as vampires. The traditions behind Ruthven, Varney and Dracula are clearly East European. Apart from this however, the mood of *Varney* is right and from a dramatic beginning the story gallops recklessly ahead with all the elements one has come to expect from vampire tales. The sexual undertones of vampirism are tackled without any subtlety, the vampire confessing at one stage that: 'I am much attached to the softer sex – to young persons full of health. I like to see the rosy cheeks, where the warm blood mantles in the superficial veins, and all is loveliness and life.'

For a synopsis of *Varney the Vampire* see Appendix 2 (page 220)

CARMILLA

The most famous female vampire in prose literature is *Carmilla*, created by Sheridan le Fanu in 1872 on a much higher literary plane than *Varney* but with similar intent. It was filmed almost a century later in 1970 under the title of *The Vampire Lovers*, starring Kate O'Mara and Ingrid Pitt along with Peter Cushing and others who helped make it something of a minor movie classic. Ingrid Pitt, incidentally, also starred around the same time in the Hammer Horror classic *Countess Dracula*, Hammer's take on the bloody career of Countess Elisabeth Bathory of Hungary.

Left: Sheridan le Fanu Above: *Carmilla* by D.H.Friston 1872

The original tale of *Carmilla* appeared in le Fanu's anthology of creepy stories titled *In A Glass Darkly*, the tales linked by the device of claiming them to be the case notes of one Dr Martin Hesselius. This was one of le Fanu's most successful books, published just a year before his death and still widely in print.

Considering the rarity of mainstream vampires in Irish tradition it is remarkable how great a part the Irish have played in launching them into the world's imagination. Perhaps it has something to do with the nation's troubled history and relations with its neighbouring island. The Irish connection continued with the establishment by author Leslie Shepard of the Bram Stoker Society in 1980, whose Journal for many years provided a forum for scholarly discussion and serious appreciation of Stoker's work.

Le Fanu's tale was one of the main inspirations for fellow Dubliner Bram Stoker in making vampires the theme of his own magnum opus. For a while, apparently, Stoker even considered making his central character female, basing her on the bloodthirsty Elisabeth Bathory, but no doubt this felt too much like plagiarism. As a tribute to *Carmilla* Stoker wrote a similar tale as a preamble to *Dracula*. This was dropped for publication but later published as an independent short story under the title *Dracula's Guest*.

The tale of *Carmilla* is narrated by a young Englishwoman living with her retired military father in a modest castle in Styria (Austria). Her story begins one warm, moonlit evening when they have left the castle for a stroll in the open: 'At our left the narrow road wound away under clumps of lordly trees, and was lost to sight amid the thickening forest. At the right the same road crosses the steep and picturesque bridge, near which stands a ruined tower which once guarded that pass; and beyond the bridge an abrupt eminence rises, covered with trees, and showing in the shadows some grey ivy-clustered rocks. Over the sward and low grounds a thin film of mist was stealing, like smoke, marking the distances with a transparent veil; and here and there we could see the river faintly flashing in the moonlight.'

Suddenly down the road from the mountains comes galloping out of control a grand carriage that overturns almost in front of them. From the wreckage crawls a noble lady, weeping for her daughter who lies unconscious within. The girl is carefully brought out and, though still uncon-scious, seems to have come to no great harm. But her mother cannot wait for her to recover because, she says, she is on a mission of life or death and cannot afford even an hour's delay. So our heroine's kindly father offers to take in the girl and, after a show of reluctance, her regal mother accepts, promising to return for her in three months. The carriage is righted and off she thunders with her escort into the night.

The injured girl, Carmilla, is carried into the *Schloss*, where she makes a rapid recovery. But Laura gets a shock when they are introduced. She recognizes Carmilla from what everyone had persuaded her was a dream twelve years earlier.

Then, at the age of about six, Laura had woken one night to find her nurse and maid absent from the nursery. She was about to call out when, to her surprise: 'I saw a solemn, but very pretty face looking at me from the side of the bed. It was that of a young lady who was kneeling, with her hands under the coverlet. I looked at her with a kind of pleased wonder, and ceased whimpering. She caressed me with her hands, and lay down beside me on the bed, and drew me towards her, smiling; I felt immediately delightfully soothed and fell asleep again. I was wakened by a sensation as if two needles ran into my breast very deep at the same moment, and I cried loudly. The lady started back, with her eyes fixed on me, and then slipped down upon the floor and, as I thought, hid herself under the bed.' The servants came running but, finding no trace of the intruder convinced the child it had only been a nightmare. Now, twelve years later, here was the same stranger, her guest in the castle and looking not a day older.

Carmilla charms away Laura's misgivings with a tale of how twelve years earlier she too had experienced a dream in which she had met Laura looking just as she did now, and so it seemed they must have been destined to be friends. And firm friends they become, though Laura is puzzled by some aspects of their guest. Carmilla will say nothing about her family or background. Even when this reduces Laura to tears, she will not give way but soothes her by saying things like: 'Dearest, your little heart is wounded; think me not cruel because I obey the irresistible law of my strength and weakness; if your dear heart is wounded, my wild heart bleeds with yours. In the rapture of my enormous humiliation I live in your warm life, and you shall die – die, sweetly die – into mine. I cannot help it; as I draw near to you, you, in your turn, will draw near to others, and learn the rapture of that cruelty, which yet is love; so, for a while, seek to know no more of me and mine, but trust me with all your loving spirit.'

Such speeches, and the passionate kisses that accompany them, trouble Laura, as does Carmilla's habit of locking herself in her bedroom and never rising before noon, but these oddities are too trifling to spoil their friendship. No immediate connection is made between Carmilla's arrival and a spate of violent deaths of young women in the neighbourhood, about which she seems curiously and coldly indifferent.

Then a picture-cleaner arrives at the castle and to everyone's amazement reveals a portrait of a long-dead Countess, one Mircalla Karnstein, to be the spitting image of Carmilla. She passes it off as a quaint coincidence but the truth gradually strains to become known. Laura herself is attacked one night by something that in her half sleep seems a cross between a large cat and a dark female. Then her health begins to fail rapidly, something she tries to hide from her father for fear, or so she tells herself, of alarming him: 'A strange melancholy was stealing over me, a melancholy that I would not have interrupted. Dim thoughts of death began to open, and an idea that I was sinking took gentle and somehow not unwelcome possession of me. If it was sad, the tone of mind which this induced was also sweet. Whatever it might be, my soul acquiesced in it. I would not admit that I was ill, I would not consent to tell my papa, or to have the doctor sent for. Carmilla became more devoted to me than ever, and her strange paroxysms of languid adoration more frequent. She used to gloat on me with increasing ardour the more my strength and spirits waned. This always shocked me like a momentary glare of insanity.

'Certain vague and strange sensations visited me in my sleep. The prevailing one was of that pleasant, peculiar cold thrill which we feel in bathing, when we move against the current of a river. This was soon accompanied by dreams that seemed interminable, and were so vague that I could never recollect their scenery and persons, or any one connected portion of their action. But they left an awful impression, and a sense of exhaustion, as if I had passed through a long period of great mental exertion and danger. After all these dreams there remained on waking a remembrance of having been in a place very nearly dark, and of having spoken to people whom I could not see; and especially of one clear voice, a female's, very deep, that spoke as if at a distance, slowly, and producing always the same sensation of indescribable solemnity and fear. Sometimes there came a sensation as if a hand was drawn softly along my cheek and neck. Sometimes it was as if warm lips kissed me, and longer and more lovingly as they reached my throat, but there the caress fixed itself. My heart beat faster, my breathing rose and fell rapidly and full drawn; a sobbing that rose into a sense of strangulation supervened, and turned into a dreadful convulsion in which my senses left me, and I became unconscious.'

All is looking very grim when a champion arrives on the scene in the guise of an old friend and neighbour, General Spielsdorf, who happens to know a great deal about vampires because his own beloved foster-child had died after befriending someone who sounds suspiciously like Carmilla. Moreover, she had come to be the General's guest in very similar circumstances, giving her name as Millarca. The General immediately grasps what is going on and, finding herself recognized, Carmilla disappears. The local authorities are roused and, after various dramas, everyone converges on the Karnstein cemetery nearby where, after a search through the Gothic ruins, the lost tomb of the supposedly long dead Countess Karnstein is discovered. The description of what follows might have been (and probably was) taken word for word from one of the many published accounts of vampire hunting in Eastern Europe in the eighteenth century:

'The grave of the Countess Mircalla was opened; and the General and my father recognized each his perfidious and beautiful guest in the face now disclosed to view.

The features, though a hundred and fifty years had passed since her funeral, were tinted with the warmth of life. Her eyes were open; no cadaverous smells exhaled from the coffin. The two medical men, one officially present, the other on the part of the promoter of the enquiry, attested the marvellous fact that there was a faint but appreciable respiration, and a corresponding action of the heart. The limbs were perfectly flexible, the flesh elastic; and the leaden coffin floated with blood, in which to the depth of seven inches, the body lay immersed. Here then were all the admitted signs and proofs of vampirism. The body, therefore, in accordance with the ancient practice, was raised and a sharp stake driven through the heart of the vampire, who uttered a piercing shriek at the moment, in all respects such as might escape from a living person in the last agony. Then the head was struck off, and a torrent of blood flowed from the severed neck. The body and head were next placed on a pile of wood and reduced to ashes, which were thrown upon the river and borne away, and that territory has never since been plagued by the visits of a vampire.'

* * *

Another literary vampire who may well have influenced Bram Stoker to a small extent was Count Vardalek in *A True Story of a Vampire* by Count Eric Stanislaus Stenbock, although Stoker's planning of *Dracula* was quite well advanced when this story appeared in 1894. Possibly Stenbock just tapped into the same vein of the *zeitgeist* that Stoker was mining, giving his vampire the same aristocratic title and surface charm.

The short story is again set in Styria and the opening is also very reminiscent of *Carmilla*, the narrator again being a girl. This time the vampire arrives as a male guest of her father after being stranded by a missed train: 'He was rather tall with fair wavy hair, rather long, which accentuated a certain effeminacy about his smooth face. His figure had something – I cannot say what – serpentine about it. The features were refined; and he had long, slender, subtle, magnetic-looking hands, a somewhat long sinuous nose, a graceful mouth, and an attractive smile, which belied the intense sadness of the expression of the eyes. When he arrived his eyes were half closed – indeed they were habitually so – so that I could not decide their colour. He looked worn and wearied. I could not possibly guess his age.'

In this story though, the target is the narrator's angelic brother Gabriel, who is enchanted by their guest but quickly begins to waste visibly away. The point comes when in the middle of the night his sister overhears Vardalek saying to the boy: 'My darling, I fain would spare thee; but thy life is my life, and I must live, I who would rather die. Will God not have any mercy on me? Oh, oh! life; oh, the torture of life! . . . . O Gabriel my beloved! My life, yes, life – oh, my life? I am sure this is but a little I demand of thee. Surely the superabundance of life can spare a little to one who is already dead.' This recrimination however does the boy little good and upon his expiry Count Vardalek mysteriously vanishes.

BRAM STOKER

It was against this broad literary background that *Dracula* was conceived and written. Bram Stoker at the time was almost fifty years old, having been born in November 1847 at 15 The Crescent in Clontarf on the north side of Dublin Bay. This was in a modestly genteel terrace of Georgian houses with a clear view over the bay that has since been obscured. Stoker's parents belonged to the cultured middle class but were not particularly wealthy. Abraham senior worked as a clerk in Dublin Castle, which is where Bram got the idea later.

Two interesting features of Stoker's home neighbourhood may later have fed into his masterpiece. The first is that his family had a private vault in St Michan's Church nearby, which was and still is famous for the preservative properties of its vaults. Bodies are naturally mummified there and to this day one can view many of them through bars in the vault, the jumbled coffins lying open to show their leather-skinned occupants like so many sleeping vampires.

St Michan's Church is one of Dublin's oldest, being built on the site of an early Danish chapel dating from 1095 that was built to serve the Viking community expelled from within the walled city. Until the seventeenth century it was also the only parish church in Dublin north of the Liffey River. The preservative properties of its limestone vaults are probably a happy accident but were remarked upon from the beginning. In the words of *The Dublin Penny Journal* for 4 January 1834: 'The adjoining cemetery was for many years a favourable burying place; the ground in its vicinity, and especially the vaults underneath the building, possessing to a remarkable degree the quality of resisting the process of corruption and decay. Bodies said to have been "deposited here some centuries since, are still in such a state of preservation that their features are nearly discernible, and the bones and skin quite perfect . . . In one vault are shown the remains of a nun, who died at the advanced age of 111; the body has now been thirty years in this mansion of death; and although there is scarcely a remnant of the coffin, the body is completely preserved as if it had been embalmed, with the exception of the hair. In the same vault are to be seen the bodies of two Roman Catholic clergymen, which have been fifty years deposited here, even more perfect than the nun."'

The other interesting feature of the neighbourhood for the morbidly inclined is that by the crossroads at Ballybough, only about half a mile from Stoker's childhood home, was a field where suicides were long buried with wooden stakes driven through their hearts.

Bram Stoker was born the third of seven children and was his parents' favourite, possibly because he was not expected to live long. In his *Reminiscences of Henry Irving* he remarks: 'In my babyhood I used, I understand, to be often at the point of death. Certainly till I was about seven years old I never knew what it was to stand upright. This early weakness, however, passed away in time and I grew into a strong boy.' The cause of this illness has never been explained and his recovery was remarkable because he grew into a robust six foot two athlete. At the age of sixteen he went to Trinity College, Dublin, where he became the university athletics and walking champion, besides playing football and any other sport going. He threw himself equally into the cultural life of the college, displaying a boundless energy that was later to serve him well. Walt Whitman was later to say of him when they met in the United States: 'My gracious he knows enough for four or five ordinary men; and what tact! He's like a breath of good, healthy, breezy sea air.'

Both parents had a great influence on Bram, and their house was crammed with books that fed his young imagination. His mother Charlotte, when not preoccupied with her large family, was a formidable personality and vigorous campaigner for women's social welfare and rights. She was also steeped in Irish legend and told first hand accounts of the horrific cholera plague which swept Europe in her youth, reaching Sligo in the west of Ireland in 1832, emptying whole villages and towns and unleashing a nightmarish anarchy upon the region, during which the living were often buried with the dead and looters ransacked abandoned homes and terrorised other survivors. At the age of twenty-four and towards the end of this period Charlotte had herself chopped off the hand of one of them reaching in through a skylight of their barricaded and fumigated house. Many of her tales formed the basis of later stories by Stoker and must have encouraged his fascination with disease, darkness and evil. His father's great love was the theatre, in which young Bram was happy to follow him.

Henry Irving

On leaving Trinity in 1870 with an honours degree in Science, Bram reluctantly followed his father into Dublin Castle as a clerk. He had no time to look round for something more interesting because his parents' modest fortune had been drained by the demands of educating itheir large family (very successfully too, as all the sons went on to glittering careers, mostly in medicine). To relieve the boredom Bram took an interest in the theatre, while continuing to study for a Master's degree and taking an active part in student life, being elected leader of both the Philosophical and Historical Societies of the University.

Of all these interests, the theatre was to prove his way forward. After being enthralled by one of Henry Irving's early performances at Dublin's Theatre Royal, Stoker (who was then nineteen, ten years younger than Irving) was amazed by the lack of reviews in the next day's papers. Taking his complaint to the editor of the *Dublin Mail,* he found himself being offered the job of unpaid (and uncredited) theatre critic for the *Mail,* and then other journals. Some five years later when Irving returned to Dublin, Stoker was able to make amends. His glowing review led to an immediate and lifelong friendship with Irving, and over the next couple of years they met regularly on both sides of the Irish Sea. Then in 1878 when Irving took over the Lyceum Theatre in London, he invited Stoker to join him as manager of both the theatre and his own affairs, beginning a partnership that was to last nearly thirty years until the great actor's death.

The Lyceum venture was an enormous success and brought Stoker to the front of London Society, but he always remained in Irving's shadow and seemed oddly content with this position. There have been suggestions that Irving's character was one of the blueprints for Dracula, and there was indeed a vampirish quality to the way Irving managed to dominate and feed off the energy of everyone around him, not least Stoker himself. Quite probably Irving was the model in the sense that Stoker visualised him acting the role of Dracula while writing the story and tailored the character accordingly, but Stoker was no Polidori. No secret envy or sly revenge against Irving can be read into his portrayal of the monstrous Dracula. If any was present it was deeply unconscious. If Irving took advantage of Stoker, he submitted to it willingly, almost as in an ideal marriage where two complementary personalities fuse so that to an outsider it is impossible to tell where one ends and the other begins.

This quasi-marital aspect of the relationship has led to much speculation about whether Bram Stoker was a repressed homosexual. There are other possible pointers — when at Trinity he had championed the poetry of Walt Whitman at a time when it was widely condemned as being morally offensive, hymning as it did the special rapport sometimes possible between male friends. Stoker's pursuit of a correspondence with the great poet (whom he eventually visited in America) shows a tendency towards hero-worship that could have masked a stronger attraction towards other males.

People have pointed also to his emotional approach to befriending Henry Irving, which to some eyes looks very much like someone falling in love. In the review of *Hamlet* that first caught Irving's eye Stoker wrote: 'In his fits of passion there is a realism that no one but a genius can ever effect.' Flattered, Irving invited him to dinner and deliberately set about winning him over completely with a recital of Thomas Hood's *Dream of Eugene Aram* delivered with such spellbinding passion it left both actor and critic on the verge of collapse. Irving retreated to a bedroom to recover, finally emerging with a photograph signed: 'My dear friend Stoker. God Bless You! Henry Irving, Dublin, December 3 1876.' Years later in his *Personal Reminiscences of Henry Irving* (1906) Stoker wrote of this encounter: 'In those moments of our mutual emotion he too had found a friend and knew it. Soul had looked into soul! From that hour began a friendship as profound, as close, as lasting as can be between two men.' Later he adds 'I never found his appearance, bearing or manner other than the best'; and 'my love and admiration for Irving were such that nothing I could tell to others – nothing that I can recall to myself – could lessen his worth.'

There is also the coincidence of Oscar Wilde having been a family friend, and of Oscar having also once courted Florence Stoker who was perhaps blind to homosexuality, unsurprising in an age when there were no laws against lesbianism because Queen Victoria did not believe such a thing possible. There was Stoker's loyal visit to Wilde in his disgraced exile in Paris – all of which suggest at the very least an awareness and tolerance of homosexuality. Ever since Ernest Jones in 1933 started the trend for reading all kinds of polymorphous Freudian sexuality into *Dracula*, one of the most commonly quoted signals of homosexual intent in the novel is that of the Count when he rescues Jonathan Harker from the three brides of Dracula crying: 'This man belongs to me!' There are also rumours that Bram's wife Florence refused to sleep with him again after the birth of their son Noel in 1879, suggesting sexual problems that could as easily be his or hers.

But despite these and many other hints that have been picked up or imagined over the years in Bram Stoker's life and writing, there is not the faintest shred of evidence to suggest that an inclination towards homosexuality was ever more than possibly latent. The suggestion that he was homosexual probably would have startled him as much as Lewis Carroll if he had been accused of being a paedophile, as we understand the term today.

* * *

Those who got to know Bram Stoker in his Lyceum years found a tall, sturdy, jovial man with a flaming red beard that contrasted strangely with the darker hair of his head. He was an enormously loyal friend and a scrupulously fair businessman and employer. He was endlessly energetic and always ready to lend a hand to those who needed it. He was brave too and was briefly famous in the London papers and recipient of a Royal Humane Society medal for gallantry for leaping into the Thames from a riverboat to rescue (unsuccessfully as it turned out) an old soldier trying to drown himself.

It is clear from all accounts that *Dracula* was not the product of some morbid, tortured soul like Edgar Allen Poe. Stoker must have had a dark side to draw on for *Dracula*. It showed in his ongoing fascination with the bizarre and weird, but few of his friends would have noticed had he lacked any such interest. To most people he appeared a complete extravert preoccupied with the business of his theatre. Whatever wrestling with demons he did was within his writing and the little free time his other affairs left him.

Stoker had his hands full running the Lyceum and organizing tours of Europe and America which often involved a hundred actors and crew, several tons of equipment and up to 1,100 wigs. He effectively managed both Irving's private and professional lives, yet somehow he managed to keep up his writing and other interests, even qualifying as a barrister in 1890 (though without ever putting this accomplishment into practice). In 1881 he published a collection of dreamy, allegorical and rather spooky children's stories, which largely originated from his postgraduate student days. *Under the Sunset*, the title referring to the fabled Celtic otherworld beyond the western ocean, received favourable reviews in all the main British newspapers and sold well enough to encourage further books. Then in 1890 came *The Snake's Pass*, a novel set in the west of Ireland. This received high praise not only from critics but even the Poet Laureate Tennyson (with whom he later became great friends), and the Prime Minister Gladstone. Among the short stories Stoker also published at this time was one titled *The Squaw*, which featured Countess Elisabeth Bathory's infamous Iron Maiden, which he had seen on a working visit to Nuremburg. In fact most of Stoker's stories, apart from the Transylvanian episodes of *Dracula*, were inspired by places he visited on holiday or during snatched breaks from work.

Then in 1895 came two critical disasters, *The Watter's Mou* set in Cruden Bay on the east coast of Scotland, and *The Shoulder of Shasta* set in California. These received almost universal panning in the press for being over-melodramatic and carelessly written, their only saving grace, according to one review, being a few 'fine descriptive passages'. (*The Watter's Mou* incidentally was published as a companion volume to Conan Doyle's *The Parasite*, the tale of a 'psychic vampire' that is counted among the influences on *Dracula*.)

Stoker however took little notice because he was deep in the throes of creating his masterpiece.

DRACULA

Years before, during his postgraduate years in Dublin, Stoker had been inspired by *Carmilla* to want to write something similar, but it was a lucky encounter in 1890 which is popularly credited with having set him on the right track.

The Lyceum Theatre had some store-rooms that had once been the home of the Sublime Society of Beefsteaks, founded by Sheridan. On taking over, Irving and Stoker had refurbished these as the Beefsteak Room for entertaining the cast and guests after shows, or simply for chewing over ideas on their own till the small hours of the morning, a habit they maintained throughout their long partnership. Invitations to dine in the Beefsteak Room were highly sought after and guests included the Prince of Wales, Randolph Churchill and Sarah Bernhardt (famed for her habit of sleeping in a coffin). In 1890 they also included a travelling Professor of Oriental Languages from Budapest University, Arminius Vambery, who entertained the company with colourful and probably exaggerated tales of his adventures as a spy in the Middle East. Vambery is also believed to have told Stoker about the infamous Vlad the Impaler, also known as Dracula, the fifteenth century defender of Romania against the Turks, the terror of friends and foes alike.

On his departure the professor apparently kept Stoker supplied with fresh information about Dracula and vampires, themes that were both strong in Eastern Europe though not previously linked. Before Stoker's novel there had never been any suggestion that the original Dracula was considered a vampire in his native land, which is somewhat surprising as he fitted many of the requirements perfectly. Exactly how much information Vambery supplied is not clear. It has been suggested that he did no more than fire Stoker's imagination one night and that Stoker learned most about Vlad Dracula from one of his brothers who served as a surgeon in the Turkish army.

In fact there is a minor academic industry dedicated to proving that *Dracula* was inspired by almost anyone but Vambery. One of the more plausible theories is that Stoker in fact first found the name Dracula and its punning association with the devil in Whitby Library while holidaying there in 1890; in William Wilkinson's *An Account of the Principalities of Wallachia and Moldavia* in fact, first published in 1820, which mentions a 'Voivode Dracula' who crossed the Danube to wage war successfully on the Turks. In a footnote Wilkinson also mentions that 'Dracula in Wallachian language means Devil' which almost certainly did suggest a name for his antihero because previously Stoker had simply been calling him Count Wampyr. But whatever the exact truth of the matter, Stoker felt he owed enough to Vambery to mention him in the novel as an authority on Dracula and vampires, while in gratitude to Whitby Library

he made that the scene for his imaginary Count Dracula's landing in England in the shape of a wolf.

Stoker also made extensive researches in the British Museum Library where, like Van Helsing in the novel, he 'studied over and over all the papers relating to this monster.' Stoker was fond of claiming that *Dracula* sprang from a nightmare brought on by too much dressed crab one dinner. Possibly this was so (a nightmare did at least provide the scene where Jonathan Harker is nearly devoured by three voluptuous female vampires) but the book was also well-rooted in research. He studied histories and travel books so effectively that it was assumed, quite wrongly, that his descriptions of Transylvania came from first-hand experience, an idea that as a showman he did little to discourage.

Reading Bram Stoker's *Dracula* today is surprisingly rewarding, given that it is one of those books that is far more famous than it is read. The style may be cumbersome and long-winded in places, the characters two-dimensional (particularly the females) and the plot held together by coincidences that would make Dickens blush, but many of these handicaps were simply conventions of the time. Once you allow for them, what remains is vivid stuff and still well worth the read. An aspect of the book that is sometimes overlooked by modern readers is the sharp contrast Stoker wanted to draw between the modern (in his day) methods of rational science and the ancient superstitions which Dracula drew upon for his terrible existence. This is because Victorian science has itself acquired a kind of gothic sheen. So the use of typewriters, telegraphs and wax cylinder recordings no longer strikes our perceptions as dazzlingly cutting edge but just kind of blend into the background of the romanticised, costume drama past.

When *Dracula* was published in May 1897, some London critics were enthusiastic and many were astonished. *The Pall Mall Gazette* said: 'It is horrid and creepy to the last degree. It is also excellent, and one of the best things in the supernatural line that we have been lucky enough to hit upon.' The *Daily Mail* recognised that a classic had been born and commented: 'In seeking a parallel to this weird, powerful and horrible story, our minds revert to such tales as "The Mysteries of Udolpho", "Frankenstein", "Wuthering Heights", "The Fall of the House of Usher" and "Marjery of Quelher". But "Dracula" is even more appalling in its gloomy fascination than any one of these!' Even hostile comments like those in the *Athenaeum* were tempered with respect for the sheer courage and compelling-ness of the tale.

The critical success of *Dracula*, even though it was not immediately matched by sales, came as some consolation to Stoker because shortly afterwards a series of disasters came along to ruin his life. The first was a fire in Southwark in 1898 that largely destroyed the Lyceum's store of costumes and scenery. This was a fatal blow as insurance covered less than a tenth of the loss. The company was immediately unable to stage most of its repertoire and was sold to a syndicate that managed to keep the Lyceum open for a few more years, but basically the fire marked the end of a glorious theatrical era. Stoker continued to work for Irving but on a much-reduced scale. Irving's health also went into serious decline.

Paradoxically, while Irving's life took a nosedive he was being showered with awards and honours, including the first ever British theatrical knighthood. Only those in his inner circle knew how desperate his circumstances had become. He struggled on for a while against both ill health and financial ruin. Stoker remained faithful to the end, despite having been shabbily betrayed by Irving at a crucial stage of the financial wrangling when he had sold the company. Stoker even accompanied him on his farewell tour of the provinces during which Irving appeared as Becket at the Theatre Royal, Bradford on 13 October 1905. Shortly after proclaiming Becket's dying words: 'Into thy hands, O Lord, into thy hands,' he had a stroke, but not before parting from Stoker with an unusually affable handshake and the words: 'Muffle up your throat old chap. Take care of yourself. God bless.' An hour or so after their parting Irving collapsed and died in the foyer of the Midland Hotel.

Then Stoker found himself cast adrift and having to rely on his pen for a living. A year later he also had a stroke that impaired his eyesight and mobility, though not enough to quench his remarkable energy.

After *Dracula* he wrote ten further books, mostly novels, which were quite successful though without ever threatening to make him rich. The one that came closest to rivalling *Dracula* was his last, *The Lair of the White Worm*, which sold vigorously from 1911 until the Second World War. It has been intermittently in print ever since and was filmed in 1988 by Ken Russell in typically outrageous style, starring Hugh Grant and Amanda Donohoe. It is not generally rated one of Russell's best films (except among some horror buffs) but is credited with having helped launch Hugh Grant onto our screens. Other Stoker books of note are *The Mystery of the Sea*,

The Jewel of Seven Stars and *The Lady of the Shroud*, but it is unlikely that any would now be remembered as more than literary footnotes without *Dracula*.

Apart, perhaps, from *The Jewel of Seven Stars*; this is often claimed to have inspired the whole genre of Egyptian mummy stories that continue to enliven our cinema screens. Published in 1903, the story tells of an embalmed Egyptian princess who returns to life with devastating consequences. It was inspired by a real mummy (supposedly of an Egyptian princess) that Stoker had seen while on holiday in Whitby some ten or fifteen years earlier. This was owned by George Elliot MP who had acquired it along with other antiquities during a spell of duty as advisor to the Ottoman viceroy of Egypt. It was perhaps not a coincidence that when Stoker's scary book was published Elliot donated the mummy to Whitby museum, who in turn passed it on to the museum in Hull where it remains, having survived a bombing in the Second World War.

Chief among Stoker's non-fictional works is his *Personal Reminiscences of Henry Irving*. His *Famous Imposters* also did well. Among other tales it uncovered a remarkable local legend in the village of Bisley, Gloucestershire. This tells how in childhood Princess Elizabeth, daughter of Henry VIII, was sent to convalesce in Overcourt Manor nearby, and died of a sudden fever. In panic, as her father was due for a visit, Elizabeth's servants dressed up a local boy in her place and somehow never quite plucked up the courage to confess the truth. Which explained, to the villagers of Bisley at least, why Queen Elizabeth I never married or had children . . .

These books enabled Stoker almost to fulfil his original ambition of being a professional author. They at least helped keep the wolf from the door until his death in 1912 at the age of 64 while living at 26 St George's Square, London (now a modern school). Although actual poverty was kept at bay, life was never as comfortable or exciting as during the Lyceum's heyday. To the end, even when dogged by ill health, depression and growing eccentricity, Stoker was driven by restless energy and died with the outlines of several new projects in mind. The cause of death noted on the certificate by his doctor was 'exhaustion'.

Daniel Farson, Stoker's great-nephew suggested in his 1975 biography that 'exhaustion' was a euphemism for a specific, scandalous and very unpleasant sexual disease (syphilis in fact, which was rife at the time) that Stoker may have contracted in Paris while visiting Oscar Wilde in exile. This notion is based largely on assurances Farson received from medical experts that the technical term 'Locomotor Ataxy' which appears on Stoker's death certificate as the cause of death was equivalent to 'tertiary syphilis'. While this is true, it depends on the accuracy of the doctor's diagnosis and, given that Stoker had already had two strokes and suffered from Bright's disease, it would be reckless to rely too much on it.

Whatever the truth, 'exhaustion' seems an apt cause of death. Stoker led an astonishingly active life and the wonder is that he didn't burn out sooner, especially given his unpromising start to life. His long-suffering wife Florence was luckier and lived to see the runaway success of *Dracula* on stage and screen, and to reap some of the financial rewards.

DRACULA ON STAGE

Soon after *Dracula* was published in 1897, Bram Stoker presented a stage version at the Lyceum theatre; but with something like fifty scenes it was little more than a public reading of the novel to establish copyright over future performances (as the law then required). Sadly, given his love of the theatre, it was the only performance Stoker was ever to see. Equally sad was Irving's expressed opinion to him that it was 'dreadful'.

Dracula's success in the theatre, and thence the cinema, began with an adaptation by Hamilton Deane, another Irishman whose grandfather happened to have been the Stokers' neighbour in Dublin. Bram Stoker and Hamilton Deane's mother had even been great friends in their youth and had discussed way back then the possibility of one day producing a vampire play.

Hamilton Deane was manager of a touring theatrical company which played to packed houses around Britain, everywhere but London where with true metropolitan snobbery he was dismissed as a provincial ham. Seeing the stage potential of *Dracula*, Deane acquired the rights from Florence Stoker and set about adapting the novel. The first production opened in Derby in June 1924 and within two years *Dracula* was dominating the company's performances, prompting Deane to say: 'By that time I was simply coining money with the play. I could not go wrong with it anywhere.' In 1927 he boldly took his production to London where the critics poured acid on his presumption, but the audiences flocked in and the show ran to almost 400 performances, at which

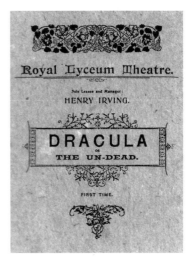

fainting in the aisles became a regular feature (there were health warning notices proudly displayed in some theatre foyers, and even sometimes a uniformed nurse, as much to entice customers as actually to warn off the faint-hearted). Thereafter *Dracula* became a staple of Deane's repertoire for almost the rest of his life, although it was a few years before he took on the title role himself.

In America the play opened on Broadway in 1927 with the unknown Hungarian Bela

Lugosi taking the title role, little realizing that he also was embarking on almost a lifetime's career in the part. Both Canada and the United States were taken by storm and the enthusiasm for stage vampires has continued more or less down to the present day, with only mild cyclical ups and downs.

The success of *Dracula* in the theatre would have delighted Bram Stoker had he lived to see it, particularly Hamilton Deane's 1939 production at the Lyceum where it ran in tandem with *Hamlet*. But the Count's success on the silver screen is of course what has made him a household name around the world. The first noteworthy production was F.W. Murnau's famous, thinly disguised version titled *Nosferatu*, filmed in Berlin in 1922 by Prana Films with the action transposed from England to Bremen in Germany, and starring Max Schreck as the startlingly grotesque vampire count. As Murnau had neglected to get permission he was successfully sued for

breach of copyright by Florence Stoker and all copies of the film were ordered to be destroyed. Luckily at least one survived to become a silent classic that was successfully remade in 1979 by Werner Herzog and starring Klaus Kinsky and Isabelle Adjani.

After Murnau's false start, the real genesis of *Dracula* on the silver screen was the Universal Pictures version of 1931, for the rights to which the studio paid Florence Stoker $40,000. Tod Browning directed the film, which starred Bela Lugosi in the role he made his own till Christopher Lee came along. In the climate of the Great Depression, the escapism of Browning's *Dracula* was an immediate and rampant success, particularly among women. Despite the villain's necessary demise at the end, it created an insatiable appetite for sequels that film-makers have been happy to feed ever since, reviving the Count in endless ingenious ways.

Curiously, given that vampirism has often been read as a metaphor for drug abuse

(among many other vices), Lugosi claimed it was the pressures of filming *Dracula* that set him on the path of morphine addiction that was eventually to kill him, though admittedly he was 73 when he died. At the request of his son and fifth wife, he was buried in his Dracula cloak in 1956, the same year that Christopher Lee took on the role for Hammer Films in Britain. At Lugosi's funeral it is rumoured that Peter Lorre looked over at Vincent Price and said: 'Should we stick a stake in his heart just to be sure?'

Christopher Lee's own theory about Dracula's universal fascination, especially in his own portrayal, is that: 'He is a superman with an erotic appeal to women, who find him totally alluring. He is everything people would like to be. Men are attracted because of the irresistible power he wields. For women, there is the complete abandonment to the power of a man.' Anne Rice, creator of the vampire Lestat has said: 'I think the vampire is a romantic, enthralling image … the image of this person who never dies and takes a blood sacrifice in order to live and exerts a charm over people; a handsome, alluring, seductive person who captivates us, then drains the life out of us so that he or she can live. We long to be one of them and the idea of being sacrificed to them becomes rather romantic.'

Anne Rice's own fascination with vampires began, when very young, by seeing *Dracula's Daughter*, Universal's 1936 sequel to Tod Browning's movie starring Gloria Holden: 'I loved the tragic figure of the daughter as a regretful creature who didn't want to kill but was driven to it. Vampires are tragic; they are not pure evil. They have a conscience, they suffer loneliness. The vampire is a cerebral image that transcends gender. I always saw them as romantic and abstract. In Bram Stoker's *Dracula*, they're presented as close to animals, but I always saw them as angels going in another direction – finely tuned imitations of human beings imbued with this evil spirit.'

CHAPTER II

THE ANCIENT EVIL

*S*O I RAISED THE LID *and laid it back against the wall; and then I saw something which filled my very soul with horror. There lay the Count, but looking as if his youth had been half-renewed, for the white hair and moustache were changed to dark iron-grey; the cheeks were fuller and the white skin seemed ruby-red underneath; the mouth was redder than ever, for on the lips were gouts of fresh blood which trickled from the corners of the mouth and ran over the chin and neck. Even the deep, burning eyes seemed set amongst swollen flesh, for the lids and pouches underneath were bloated. It seemed as if the whole awful creature were simply gorged with blood; he lay like a filthy leech, exhausted with his repletion.*

Jonathan Harker in Bram Stoker's *Dracula*

VAMPIRES ARE A CURIOUSLY AMBIVALENT EVIL. They tap into our deepest nightmares, those childhood terrors when the wind howls in the night and the creaking of timbers and scratching of twigs at the window sounds horribly purposeful. And what makes vampires more terrifying than other night prowlers is that they are not just after your life, but your very soul. Once bitten, you become one of them, immortal but an outcast and slave to a sacrilegious thirst. Even to those lacking in religion some relic of this dread remains, along with a secret fascination.

Because the thing is that vampires also have (at least in fiction) a certain glamour that eludes most other monsters, including werewolves to whom they are closely related – it being a common belief in the Balkans that werewolves become vampires after death. The 1994 film *Wolf* starring Jack Nicholson and Michelle Pfeiffer went somewhat against the norm, with Pfeiffer introducing a certain sexiness to the condition towards the end; but on the whole werewolves are just savage monsters most people would want to keep well away from, while the vampire's victims are often enslaved long before those sharp fangs have delivered their fatal jugular kiss. They have as often to be rescued from their own secret, complicit desires as from the monster itself. Vampires cannot enter a house without first being invited, but rarely lack invitations. People open their doors and windows to the night of their own half-conscious accord to let the demon in.

This glamour is largely the invention of fiction since the nineteenth century because most of the old East European folk tales upon which our idea of the vampire is based speak mainly of the simple horror of the marauding undead; there is little glamour in most of the tales. The sexual allure mainly came from combining the dead rising from their graves with their cousins, the sirens of many cultures – the German Lorelei, the Russian Rusalki and other quasi-vampires whose beauty is their fatal lure. The ancient Roman bloodsucker, the lamia, was also famous for her scorching beauty, as were her ghoulish cousins from the Near to the Far East, plus of course the famous sirens from Homer's *Odyssey* against whose beguiling songs he had his crew's ears stopped with beeswax.

Underlying the sexual allure of the vampire is the often powerful instinctual connection between biting and kissing – a topic that has been well explored in many psychological studies of vampirism. Havelock Ellis for example wrote: 'The impulse to bite is the origin of the kiss,' and 'the love bite is so common and widespread that it can be considered as a habitual variant of the kiss, especially practised by women.' The *Kama Sutra* devotes a chapter to the love-bite, which it breaks down into six distinct categories, as does the *Perfumed Garden* of Sheikh Nefzaoui.

BEYOND DEATH

Vampires are the undead. Or, strictly speaking, they are the dead who seize an unnatural extension of their earthly existence by feeding upon the lifeblood of others. They are undoubtedly evil but for the most part they get away with it and live beyond the bounds of normal existence. They have supernatural powers and within certain limits can come and go as they please. Who can deny the secret appeal of such an existence? Moreover, vampires can make others like themselves and that is part of their secret allure. Creatures of the night, they appeal to our own shadow side, that part of us which rages against the limitations of life and its endless obligations, that sump of pent-up grievances and suppressed urges at the back of all our beings. Vampires suffer from none of this because they care only for their own gratification and as they sink their fangs into their prey they tease with the notion that they may be offering something in return – ecstasy beyond imagination and possible entry into a new plane of being. It's no wonder that vampirism has so often been likened to heroin, crack cocaine and other serious drug addiction because the parallels are so close – the unearthly, inexpressible pleasure accompanied by a separation from normal human habits and a desperate hunger that takes little account of the cost to those on whom the addict preys to feed that hunger, or even the cost to themselves.

Virtue alone is no great defence against the vampire because virtue usually requires the suppression of many natural as well as unnatural urges, which the vampire can

secretly tap into. In fact it is probably safe to say that any virtue that has been won through great effort and self-denial creates a hook which the vampire can secretly latch onto, or whole nests of repressed instincts that are open to temptation. Bram Stoker seems to have understood this very well, whether consciously or not, from the way he charts Lucy Westenra's descent into vampirism. At the outset she is a lively and flirtatious character but well within the bounds of the Victorian ideal of femininity, complete with suppressed sexuality. But once she has fallen under Dracula's spell what emerges in her behaviour is a growing sensuality and even wanton lust that shocks her friends as much as anything else.

This shows when she is lying ill in what is to become her death-bed, and is visited by her fiancé Arthur. In Dr Seward's words: 'gradually her eyes closed, and she sank to sleep. For a little bit her breast heaved softly, and her breath came and went like a tired child's. And then insensibly there came the strange change which I had noticed in the night. Her breathing grew stertorous, the mouth opened and the pale gums, drawn back, made the teeth look longer and sharper than ever. In a sort of sleep-waking, vague, unconscious way she opened her eyes, which were now dull and hard at once, and said in a soft voluptuous voice such as I had never heard from her lips:

"'Arthur! Oh my love, I am so glad you have come! Kiss me!" Arthur bent eagerly over to kiss her; but at that instant Van Helsing, who like me had been startled by her voice, swooped upon him, and catching him by the neck with both hands, dragged him back with a fury of strength which I never thought he could have possessed.'

Then there is the question of the vampire's immortality, unless a Van Helsing catches up with them. Even without any pent-up grievances or desires to play upon, there is always the oldest human fear of all – that of death, which is the vampire's trade and to which he holds an antidote more tangible than is offered by any religion. Unlike Christians, Muslims and others, vampires are not required to take their fate after death on trust, or wait until Judgement Day before rising again from the grave. The vampire's baptismal transformation is immediate and tangible. And in an age when growing numbers of people no longer seriously believe in heavenly immortality anyway, the vampire's appeal is greater than ever. Even for those who do believe, as did most of *Dracula*'s first readers, the immortality teasingly offered by fictional vampires is literally more tangible because the vampire is there in the flesh.

* * *

To study the vampire is to study peoples changing attitudes, beliefs and fears about dying and the dead; and although we spend much of our lives determinedly not thinking of how or when they will end, such thoughts do of course inevitably and increasingly prey upon our minds as time passes and the inevitable becomes, well, ever more inevitable. We are all to some degree unable to resist the glowing, mesmeric gaze of the dark stranger at the window who is immune to this fear. We all sometimes feel the temptation to turn away from the sun and gaze into the dark navel of the night in the hope of finding there some redemption from our deepest fears.

The vampirism we are talking about is mostly imaginary of course. We are considering the idea of vampires much more than their reality. But there is more substance to the vampire legend than one might imagine. With hindsight many claimed cases of vampirism can easily be explained in other ways. For instance, the dying often dream that they are being visited by the recently deceased and can be forgiven for imagining they are being dragged by them into the shadows. Victims of tuberculosis, or consumption, often feel in the night as if something is sitting on their chests (like the wolf in Stoker's posthumous short story *Dracula's Guest* or the hideous goblin in Henri Fuseli's painting *The Nightmare*) after which the vitality drains out of them as dramatically as if a vampire really were at work. This sense of something sitting on one's chest is also a feature of night paralysis, in which the sufferer is conscious but unable to   move – a mild form of catalepsy. Anaemia and haemophilia have also often been mistaken for the work of vampires, as has porphyria, a rare hereditary blood disorder that causes an aversion to sunlight and leads some sufferers to crave blood, although drinking it is no cure. Also, it is worth noting that outbreaks of 'vampirism' have often occurred in times of plague and, according to Bernard Davies, Chairman of the British Dracula Society in 1997, 'Vampyr' does not mean "undead" as Stoker claimed but "plague-carrier."'

Then there is catalepsy, the death-like trance that often leads to premature burial, instances of which continue to crop up in the news with worrying regularity. In more primitive times the commonness of premature burial and hence noises in the grave and even the odd angry unfortunate struggling out of the tomb full of fury at his nearest and dearest, hardly bears thinking about. In Victorian times there was even a passing vogue for fitting coffins with bells or speaking tubes to prevent this. However, much remains that cannot easily be explained, enough to suggest that the eighteenth century vampire epidemics of Eastern Europe, for example, may not just have been just the product of ignorance and hysteria, even though no single, solid, scientific explanation satisfactorily explains them all.

EIGHTEENTH CENTURY:
A PLAGUE OF VAMPIRES

In Western Europe the native vampire tradition largely died out around the fifteenth century, but in the east people kept right on believing in the undead from medieval to modern times. In the seventeenth and eighteenth centuries this belief threatened to get completely out of control and caught the worried attention of many academic, Church and legal authorities who attempted to get to grips with the problem in various, often counter-productive, ways. The French journal *Mercure Galant* was typical of the media that spread news of the strange goings-on in the east to a puzzled wider audience. In its 1693-4 issue, drawing on travellers' tales, it reported: 'The vampires appeared after lunch and stayed till midnight, sucking the blood of people and cattle in great abundance. They sucked through the mouth, the nose but mainly through the ears. They say that the vampires had a sort of hunger that made them chew even their shrouds in the grave.'

Another popular source for rumour was the Encyclopaedia of Baron von Valvasor in which he tells the tale of the Vampire of Kring: 'In 1672 there dwelt in the market town of Kring, in the Archduchy of Krain [now Kringa in Croatia], a man named Jure Grando, who died, and was buried by Father George, a monk of St. Paul, who, on returning to the widow's house, saw Grando sitting behind the door. The monk and the neighbours fled. Soon stories began to circulate of a dark figure being seen to go about the streets by night, stopping now and then to tap at the door of a house, but never to wait for an answer. In a little while people began to die mysteriously in Kring, and it was noticed that the deaths occurred in the houses at which the spectred figure had tapped its signal. The widow Grando also complained that she was tormented by the spirit of her husband, who night after night threw her into a deep sleep with the object of sucking her blood. The Supan, or chief magistrate, of Kring decided to take the usual steps to ascertain whether Grando was a vampire. He called together some of the neighbours, fortified them with a plentyful supply of spirituous liquor, and they sallied off with torches and a crucifix.

'Grando's grave was opened, and the body was found to be perfectly sound and not decomposed, the mouth being opened with a pleasant smile, and there was rosy flush on the cheeks. The whole party were seized with terror and hurried back to Kring, with the exception of the Supan. The second visit was made in company with a priest, and the party also took a heavy stick of hawthorn sharpened to a point. The grave and body were found to be exactly as they had been left. The priest kneeled down solemnly and held the crucifix aloft: "O vampire, look at this," he said; "here is Jesus Christ who loosed us from the pains of hell and died for us upon the tree!"

'He went on to address the corpse, when it was seen that great tears were rolling down the vampire's cheeks. A hawthorn stake was brought forward, and as often as they strove to drive it through the body the sharpened wood rebounded, and it was not until one of the number sprang into the grave and cut off the vampire's head that the evil spirit departed with a loud shriek and a contortion of the limbs.'

This story has become so famous that the town sign of Kringa boasts that it is the home of the 'LEGENDA O VAMPIRU JURE GRANDO 1672'.

Possibly the most influential book in the vampire debate was *Magia Posthuma* by Charles Ferdinand de Schertz published in 1706. Although warning against accepting exaggerations, this presented a number of vampire stories as largely believable, including the now famous case of Peter Plogojovitz. As a lawyer, Schertz argued for suspected vampire cases to be processed by the courts of law, calling on the advice of doctors, theologians and other authorities instead of leaving it to the whims of village mobs. This admirable recommendation was often taken up but far from quelling the rumours they only fed them with more and more closely documented tales of apparent vampires being unearthed from their graves.

This book was attacked from all sides but continued to be quoted as a plausible authority well into the nineteenth century. One of the books attacking it was the *Dissertazione sopra I Vampiri* written by Guiseppe Davanzati, Archbishop of Florence in 1744. Davanzati did not believe in vampires at all and one way he tried to prove his case was to engage in debate with Cardinal Schtattembach, the Bishop of Olmutz in Moravia (now the eastern part of the Czech Republic) who did believe in them as they were apparently being dug up left, right and centre in his jurisdiction. Unfortunately for Davanzati people often gave more weight to the Cardinal's opinions than his own, perhaps because he was writing from the scene of events:

'The ministers received exact information, and forming a juridicial assembly, pronounced a final sentence against the so-called Vampire, by which, according to all due forms it was solemnly and legally decreed that the public Executioner should go to the place where the vampire was, open the tomb, and with a saw or long sword, and in sight of all the public spectators, should cut off the vampire's head and then open his chest with a lance and transfix the vampire's heart with an iron stake, striking through the breast, and then closing the tomb again. In this way, the Cardinal told me, the Vampire would cease to appear, while many others who had not yet been judged or executed were still appearing and producing calamitous results like the first. But what was worth noticing, and marvelling at, according to the same author, was that many of these adjudged vampires were found full of colour, rosy-cheeked, eyes open and full of living blood, as though they were actually alive and in good health, so that when they were struck with a lance, as sentence was being inflicted upon them, they uttered a horrifying shriek, and a copious stream of blood shot out from their chest that not only filled the grave but spurted outside and soaked the nearby ground.'

The most famous scholar to study the phenomenon of eighteenth century vampirism was the French Benedictine Dom Augustin Calmet, abbé of Senones in Lorraine, who in 1749 published one of the most thorough investigations into vampires, his treatise on *The Appearance of Spirits and on Vampires*:

Dom Augustin Calmet

'For about the last sixty years, we have been witnesses of new extraordinary incidents in Hungary, Moravia, Silesia, Poland. In those places, we are told, men dead for several months return from the tomb, speak, walk about in hamlets and villages, and injure men and beasts, whose blood they drain, causing illness and death. The only cure for these horrible attacks is to dig up the corpses, drive a sharp stake through the bodies, cut off the heads, tear out the hearts, or burn the bodies to ashes. The name of these ghosts is Oupires or Vampires, which in the Slavonic language means bloodsuckers. The details of the actual cases are so well-attested and legally documented that it seems impossible not to accept them.

'It is asserted by the modern Greeks . . . that the bodies of excommunicated persons never rot, but swell up to an uncommon size, and are stretched like drums, nor ever corrupt or fall to dust till they have received absolution from some bishop or priest. And they produce many instances of carcasses which have afterwards putrefied, as soon as the excommunication was taken off.

'They do not deny that a body's not corrupting is sometimes a proof of sanctity, but in this case they expect it to send forth an agreeable smell, to be white and ruddy, and not black, stinking and swelled like a drum, as the bodies of excommunicated persons generally are.'

One of Dom Calmet's informants was the Count of Cabreras, a Holy Roman Imperial officer charged with conducting vampire investigations. His stories, told to a Freiburg University professor in 1730 and thence relayed to Calmet, were typical of the hundreds of similar cases in Hungary at the time:

'It is now fifteen years since a soldier, who was quartered in the house of a Haidamack peasant, upon the frontiers of Hungary, saw as he was at table with his landlord, a stranger come in and sit down by them. The master of the house and the rest of the company were strangely terrified but the soldier knew not what to make of it. The next day the peasant died, and upon the soldier's enquiring into the meaning of it, he was told that it was his landlord's father, who had been dead and buried for over ten years, that came and sat down at the table and gave his son notice of his death.'

News of the strange incident reached the soldier's superiors who commissioned the Count of Cabreras to enquire further into it, which he did with several other officers, a surgeon and a notary. After taking statements from everyone involved, who were unanimous in supporting the soldier's tale, the party dug up the grave of the alleged spectre and found it to be 'in the same state as if it had been just dead, the blood like that of a living person.' The Count ordered its head to be cut off and the body reburied. He then investigated other similar cases, including that of a man who had been dead over thirty years. Despite this he was alleged to have appeared several times in his own house at dinner: 'At his first visit he had fastened upon the neck of his own brother and sucked his blood; at his second, he had treated one of his children in the same manner, and the third time, he fastened upon a servant of the family; and all three died instantly.' When the alleged culprit was dug up his corpse again seemed full of blood like a living person so 'a great nail was driven through his temples and he was buried again.'

The Count's report on his investigations prompted the Holy Roman Emperor Charles VI to order the setting up of an Imperial Commission comprising army officers, lawyers, doctors and priests to investigate further, unearthing dozens more similar cases.

Calmet's work remains a classic study and a great source of strange and wonderful tales, but again it had almost the opposite effect to the one he hoped for. Calmet himself was basically sceptical about vampires but nevertheless he was scrupulously fair in reporting the tales he heard, presenting them as true stories while saving his own arguments for later chapters of the book where they were often overlooked. Here's a sample of his quizzical attitude towards the whole subject:

'Supposing, indeed there were any truth in the accounts of these appearances of vampires, are they to be attributed to the powers of God, to the angels, to the souls of those who return in this way or to the Devil? If we adopt that prevalent last hypothesis it follows that the Devil can imbue these corpses with subtlety and bestow upon them the power of passing through the earth without any disturbance to the ground, of gliding through the cracks and joints of doors, of slipping through a keyhole, of increasing and diminishing, of becoming rarefied as air or water to penetrate the earth; in short, of enjoying the same properties as we believe will be possessed by the blessed after Resurrection, and which distinguished the human body of Our Lord after the first Easter Day, inasmuch as he appeared to those to whom he would show himself.

'Yet even if it be accepted that the Devil can re-animate dead bodies and give them movement for a certain time, can he also bestow these powers of increasing, diminishing, becoming rarefied and also so subtle that they can penetrate the earth, doors, windows?

'We are not told that God allows him the exercise of such powers, and it is hard to believe that a material body, gross and substantial, can be endowed with this subtlety and spirituality without some destruction or alteration of the general structure and without damage to the configuration of the body. But this would not be in accord with the intention of the Devil, for such change would prevent this body from appearing, from manifesting itself, from motion and speech, indeed, from being eventually hacked to pieces and burned as so often happens in the case of vampires in Moravia, Poland and Silesia.'

Such reservations however carried less weight than many of the eyewitness reports Dom Calmet relayed and as a result he has often been accused quite wrongly of being a gullible reporter of unproven marvels – which was the opinion of the great Voltaire when he joined the debate in his *Dictionnaire Philosphique*, drawing attention to the conflicting views of Eastern and Western Christianity: 'For a long time the Christians who practised the Greek ritual believed that the corpses of those Christians who practised the Latin ritual would not decompose when buried in Greece, because they were excommunicated. This is precisely the contrary of what we, the Christians of the Latin ritual, think. We believe that corpses that remain intact bear the mark of eternal felicity.'

So despite the best efforts of many scholars and theologians the idea of there being a vampire plague in Eastern Europe spread anyway. And what followed from that was the notion that if it was happening in the east, might it not also spread westwards?

* * *

A good example of how effectively the idea of vampires caught on in the west is the apparently true story told to Napoleon Bonaparte by his head of security and Minister for Police, Joseph Fouché. It concerned extraordinary events at the Hotel Pepin, Rue Saint-Eloi in Paris that were retold in Baron Langon's *Evenings with Prince Cambaceres, Second Consul* 1837, currently available as a reprint by Kessinger Publishing. The story goes that a certain M. Rafin moved into the hotel. He was well-dressed and handsome, if in a slightly unsettling way, but it was his odd habits that drew attention. At exactly eleven each evening he left the hotel and did not return till the morning. Fouché's agents followed him but learned little because each night he disappeared into the Père Lachaise cemetery and did not show himself again till four in the morning. No matter how hard they tried, the police could learn no more because they lost the trail in that labyrinthine place. They searched his rooms in his absence but found nothing suspicious and his papers were in order.

Rumours began to spread about the enigmatic stranger. A young milliner he visited had become pale and sickly and the same happened to a 'stout and ruddy' widow. So one night the police stopped Rafin near Père Lachaise. He reacted violently. With one punch he felled two of them with a blow 'like a bar of iron'. The rest overpowered him and he calmed down, offering to pay a tip for the agents' inconvenience. As his papers were in order they had no grounds to hold Rafin, but the officers who searched him commented on the dreadful stench that came from his body.

Rafin continued his nocturnal routine undeterred till one afternoon an agitated young man came to the hotel asking for him. As he was out, the young man awaited his return and when Rafin came in, the young man immediately attacked him shouting 'Assassin! Monster!' Pulling out a knife he stabbed Rafin once in the side; upon which Rafin fell dead to the floor and his attacker fled. Four witnesses clearly saw that there had been but a single blow, but when a surgeon examined the body he found six bleeding wounds — two in the neck, two in the right side and two in the abdomen.

The killer was soon caught and told a tragic tale of how his sweetheart had been seduced away from him by Rafin, how soon afterwards her health had begun to fade and she had begun to suffer terrible nightmares in which 'her blood was nightly sucked by a being of hideous appearance' who bore a resemblance to Rafin. That very morning the young man had watched her die and had gone to the Hotel Pepin for revenge on the monster he believed had killed her.

That should have been the end of the matter but, so Fouché the Minister for Police told Napoleon, there was more to come. The body with its six wounds lay at the hotel

The Dutch *Gleaner* magazine No 18 in 1732 carried the following article about two of the most famous vampire cases.

In a certain town of Hungary, which is called, in Latin, Oppida Heidonum, on the other side of Tibiscus, vulgarly called the Teysse, that is to say, the river which washes the celebrated territory of Tokay, as also a part of Transylvania, the people known by the name of Heydukes believe that certain dead persons, whom they call Vampires, suck the blood of the living, insomuch that these people appear like skeletons, while the dead bodies of the suckers are so full of blood, that it runs out at all the passages of their bodies, and even at their very pores. This old opinion of theirs they support by a multitude of facts, attested in such a manner, that they leave no room for doubt. We shall here mention some of the most considerable.

It is now about five years ago, that a certain Heyduke, an inhabitant of the village of Medreiga [Medwegya or Meduega], whose name was Arnold Paul [or Paole], was bruised to death by a hay-cart, which ran over him. Thirty days after his death, no less than four persons died suddenly in that manner, wherein, according to the tradition of the country, those people generally die who are sucked by Vampires. Upon this, a story was called to mind that this Arnold Paul had told in his lifetime, viz, that at Cossovia [Kosice in Hungary], on the frontiers of the Turkish Servia, he had been tormented by a Vampire; (now the established opinion is, that a person sucked by a Vampire becomes a Vampire himself, and sucks in his turn;) but that he had found a way to rid himself of this evil by eating some of the earth out of the Vampire's grave, and rubbing himself with his blood. This precaution, however, did not hinder his becoming a Vampire; insomuch, that his body being taken up forty days after his death, all the marks of a notorious Vampire were found thereon. His

complexion was fresh, his hair, nails, and beard were grown; he was full of fluid blood, which ran from all parts of his body upon his shroud. The Hadnagy or Bailiff of the place, who was a person well acquainted with Vampirism, caused a sharp stake to be thrust, as the custom is, through the heart of Arnold Paul, and also quite through his body; whereupon he cried out dreadfully, as if he had been alive. This done, they cut off his head, burnt his body, and threw the ashes thereof into the Saave. They took the same measures with the bodies of those persons who had died of Vampirism, for fear that they should fall to sucking in their turns.

All these prudent steps did not hinder the same mischief from breaking out again about five years afterwards, when several people in the same village died in a very odd manner. In the space of three months, seventeen persons of all ages and sexes died of Vampirism, some suddenly, and some after two or three days' suffering. Amongst others, there was one Stanoska, the daughter of a Heyduke, whose name was Jovitzo, who, going to bed in perfect health, waked in the middle of the night, and making a terrible outcry affirmed, that the son of a certain Heyduke, whose name was Millo, and who had been dead about three weeks, had attempted to strangle her in her sleep. She continued from that time in a languishing condition, and in the space of three days died. What this girl had said, discovered the son of Millo to be a Vampire. They took up the body, and found him so in effect. The principal persons of the place, particularly the physician and surgeons, began to examine very narrowly, how, in spite of all their precautions, Vampirism had again broke out in so terrible a manner. After a strict inquisition, they found that the deceased Arnold Paul had not only sucked the four persons before mentioned, but likewise several beasts, of whom the new Vampires had eaten, particularly the son of Millo. Induced by these circumstances, they took a resolution of digging up the bodies of all persons who had died within a certain time. They did so, and amongst forty bodies, there were found seventeen evidently Vampires. Through the hearts of these they drove stakes, cut off their heads, burnt their bodies, and threw the ashes into the river. All the informations we have been speaking of were taken in a legal way, and all the executions were so performed, as appears by certificates drawn up in full form, attested by several officers in the neighbouring garrisons, by the surgeons of several regiments, and the principal inhabitants of the place.

till the day of burial, but when the funeral directors came it had mysteriously vanished. Then, six weeks later M. Rafin walked back into the Hotel Pepin as right as rain. By way of explanation he told a tale of having miraculously revived on the point of being dissected by medical students, who had received their cadaver illegally from body-snatchers and therefore wished to remain anonymous.

Everyone believed this tale save Fouché himself who had Rafin arrested and tried. Then, by way of experiment and in front of eleven witnesses including the eminent scientists Baron Georges Cuvier and Antoine Fourcroy, he cut the prisoner's flesh with a scalpel to draw blood. As soon as the first drop appeared, Rafin's other six wounds reopened and bled so profusely that before the blood could be staunched, the prisoner died.

To be on the safe side, he was buried in an iron coffin with his head, hands and feet cut off. A year later he was exhumed and the body was found to have decomposed normally; and M. Rafin made no more appearances on the streets of Paris. Fouché's comment on the case was: 'We are in the nineteenth century and we beheld before us a vampire, a bloodsucker. I cannot admit the reality of vampires, yet it is certain that I witnessed the facts I have declared.'

* * *

Père Lachaise cemetery has been the scene of many other strange nocturnal dramas, as befits one of the most famous and romantic cemeteries in the world. At around 120 acres and with many tombs the size of small houses, it is virtually a city of the dead, inhabited otherwise only by their visiting relations, the curious and cats who pad about its paved streets on their own mysterious business. Among its famous dead residents are, in no particular order, Abélard and Héloïse, Molière, Oscar Wilde, Honoré de Balzac, Sarah Bernhardt, Eugène Delacroix, Isadora Duncan, Stéphane Grappelli, Marcel Marceau and Alice B. Toklas. The most visited grave though belongs to rock singer Jim Morrison of the Doors. Almost forty years after his death fans from around the world still come to lay flowers on his grave, often to the annoyance of other visitors and at least partly because of the abundant graffiti pointing the way (often incorrectly) to his tomb.

In the annals of vampirism one of the most famous cases is that of Sergeant Bertrand, known throughout France as 'The Vampire' at the time of his trial in 1849, although he was less a vampire than a necrophiliac or necrophagist. He attributed his behaviour to a kind of werewolfism or lycanthropy.

The trouble began at Père Lachaise cemetery where watchmen began to notice a shadowy figure flitting through the tombs at night. Then several graves were found to

have been disturbed and their occupants horribly mutilated, their entrails being torn out and the bodies being otherwise hideously mutilated as if by a wild beast. Then the activity moved to a remote suburban cemetery where the body of a seven year old girl was found dug up and desecrated the day after her funeral. According to *Reynold's Miscellany* for 30 November 1850: 'Every means were taken to discover the criminal; but the only result of the increased surveillance was that the scene of profanation was removed to the cemetery of Mont Parnasse, where the exhumations were carried to such an extent that the authorities were at their wit's ends. Considering, by the way, that all these cemeteries are surrounded by walls and have iron gates, which are kept closed, it certainly seems strange that any ghoul or vampire of solid flesh and blood should have been able to pursue his vocation so long undisturbed'.

At last however the marauder was caught by a mechanical man-trap set by the Montparnasse cemetery keepers. They shot him, but he escaped, leaving a trail of blood and some scraps of military uniform. Then word came from the sappers of the 74th Regiment that one of their sergeants had returned shortly after midnight with gunshot wounds, and had been taken to Val de Grace military hospital where he was arrested and then brought to trial. The courtroom was packed; not least, as journals commented at the time, with curious ladies. In his defence Bertrand claimed he committed his outrages while in the grip of a kind of dementia which compelled him to dig up, often with his bare hand, and violate the corpses, after which he fell into a kind of trance or coma: 'When a fit seized me, whether it were midday or midnight, I had to go off, there was no postponing it.' Despite this, he was judged sane and sentenced to a year's imprisonment, the maximum permitted by law, after which he disappears from the record. Commenting on the case in *Vampirisme, Necrophilie, Necrosadisme* 1901, Dr Alexis Epaularde commented: 'All in all, Bertrand was a vampire just as other people are drinkers.'

Another apparently true case of vampirism in France is told by Jessie Adelaide Middleton in *Another Grey Ghost Book* 1914. She tells of a Viscount de Moreive who was one of the few nobles to hold onto their estate during the French Revolution. According to Middleton he was an extraordinary looking man — very tall and thin with a high, pointed forehead and four very protruding teeth. Despite a gracious manner he was capable of ferocious cruelty, as he showed when the revolutionary fervour had cooled in the country. Rounding up those he considered the chief troublemakers under his rule, he interviewed them one by one and then had their heads chopped off. The revolutionary fervour had not died completely however and before long some peasants rose up and killed him in turn.

Soon after the Viscount's burial a large number of children began to die in the neighbourhood, many with bite marks at the throat. At the height of the savagery nine children died in a single week. In varying degrees this went on for seventy-two years until the old Viscount's grandson inherited the estate. Learning of the rumours, the new lord decided to lay either them or his grandfather to rest. Hiring a respected vampire hunter and in the presence of witnesses the vault was opened. All the bodies within were found to have decomposed normally save that of the old Viscount who lay plump and sleek, with a flushed face, blood in his veins and long fingernails which had continued growing in the tomb. The old vampire was thereupon impaled through the heart with a whitethorn stake, upon which the corpse screeched and blood and water flowed from the wound. The body was then burned on the sea shore and from that day the child slaughter ceased.

Middleton goes on to quote many other examples of vampirism, including the famous case of Arnold Paul of Meduega mentioned earlier and that of Grando, the Vampire of Kring. Finally, Middleton mentions the case of a vampire whose confession was apparently carefully preserved by the Cistercians of Palermo. The singularity of this case was that the man apparently became a vampire through being bitten by a vampire bat while in the tropics. Though it casts some doubt on the plausibility of her other stories, it deserves mention if only as an example of how ideas about vampires had spread and taken shape the previous century. After being bitten by a vampire bat the man in question had begun, in unspecified ways, to act like a vampire. This had not, however, granted him immortality because on his deathbed he swore on oath to a priest that he was surrounded by five spectral, horribly laughing women with protruding teeth and very red lips who were stretching out their hands as if to receive him. For several years after death his body showed no sign of decay and there were other signs of vampirism, so finally he was despatched in the traditional way with garlic and wooden stake.

THE LAND BEYOND THE FOREST

Although Jessie Middleton's stories were written after Bram Stoker had completed *Dracula*, most of them, or ones very similar, were in circulation long before that and were the kind of thing that coloured his own creation. One of his main sources though for the Transylvanian chapters of *Dracula* was *The Land Beyond the Forest* by Madame Emily de Laszowska Gerard (1849-1905), published in 1885 and written while Gerard was stationed in Transylvania with her Austro-Hungarian cavalry officer husband. This Baedeker travel guide provided many of Stoker's convincing descriptions of both the land and its natives, including their superstitions. Here is to be found an explanation of the strange lights Jonathan Harker sees during his wild and ghostly ride to Dracula's castle at the opening of the tale:

'This same night is the best for finding treasures and many people spend it in wandering about the hills trying to probe the earth for the gold it contains. Vain and futile as such searches usually are, yet they have in this country a somewhat greater semblance of reason than in most other parts, for perhaps nowhere else have so many successive nations been forced to secrete their riches in flying from an enemy. Not a year passes without bringing to light some earthen jar containing old Dacian coins, or golden ornaments of Roman origin . . . In the night of St George's Day (so say the legends) all these treasures begin to burn, or, to speak in mystic language, to "bloom" in the bosom of the earth, and the light they give forth, described as a bluish flame resembling the colour of lighted spirits of wine, serves to guide favoured mortals to their place of concealment. The lights seen before midnight denote treasures kept by benevolent spirits, while those which appear at a later hour are unquestionably of a pernicious nature.'

Of the country in general Gerard observes: 'Transylvania might well be termed the land of superstition, for nowhere else does this curious crooked plant of delusion flourish as persistently and in such bewildering variety. It would almost seem as though the whole species of demons, pixies, witches and hobgoblins, driven from the rest of Europe by the wand of science, had taken refuge within this mountain rampart, well aware that here they would find secure lurking-places, whence they might defy their persecutors yet awhile. . . The spirit of evil (or, not to put too fine a point upon it, the devil) plays a conspicuous part in the Roumenian code of superstition, and such designations as the Gregynia Drakuluj (devil's garden), the Gania Drakuluj (devil's mountain), Yadu Drakuluj (devil's abyss) &c &c, which we frequently find attached to rocks, caverns, or heights, attest to the fact that these people believe themselves to be surrounded on all sides by a whole legion of evil spirits.'

All of which must have been music to Stoker's ears when it came to defining his champion of blasphemous evil against both science and religion. Among the many marvels and terrors the locals believed in, according to Gerard, were dragons which dwelt in remote mountains lakes, issuing forth in clouds of thunder and lightning when disturbed. She also mentions something that Stoker placed almost straight into Van Helsing's mouth in describing the place where Count Dracula supposedly acquired his occult powers. 'The Scholomance, or school supposed to exist somewhere in the heart of the mountains, and where all the secrets of nature, the language of animals, and all imaginable magic spells and charms are taught by the devil in person. Only ten scholars are admitted at a time, and when the course of learning has expired and nine of them are released to return to their homes, the tenth scholar is detained by the devil as payment. Mounted upon an Ismeju (dragon); he becomes the devil's aide-de-camp, and assists him in "making the weather", that is to say, preparing the thunderbolts.'

After considering the funeral rites of Romanians, and their belief that if they are neglected the dead cannot rest in their graves, Gerard goes on: 'these restless spirits, called Strigoi, are not malicious, but their appearance bodes no good, and may be regarded as omens of sickness and misfortune.' Then: 'more decidedly evil, however, is the vampire, or nosferatu, in whom every Roumenian peasant believes as firmly as he does in heaven or hell. There are two sorts of vampires – living and dead. The living vampire is in general the illegitimate offspring of two illegitimate persons, but even a flawless pedigree will not ensure anyone against the intrusion of a vampire into his family vault, since every person killed by a nosferatu becomes likewise a vampire after death, and will continue to suck the blood of other innocent people till the spirit has been exorcised, either by opening the grave of the person suspected and driving a stake through the corpse, or firing a pistol shot into the coffin. In very obstinate cases it is further recommended to cut off the head and replace it in the coffin with the mouth filled with garlic, or to extract the heart and burn it, strewing the ashes over the grave. That such remedies are often resorted to, even in our enlightened days, is a well-attested fact, and there are probably few Roumenian villages where such has not taken place within the memory of the inhabitants.'

What Gerard thought about Stoker's plundering of her researches for Dracula is unknown. Quite possibly she was unaware of it as she died in 1905, well before the novel really took off.

BALKAN VAMPIRES

In one form or another, vampires have stalked the nightmares of people throughout the world, but the vampire most people immediately think of today originates in Eastern Europe and the Balkans where, as we have seen in Emily Gerard's observations, circumstances conspired to produce an astonishingly powerful belief in the sharp-toothed prowler of the night. Travellers until recently found that even the smallest villages had their local tales of the dead rising from the grave to terrorise and feed upon the living. Where in other parts of the world people told tales of ghosts around their winter fires, in the Balkans they spoke in hushed tones of vampires, and probably still do in places, if this news story is anything to go by:

The Scottish *Sunday Herald* on 11 March 2007 reported a bizarre incident that had just taken place in Pozarevac, Serbia – birth and burial place of former dictator Slobodan Milosevic. With the anniversary of his burial approaching on 18 March, local self-proclaimed vampire hunter Miroslav Milosevic (no relation) broke into his vault in the middle of the night and impaled his namesake through the heart with a metre-long hawthorn stake to prevent him rising from the grave. He then called the police on his mobile phone, confessed what he had done and later presented himself at the police station to be charged. He said: 'Driving a hawthorn stake through the body was my duty carried out in the name of the Pozarevac Resistance.'

Much of the vampire folklore in Russia and the Balkans was due to the religious beliefs of the area, and in particular the doctrines of the Orthodox Church regarding the continued influence of a departed soul on the body left behind. These ideas are probably much more ancient than Christianity because archaeological digs in prehistoric graveyards, in

Greece particularly, often reveal corpses that have been nailed to their coffins, had their heads removed and garlic stuffed in the neck, wooden stakes driven through their hearts, their bodies eviscerated and filled with vinegar and so on – all measures taken against vampires much later. So these ideas were probably not the invention of Orthodox Christianity, but by being incorporated into official dogma they were given respectability and credence and spread to regions where they might otherwise not have been strongly held.

It became Church dogma, for instance, that the corpses of people who had been excommunicated did not decompose in the ordinary way because their spirits were still bound to them. They were then liable to rise again as vampires, desperately seeking refreshment from the blood of the living until laid to rest, either by lifting the excommunication or by the time-honoured means of beheading, impaling and/or cremating the body.

Murderers and suicides were also liable to become vampires, as were warlocks, witches and anyone who died with un-confessed mortal sins on their conscience. Plus of course anyone who had been the victim of a vampire, or any corpse over which a cat

or wild animal had jumped, because the beast's feral nature might have infected the still delicate, lingering soul of the deceased. Further, anyone dying under a curse, even their own, was unable to rest in the grave, which must have given people pause for thought before saying 'damn me'. Other widely-believed causes include being born with a caul (membrane enclosing a foetus) attached, or with teeth or tail; or even simply being born on Christmas Day, which for some reason was considered particularly unlucky at one time in Greece, perhaps because it was seen as impiously intruding on the Saviour's birthday. To prevent the baby growing into a goblin or vampire, it had to be baptised immediately. A baby weaned too early from its mother's breast was also likely to turn into a vampire. Conversely, a powerful deterrent to vampires was to eat a cake made with the blood of three young mothers.

Children that have died without being baptised, especially unwanted children who have been strangled at birth, are liable to turn into a particularly nasty form of vampire-goblin called Callicantzari. They carry a piece of charcoal in their mouths and spit fire. They also creep into their mothers' beds and suckle while they sleep; and the woman will know this because she will wake in extreme pain and with her breasts smothered in blood. The vampire-goblins also like to strangle unbaptised babies and so newborn children often have the sign of the cross marked on their foreheads until baptism. Other precautions were also taken and both religious and superstitious talismans would also be hung around the windows and doors. Particularly effective was supposed to be the lower jaw of a pig hung in the fireplace to prevent goblins coming down the chimney. Some say these creatures also have wings and their cry is very like that of normal babies. Often it can be heard scratching around inside its tomb which, if opened, will reveal the child to be ruddy and bloated and its stomach filled with curdled milk. In Samos the way to destroy these little vampires was to remove their hearts and lungs and pour vinegar into the cavity.

This idea of murdered babies striking back from the grave is related to the widespread belief in Greece that a murdered person's blood can cry out from the ground until the killing is avenged. At a spot on Zakynthos this is supposed to happen to this day — every night there comes a horrible shriek from the bowels of the earth. Some locals attribute it to demons but most say it is the blood of a murdered man baying for revenge. If not this way, a murdered person has many other means of troubling the friends and relations supposed to avenge his or her death — even sometimes returning as a vampire — which has led to many blood feuds that have lasted generations. A popular ditty from Corfu tells a tale that could have fallen out of some ancient Greek tragedy: A boy comes home early to find his mother in bed with a lover. The boy threatens to tell his father and to keep his silence the mother persuades her boyfriend to kill the child. When her husband returns from hunting she makes an excuse for the boy's absence and serves up a tasty meal made from the boy's cooked liver. Perhaps she hopes to draw him into the guilt of the deed, but before the hunter can take a bite the liver moves and screams out the crime. Whereupon the husband cuts off his wife's head and has it ground to shreds at the mill.

Incidentally, the fear about cats jumping over a corpse can be found across Eurasia from the tip of Scotland to Shanghai and often a large point of keeping vigil over a corpse was expressly to prevent this happening. In nineteenth century Scotland when vampires as we think of them had largely been forgotten in folklore, the fear was of the dead rising as ghosts; but in China it was of the corpse being physically reanimated, just as in Eastern Europe. If despite precautions a cat did manage to jump over the body, various measures had immediately to be taken, such as sticking needles into the corpse or nailing it into its coffin.

Vampire-hunting in the Balkans was once a quite legitimate profession on a par with being a herbalist or tinker. In much of Greece it is believed that a successful vampire-hunter had to have been born on a Saturday, which was also the day on which exhumations were mostly performed because vampires are particularly weak on that day and cannot leave their tombs. Many hunters also claim descent from vampires themselves, which, while enhancing their claimed skills probably does not endear them much to their clients. That a vampire can have children may seem strange to us, but in that part of the world vampires did not always just attack their nearest and dearest. Often they returned from the grave in order to sleep with their spouses, which is how their wives sometimes came to produce babies more than nine months after their deaths. Of course other explanations entirely spring to the sceptical mind but one cannot always blame the widow looking for an excuse. A common practical joke still in the deep countryside is for lusty youths to visit widows wearing sheets so they will think it their dead spouse returned from the grave and not dare refuse his advances.

However, traditionally when it truly was a vampire and not just human concupiscence at work, the fruits of such unnatural liaisons were often stillborn and monstrous, but many did survive and grow into almost normal-seeming people, though they tended to be shunned by their neighbours and this probably encouraged them to think of vampire-hunting as a viable career choice.

In Serbia the son of a vampire is called a dhampir and has the power to sense the presence of vampires and see those that are invisible. This power is then transmitted to his own sons and to the sons and grandsons of his daughters. In an article in the *Journal of the Gypsy Lore Society* (1-2, 1959) Tatomir Vukanovic described the typical course of a vampire exorcism by such a dhampir at that time. The dhampir would arrive at the village to which he had been called and after solemnly sniffing the air and declaring that it smelled bad, he faced the four corners of the compass in turn, as if gauging the direction the menace came from. After this he would proceed to the village square where a crowd would be gathered, keeping a safe distance from him because anyone splashed by the vampire blood he spilled was sure to go mad and die soon afterwards. As night fell, the dhampir would begin to whistle like a hunter and search around as if hunting in a fog for something hiding among the obstacles of the village square.

Then he might strip down to his underwear and, peering through the tube of a shirt sleeve, announce that he had spotted the vampire, which could have human form or equally that of an animal, bird or snake. Then when he finally came to grips with the phantom a furious battle followed, though the spectators only saw half of it – the dhampir wrestling for his life with an invisible demon. Finally, if he succeeded in slaying the monster, the dhampir gave out a final long whistle and proclaimed his victory. A terrific stench then filled the air and a pool of blood would form at the spot where the vampire had died. This had to be immediately washed away with water.

Sometimes it took several nights of battle to slay a vampire, and occasionally the dhampir had to admit defeat and settle for banishing the ghoul to another district.

* * *

Given the multitude of possible causes of vampirism traditionally believed in by Orthodox Christians, concern for the welfare of their relations did not end with death. It was believed possible to judge the afterlife fortunes of the deceased by the condition of their corpses. Detailed lists of the signs to watch for were published by the Church, which resulted in the regular practice in Greece and Bulgaria of digging up the dead after one, two or three years to see if they had gone to heaven or hell. And indeed to check that they had not become vampires.

The fifteenth century Sultan of Turkey, Mohammed (or Mehmet) II, arch-foe of the original Vlad Dracula, was intrigued by this supposed power of excommunication amongst his Christian subjects. Summoning Maximus, the Orthodox Patriarch of Istanbul, the Sultan demanded a demonstration. A search was made for the grave of a woman famously excommunicated for promiscuity. The body was dug up and, no doubt to Maximus's great relief, found to be in the predicted condition – dark-skinned and swollen as a drum (the Greek word for vampires – vrykolakas – apparently means 'drum-like', it was borrowed from the Greeks' Slavic neighbours), but with no other sign of decomposition. Then came the real test. The coffin was carried to the palace and sealed under the Sultan's gaze. Then it was taken to church and a service of absolution performed over it by the Patriarch, witnessed by a number of trusted courtiers (though not the Sultan himself, who presumably did not wish to compromise his Islamic faith). The story goes that halfway through the service there came a rattle of bones from the coffin, and when it was opened the body was found to have been duly reduced to dust.

This is just one of the most famous cases, but countless similar tales from ancient to almost modern times from the region, sworn to by the most exalted witnesses, testify to people's fervent belief in the phenomenon of the dead turning into vampires. From this distance in time it is easy to dismiss most of them as fanciful church propaganda, but the evidence of vampiric activity in Eastern Europe from Dom Calmet and others is often hard to dismiss completely.

MONTAGUE SUMMERS

Anyone curious about the legendary background of vampires is soon bound to stumble across Montague Summers. His writing on the subject in the 1920s established him as the foremost authority of the time and, as it happens, ever since. *The Vampire: His Kith and Kin* (1928) and *The Vampire in Europe* (1929) investigated the subject and all its ramifications in almost microscopic detail, presenting a record of folk beliefs about death and vampires from around the world that is unlikely to be equalled for sheer scope and obsessive depth.

Even Summers' greatest fans, however, admit that his style is often dense and bewildering. His habit of piling up examples of any passing point often obscures the drift of his argument, however fascinating the obscure examples and anecdotes are in themselves. Summers was a clear writer on other themes and a very effective editor of other people's work, but when it came to vampires he tended just to follow the prompting of his own boundless curiosity. In tackling his books it also helps to be multilingual. Often for pages on end it is not at all clear what tongue the book is supposed to be written in, and for the more risqué passages a more than working knowledge of French is vital.

Although he was writing in the twentieth century, Summers's outlook belonged to a much earlier age, something which astonished and even shocked many reviewers at the time. In everyday life he felt himself to be a refugee from the eighteenth century but many of his views would have seemed antiquated even then. Like some medieval scholar he believed that in chronicling vampires he was studying a terrifying reality, not just some fiction or quaint superstition belonging to exotic and distant cultures.

To the sceptic he may seem over-trusting of his sources, particularly ecclesiastical ones. If a Church dignitary speaks of vampires and quotes witnesses he believes reliable, Summers appears to take the testimony at face value. But this is no great handicap.

He may have lacked the detachment expected of modern scholars, but he is meticulous in naming his sources and he succeeds in conveying powerfully what it feels like to believe in such things as vampires, as most people have throughout history. And still do in many parts of the world, as shown by the bizarre modern outbreaks of vampire hysteria.

Alphonsus Joseph-Mary Augustus Montague Summers (1880-1948) was a fascinating character in himself. Throughout his life he was described by acquaintances as kind, courteous, generous and outrageously witty; but those who knew him well sensed an underlying discomfort and mystery. In appearance he was plump, round cheeked and generally smiling. His dress resembled that of an eighteenth century cleric, with a few added flourishes such as a silver-topped cane depicting Leda being ravished by Zeus in the form of a swan. He wore sweeping black capes crowned by a curious hairstyle of his own devising which led many to assume he wore a wig. His voice was high pitched, comical and often in complete contrast to the macabre tales he was in the habit of spouting. Throughout his life he astonished people with his knowledge of esoteric and unsettling occult lore. Many people later described

Montague Summers

him as the most extraordinary person they had known in their lives.

Despite his cherubic demeanour and affability some people found him sinister, a view he delighted in encouraging. On one occasion in Oxford a Jesuit sprinkled him with holy water, looking for a negative reaction. The only one he did get was Summers's amused comment: 'If you had sprinkled me on consecrated ground I should have spun.'

It was always hard to tell how much Summers was putting on a show when in company, particularly in his early life, but he does appear to have been driven by demons, not least of them being those arising from having homosexual tendencies in an intolerant age. And although in everyday life he was kind and considerate, when engaged in academic debate he was furiously intolerant. There were also rumours that in his youth Summers had dabbled in black magic. If true, the only effect seems to have been to turn him completely against such meddling later. He may have been fascinated, even obsessed by witches, vampires, werewolves and the like but the tone of his writings is consistently hostile towards them.

Montague Summers grew up in a wealthy family living at Tellisford House on Clifton Down, near Bristol. Religion always played a large part in his life and his interest in the supernatural was probably encouraged by several unusual experiences he had there, as told in his autobiography *The Galanty Show* ('galanty' meaning a shadow-play). One occurred while he was home at Easter while an undergraduate at Oxford. One midnight he was on his way upstairs when he saw a woman in a Paisley shawl and wearing a Quaker style bonnet hurrying along a gallery. She disappeared into a bathroom at the end of a corridor and, thinking her a servant sneaking out to meet her lover, Summers gave chase. Throwing open the bathroom door, he found the place empty and the only window barred. His mother, who had seen the ghost several times, said it was the shade of an eccentric old lady who had lived at Tellisford House fifty years earlier. On another occasion a family friend from Bath entered the room and then suddenly left, as if having forgotten something, closing the door behind her. A search of the house showed no sign of the visitor but the next day a note arrived informing the family of Miss Teviot's death. Of such incidents Summers commented: 'We get little glimpses through a chink, as it were, of the spiritual world, and it is pure egotism to assume or argue that they are designed for our information. They may very well have to do with affairs and business of which we know nothing at all.'

Summers was raised as an evangelical Anglican but his love of ceremonial and sacraments drew him to the High Church. After graduating in Theology at Oxford he took the first steps towards holy orders at Lichfield Theological College and entered his apprenticeship as a curate in the diocese of Bitton near Bristol. This ended in a cloud of unproven scandal involving choirboys that was to dog him for the rest of his life. A year or so later he converted to Catholicism and by 1913 was claiming to have been ordained a Catholic priest, adopting the title of Reverend. There was doubt about the legitimacy of his orders though. He was in the habit of celebrating the Mass publicly when travelling abroad, so must have been able to produce some kind of evidence, but at home in England he only performed the sacraments in private. The truth is probably that he was ordained technically, possibly in Italy but outside the regular procedures of the Church. He therefore appeared on no clergy list in Britain, was under the authority of no bishop and therefore could not practise publicly without first submitting to such authority.

None of his close friends doubted the sincerity of his religious faith, however, no matter how blasphemous his conversation often seemed. Dame Sybil Thorndike wrote of him: 'I think that because of his profound belief in the tenets of orthodox Catholic Christianity he was able to be in a way almost frivolous in his approach to certain macabre heterodoxies. His humour, his "wicked humour" as some people called it, was most refreshing, so different from the tiresome sentimentalism of so many convinced believers.'

For a living, Summers was able to draw on a modest legacy from his father, supplemented by spells of teaching at various schools, including Hertford Grammar, the Central School of Arts and Crafts in Holborn, and Brockley School in south London where he was senior English and Classics Master. He described teaching as: 'One of the most difficult and depressing of trades, and so in some measure it must have been even well-nigh three hundred years ago when boys were not nearly so stupid as they are today.' In practice though, he was both entertaining and effective as a teacher once he had overcome initial problems with discipline, and was popular with both pupils and colleagues despite making it plain his real interests lay elsewhere.

From 1926, when he was in his mid-forties, Summers's writing and editing earned him the freedom to pursue full time his many enthusiasms and love of travel, particularly in Italy. The bulk of his activity then was related to English Restoration drama of the seventeenth century. Beginning in 1914 with the Shakespeare Head Press, Summers edited a large number of Restoration plays for various publishers, accompanied by lengthy critical introductions which were highly praised in their own right, and did much to rescue that period of literature from oblivion.

Not content with editing and introducing these plays, Summers helped in 1919 to found the Phoenix Society whose aim was to present them on stage in London. The venture was an immediate success and Summers threw himself wholeheartedly and popularly into all aspects of the productions, which were staged at various theatres. This brought him a measure of fame in London society and invitations to the most select salons, which he dazzled with his wit and erudition. By 1926 he was recognized as the greatest living authority on Restoration drama. Some ten years later he crystallised his knowledge in *The Restoration Theatre* and *The Playhouse of Pepys* which examined almost every possible aspect of the London stage between 1660 and 1710.

Summers's twin involvement with the theatre and vampires presents a curious parallel with his near contemporary Bram Stoker. There is even a suggestion of some jealousy in the grudging praise Summers gives Bram Stoker's *Dracula* at the end of *The Vampire: His Kith and Kin,* leading to his conclusion that the novel's success owed more to Stoker's choice of subject than his skill as an author. He reached the same conclusion about Hamilton Deane's stage production and one can't help suspecting Summers felt that if only he had been born some twenty years earlier he might have written the definitive vampire novel himself, only better.

Summers's fame as an expert on the occult began in 1926 with the publication of his *History of Demonology and Witchcraft* followed by other studies of witches, vampires and werewolves. As an editor he also introduced to the public, along with many other works, a reprint of *The Discovery of Witches* by the infamous witchfinder Matthew Hopkins and the first English translation of the classic fifteenth century treatise on witchcraft,

Malleus Maleficarum. In later life he also wrote influential studies of the Gothic novel, another lifelong enthusiasm; notably *The Gothic Quest, a History of the Gothic Novel* (Fortune Press 1938) and *A Gothic Bibliography* (Fortune Press 1940).

In his introduction to Horace Walpole's *The Castle of Otranto* Summers articulated the appeal of Gothic novels, and perhaps also the appeal of all the dark mysteries which fascinated him: 'There is in the Romantic revival a certain disquietude and a certain aspiration. It is this disquietude with earth and aspiration for heaven which inform the greatest Romance of all, Mysticism, the Romance of the Saints. The Classical writer set down fixed rules and precisely determined his boundaries. The Romantic spirit reaches out beyond these with an indefinite but very real longing to new and dimly guessed spheres of beauty. The Romantic writer fell in love with the Middle Ages, the vague years of long ago, the days of chivalry and strange adventure. He imagined and elaborated a medievalism for himself, he created a fresh world, a world which never was and never could have been, a domain which fancy built and fancy ruled. And in this land there will be mystery, because where there is mystery beauty may always lie hid. There will be wonder, because wonder always lurks where there is the unknown. And it is this longing for beauty intermingling with wonder and mystery that will express itself, perhaps exquisitely and passionately in the twilight moods of the romantic poets, perhaps a little crudely and even a little vulgarly in tales of horror and blood.'

After his death at 4 Dynevor Road in Richmond, Surrey, his companion Hector Stuart-Forbes experienced poltergeist activity there and following occupants of the house found the atmosphere so oppressive that they had the place exorcised; after which one hopes that Summers's restless spirit found peace. The memorial stone over his Richmond tomb reads 'Tell me strange things', a phrase with which he often opened conversations.

British Vampires

Some of the eastern ideas about the afterlife surfaced in western Christianity, though in diluted forms. Montague Summers unearthed many colourful and stoutly sworn cases of excommunicates, murderers and suicides in Western Europe being unable to rest in their graves. In Britain, for example, fear of suicides meant that until 1824 they were required by law to be buried at a crossroads with a stake through the heart to stop them troubling the living. (This was a double insurance; they were buried at crossroads so there was only a one in four chance of them finding their way home if the stake did not work.) Similar practices regarding suicides have prevailed in many, if not most, other parts of the world, along with other elaborate rituals to prevent the restless dead from troubling the living. In most cases they were aimed at disabling the malevolent ghost of the deceased, but suicide is commonly listed as one cause of the more physical vampire.

In Scotland it was long believed that people who died prematurely remained incorrupt in the grave until the moment they should have died. As in Eastern Europe, cats and other animals were banned from proximity to corpses in Scotland, for fear of them stirring up the spirit of the dead person, a custom that continued in some areas long after this reason seems to have been forgotten.

There are some traces of vampires as we usually think of them in the folklore of the British Isles and suggestions of a once widespread belief, but for some reason this seems to have largely died out in the twelfth century. With suicides it was their restless and hungry spirits people feared more than them rising bodily from the grave. But back in the Middle Ages people did fear unnatural bodily resurrection and the plagues that seemed to follow.

Walter Map, who lived from the mid twelfth to early thirteenth centuries, was one of several chroniclers who recorded strange instances of 'revenants', of the dead rising physically from their graves to attack the living. Only tentative explanations for these events are offered. The incidents are simply presented as strange but true occurrences, Walter Map commenting about one of them:

'We know about the true circumstances of this event, but we do not know the cause.' In his one surviving book, *De Nugis Curialum* (*Trifles of Courtiers* bk.ii: 23) he tells of a complaint made by a knight, William Laudun, to his bishop:

'Lord, I take refuge with you seeking advice. A certain evil Welshman quite recently died irreligiously in my village, and immediately after four nights he took to walking back to the village each night, and will not stop calling out by name each of his neighbours. As soon as they are called they take ill, and within three days they die, so that already very few are left.'

The bishop suggested that Laudun should open the tomb and sprinkle the Welshman's corpse liberally with holy water, which was done but it made no difference, the nightly

THE ALNWICK MONSTER

A typical medieval account of the restless dead is presented as plain fact by William of Newbury in his chronicle for 1196 (*Historia Rerum Anglicarum* v.23-4). Because of the colourful language it seems worth quoting directly.

'A certain man of depraved and dishonest life, either through fear of the law or else shunning the vengeance of his enemies, left the county of Yorkshire and betook himself to Alnwick Castle, whose lord he had long known, and settled down there. Here he busied himself in lewd traffic, and he seemed rather to persevere in his wickedness than to endeavour to correct his ways. He married a wife and this soothly proved his bane, as afterwards was clearly shown. For on a day when wanton stories were whispered in his ear concerning his spouse, he was fired with a raging jealousy.

'Restless and full of anxiety to know whether the charges were true, he pretended that he was going on a long journey and would not return for several days. He stole back, however, that very evening and was secretly admitted to his wife's bedchamber by a serving wench who was privy to his design. Here he crept quietly up and lay at length upon the roof-trig which ran just over the bed, so he might see with his own eyes if she violated her nuptial faith.

'Now when he espied there beneath him his wife being well served by a lusty youth, a near neighbour, in his bitter wrath he clean forgot his perilous position and in a trice he had tumbled down, falling heavily to the ground just at the side of the bed where the twain were clipping at clicket. The young cuckold-maker beat a hasty retreat; but his wife hastened to raise him gently from the floor.'

Harsh words followed but before the husband could carry out any of his threats he died of his injuries. Despite being so full of unconfessed sin he was given a Christian burial, but was soon seen during the hours of night: 'to come forth from his tomb and wander about all through the streets, prowling round the houses whilst on every side the dogs were howling and yelping the whole night long. Throughout the whole district then every man locked and barred his door, nor did anyone between the hours of dusk and dawn dare go out on any business whatsoever. Yet even these precautions were of no avail, for the air became foul and tainted as this fetid and corrupting body wandered abroad, so that a terrible plague broke out and there was hardly a house that did not mourn its dead.

'The parish priest, the good man from whose mouth I learned this story, was grieved to the heart at this trouble which had fallen upon his flock. Accordingly upon Palm Sunday he called together a number of wise and devout men who might advise him what was the best course to take.'

While they were gathered over a meal two young men who had lost their father to the plague and were afraid for their own lives decided to take matters into their own hands: 'They armed themselves, therefore, with sharp spades and, betaking themselves to the cemetery, they began to dig. And whilst they yet thought they would have to dig much deeper, suddenly they came upon the body covered with but a thin layer of earth. It was gorged and swollen with a frightful corpulence. Its face was florrid and chubby, with huge red puffed cheeks, and the shroud in which he had been wrapped was all soiled and torn. But the young men, who were mad with grief and anger, were not in any way frightened. They at once dealt the corpse a sharp blow with the keen edge of a spade and immediately there gushed out such a stream of warm red gore that they realized this sanguisuga [vampire] had battened in the blood of many poor folk.

'Accordingly they dragged it outside the town and here they quickly built a large pyre. When this was in a blaze, they went to the priest's house and informed the assembled company what they had done. There was not a man of these who did not hasten to the spot and who was not a witness, if future testimony were required, of what had taken place. Now, no sooner had that infernal monster been thus destroyed than the plague entirely ceased, just as if the polluted air was cleansed by the fire which burned up the hellish brute who had infected the whole atmosphere.'

attacks continuing as before. This apparently proved to the Church authorities that it was not the work of a demon reanimating the dead body, but that the corpse was somehow self-driven. Laudun finally solved the problem in true knightly fashion by apparently chasing the monster back to its grave and splitting open its head down to the neck, after which it caused no more trouble. Another of Map's tales tells of another 'irreligious' man whose dead body roamed the countryside for a month till it was cornered by a crowd at the edge of their town and given a proper burial with a cross to mark the grave, after which it lay quiet.

Another chronicler, William of Newbury (or Newburgh) writing in 1196 tells several such tales in *Historia Rerum Anglicarum* (*History of the English Church*) commenting: 'Such things often happened in England' although it 'would not easily be accepted as true if there were not so many examples at hand from our own time, and if the testimony were not so abundant . . . If I wanted to write about every incident of this sort . . . it would be too complicated and onerous.' He was puzzled, though, that earlier chronicles made no mention of the phenomenon.

One incident took place in Buckingham where a 'sinful' man came back from the grave and crawled into the bed of his terrified wife, almost crushing her and lashing out furiously at the other family members who came to her rescue. They and their neighbours asked permission of their bishop to dig up and cremate the sinner's body, but the bishop proposed that they just lay a letter of absolution for the man's sins on his tomb and this rather amazingly seems to have done the trick. In another famous case in Berwick-on-Tweed a lively corpse terrified the town and set the dogs howling by prowling the streets at night until some brave local youths dug up his body, broke it up and cremated it. In yet another case the hunting, wenching chaplain of a parish near Melrose Abbey came back from the grave to pester his former mistress. She called in some young men who lay in wait near the graveyard and despatched the revenant when it returned towards dawn. Then when they later opened the grave they found the fresh-looking corpse bearing the axe wound, so they cremated it as well to be on the safe side.

* * *

A notable feature of Walter Map and William of Newbury's stories is that, as with Russian and Greek vampires, the English revenants seem to leave the grave in a tangible, physical form while their actual corpses remain buried, unless this is some kind of Chinese Whispers confusion arising from the retelling of the tales. M.R. James though, ghost storyteller and tireless investigator of the supernatural, collected very similar tales from Yorkshire dating from two centuries later around 1400. In

Twelve Medieval Ghost-Stories published in the English Historical Review vol. xxxvii in 1922 he tells several tales (translated from Latin) in which the revenant clearly has a tangible form. In one, a woman bizarrely tries to carry the thing home (perhaps she thinks it is her husband or lover risen from the dead) but according to witnesses her hands sank deeply into its flesh 'as if the flesh of the spirit were putrid and not solid, but illusory'.

While cremation or being cast adrift in water remain the trusted remedies for this phenomenon in James's stories, in one tale simple forgiveness of sins again proves up to the task: 'Concerning the spirit of Robert, the son of Robert de Boltebo of Killebourne, who was caught in the cemetery. The younger Robert died and was buried in the cemetery, but he used to go out from his grave at night and terrify and disturb the townspeople, and the dogs of the town used to follow him and howl mightily. Finally, some young men . . . decided to catch him somehow if they could, and they met at the cemetery. But when he appeared, they all fled except two, one of whom was named Robert Foxton. He seized him as he was going out from the cemetery and put him on the church-stile, while the other shouted bravely, "Hold him fast until I can get there!" But the other one answered, "Go quickly to the parish priest so that he can be conjured!" . . . The parish priest came quickly and conjured him in the name of the Holy Trinity . . . Having been conjured in this way, he answered from the depths of his entrails; not with his tongue but as if from an empty jar, and he confessed various trespasses.'

MASTCATIONE MORTUORUM (THE CHEWING DEAD)

From this distance in time it is impossible to judge the truth behind such strange tales, which are presented as facts rather than legends, but whose evidence would probably not stand up in a court of law today; but similar stories right across Europe testify to, at the least, a very real fear of the dead rising in a physical way from their graves. Practical explanations are not hard to find, as we considered earlier. In times of recurring plague especially, it is quite likely that many people were buried over-hastily and quite a few probably did struggle from the grave and wander home in a confused rage, giving rise to stories that mingled fact with superstition and fed the notion of the wicked or unfortunate being able to rise from the grave to molest the living.

Then in the build-up to the eighteenth century vampire 'epidemics' of Eastern Europe there was another related phenomenon which helped prepare the ground for the hysteria. All over Europe cases were reported of noises from the coffins of the dead; and when these were opened the bodies were disturbed and seemed to have been eating their own shrouds; or, if it was a shared grave, the shrouds and even the bodies of their neighbours.

One of the studies that helped fuel the rumours of this strange activity is the *Dissertatio Historico-Philosophica de Masticatione Mortuorum* (to give it its shortened title) by Philip Rohr, published in 1679. It is far from being the only such investigation and it quotes many other similar tracts from scholars wrestling with the same questions, but it has become the most famous and gives a good taste of the mood of the times.

Rohr opens his dissertation by declaring his intent: 'Those who have written of the history of funeral rites and of the mysteries of death have not neglected to place on record that there have been found from time to time bodies who appear to have devoured the grave clothes in which they were wound, their cerements, and while doing so have uttered a grunting noise like the sound of porkers chawing and rooting with their groyns. Now different writers have pronounced very different opinions upon this matter, and some learned men have ascribed this phenomenon to natural causes which are not clearly known to us; whilst others have only been able to explain it by assuming that there are certain animals which glut their hunger for human flesh by feeding upon corpses, but what animals these may be they do not tell; and others again have advanced yet other opinions. This phenomenon then seemed to us to be a fit subject which might

The Premature Burial 1864 Antoine Wiertz

be treated in a public and formal disputation . . . in order that we might arrive at the best explanation of this matter and to some extent at any rate elucidate it.'

As with Dom Augustin Calmet's later and similar investigation into vampirism, Rohr's aim seems to have been the admirable one of simply investigating the subject with the best academic means at his disposal to find a rational explanation of the phenomenon, and even to determine if it actually existed – to cool the fevered speculation with some rational debate in fact, but the effect of his treatise seems to have been almost the reverse because it lent weight and respectability to the subject besides apparently confirming it as a real phenomenon.

He begins with a historical survey of cases in which the apparent dead have returned to life, quoting famous examples from the Bible and classical antiquity. Moving on to more recent times, he mentions in passing the great philosopher John Duns Scotus who, on good authority, was prematurely buried after his sudden 'death' and showed signs of having revived in the tomb. Then at some length he quotes a story told by one of his own main sources, Henricus Kornmann (*De Miraculis Mortuorum*, 1610). While visiting the Church of the Holy Apostles in Cologne, Kornmann had noticed an unusual picture. On making enquiries he was told the tale it commemorated. In 1357 a certain wealthy lady in the town named Richemodia had died of the plague. Her husband loved her so much he insisted she be buried with her valuable wedding ring, which proved too much temptation for the sexton. Late that night he returned with a servant. They opened the vault and coffin, but just as they were pulling off the ring Richemodia sat up. The two thieves fled in terror, leaving their lantern behind, by whose light she found her way home to the happy astonishment of her husband and mourning friends.

There are countless similar famous and dramatic tales of course, so moving on from cases of misdiagnosis of death, Rohr then considers supernatural re-animation. It being an article of faith at the time that only God could truly bring the dead back to life, the only possible conclusion when bodies seemed to rise from the grave to no good purpose (or grunt, shuffle and chew their shrouds), was that Satan or some other demon had taken possession of them 'and just as a pilot will move a vessel so will he move them, and he will compel these dead bodies exactly to imitate the actions and gestures of living men.'

Using the term manducation (a now rarely used term for chewing) to describe what the dead do as opposed to the normal mastication of the living (which is for the purpose of nourishment, obviously impossible and unnecessary for a dead body) he then quotes a range of well documented cases of corpses having been found to have consumed their winding sheets, their own flesh or that of neighbours in the tomb, noting that such behaviour was most common in times of plague, before ending with an example very close to home. Just a few years before he was writing, a good and trustworthy friend of the author had been witness in 1672 to the exhuming of a body by villagers just three miles away from where he was writing, of a body which was found to have mostly consumed its own limbs.

Having established to his own satisfaction the reality of the phenomenon, Rohr moves on to a philosophical and theological discussion in which he ends up blaming demons for the re-animation. This, he argued, usually had nothing at all to do with the departed soul of the corpse's former tenant, or their virtues or vices; but to what purpose would a demon choose to re-animate a dead body to the limited extent of the Chewing Dead? Well, since the principal aim of demons is simply to stir up mischief and grief for the human race, Rohr argued, that is their aim here too. Lacking physical bodies of their own, demons need something to work with and dead bodies are more biddable, if less active, than most living ones. The aims could be various. Sometimes corpses might be stirred simply to blacken the character of the dead person, since it was commonly held (and still is as a figure of speech) that the wicked or unhappy dead are unable to rest peacefully in the grave. This would distress their relations especially if, as often happened, the body was exhumed, dismembered and cremated. It could also cause strife between villagers in favour of and against such a course. Most dangerously, especially in times of plague, exhuming an infected corpse could actively spread the plague to those involved in the dismemberment – hence another apparent link between plague and the restless dead – it was not just that plague led to over-hasty burials, but measures taken to make sure the dead stayed dead helped spread the plague.

This was at least a reasoned step beyond the purely superstitious link between the two – away from the idea that the Chewing Dead helped spread plague in some magical way and hence needed to be shut up – but Rohr then reverts to the spirit of his age and concludes that the best way of guarding against all perils associated with the chewing dead are those that apply to guarding against demons generally – i.e. virtue, prayer and a strict adherence to the teachings and practices of the Church. Montague Summers, who translated this tract complete for *The Vampire in Europe* in 1929, added a whole string of further precautions of the same kind, such as regular or even daily attendance at Mass, reciting the Rosary and other prayers to the Virgin Mary, the wearing of holy relics and medals, and mortifications such as the wearing of a cilice, a spiked belt or chain worn around the thigh to cause discomfort and even pain. This has recently become rather famous through its apparent popularity with the shadowy Catholic Opus Dei organisation.

With hindsight much of the phenomenon of the Chewing Dead can be explained in a rational way without resort to demons. Noises in the coffin and grave are often caused by the gases produced by decomposition which, without going into too graphic detail, might well sound like the grunting of pigs and might also disturb the body enough so as to make it seem, upon opening the grave that it has moved of its own volition. There is also the famous rumour of Henry VIII having exploded in his coffin. Although for obvious reasons this is not one of the most publicised aspects of his story, and is probably untrue, it is quite possible that his coffin exploded in slow motion due to the pressure of gases from his decomposing bulk. However there remains the odd and seemingly well-attested oddity of the dead seeming to have eaten their shrouds. Even those unfortunate enough to find themselves buried alive are unlikely to have time to do this upon waking in the coffin because they would soon die from lack of oxygen; and besides they would probably in that brief period between waking and suffocating have other priorities than hunger on their minds . . .

PREMATURE BURIAL

Determining the point of death has never been easy and in the past many ingenious methods were employed to make sure of death before consigning a person to the grave. Common tests still in use by qualified doctors in the nineteenth century include lighting a feather and blowing smoke in the nostrils, smearing cow dung on the upper lip, pouring vinegar, urine or pepper into the corpse's mouth, inserting pins under the finger- and toenails or tweaking sensitive areas of the body with tongs.

The wiser physicians of the past reached the conclusion that the only sure proof of death is the onset of decomposition, for which reason burial was often delayed until this clearly happened. One influential proponent of this was the great Parisian anatomist Jacques-Bénigne Winslow who in 1742 published *The Uncertainty of the Signs of Death* motivated by having himself apparently been mistakenly laid in his coffin twice. He also made the point with many other well-proven examples of premature burial. One of these was the case of two young Parisian lovers. The girl's father refused permission for them to marry, insisting she marry someone else. Upon which the girl sank into gloom and despair, then finally into a coma so deep she was pronounced dead and buried. Luckily her lover refused to accept this and, believing her still to be alive, he unearthed her coffin and she did indeed wake up in his arms. Also in 1742, Jean Bruhier-d'Ablaincourt, a prominent Parisian doctor, estimated that seventy-two people had been mistakenly declared dead in that year.

Unease in France about premature burial was further stirred in 1785 by the emptying of Parisian cemeteries like Les Innocents, which were blamed for spreading disease through the city. In the course of this so many corpses were found face down in their coffins, or with other signs of disturbance, that panic over premature burial spread through the population and abroad.

When George Washington died in 1799 he is said to have asked his family to delay burial for three days to make sure of it. Despite advances in medical science, fear of premature burial rose to a peak in nineteenth century Europe and America, helped by the patchy skills of the medical profession and easily spread news of cases happening all the time. For instance the *Annual Register* for 1809 reported the case of a woman called Prosser who after a long illness finally seemed to die. The body was laid out by a professional woman who, on returning about six hours later, noticed that the hands had changed position. Then when she tried to close the mouth she was startled into a fit by the supposed corpse saying: 'Do not close my mouth, for I am not quite dead.' Prosser later recovered enough to talk about her experience, during which she had been able to hear all the arrangements being made for her funeral, but was too weak to speak out or move.

When the Duke of Wellington died in 1852 his body was not buried for two months as a precaution and many other notable figures made similar provisions in their wills during the nineteenth century. Francis Douce, Keeper of Manuscripts at the British Museum, and author Harriet Martineau both requested post-mortem decapitation, or at least the severing of a jugular vein. Others like William Shakwell, a city official in Plymouth, Devon, requested the amputation of fingers or toes. Meanwhile in Germany reforms introduced by the great medical doctor Christoph Hufeland led to the widespread popularity of 'waiting mortuaries' where bodies were exposed in supervised cells, often with alarms attached in case they woke up, until they began to decay and were released for burial. By the end of the nineteenth century most German cities had at least one of these 'Temples of Rest' and Munich had ten.

On 5 January 1874 *The New York Times* looked into the subject in an article typical of those which fanned the flames of panic: 'A paragraph appeared in our impression of 1st January in reference to an extraordinary circumstance reported to have lately occurred in Missouri, where a child was rescued from being buried alive when actually in its coffin and on the way to the cemetery. Just a year ago a dreadful discovery reported in the Ottowa *Citizen*, drew attention anew to this subject. For some time the work of removing bodies from an old to a new Roman Catholic cemetery had been in progress. In the course of the process the lid of a coffin came off. It proved to be that of an uncle of the gentleman who was superintending the removal and the contents presented a terrible spectacle. "The miserable occupant had evidently lived in it. His face was contorted into an agonized expression; the arms were drawn up as far as the coffin would admit, and the head twisted round to the shoulders, which had apparently been gnawed by the wretched man himself." This apprehension of being buried alive has been the bugbear of many eminent men. Prescott, the historian, left instructions, which were carefully carried out, that his jugular vein should be severed, and, on the occasion of Lord Lytton's death we read in the London *Times* about that date: "The coffin has been made, but the body was not placed in it in consequence of a curious injunction contained in a paper which, on his lordship's death, came into the hands of his legal representatives. According to this, he stipulates that after death, or presumed death, his body shall be allowed to remain three days on the bed, where he may be untouched; after which medical men are to examine him to ascertain that he is really dead, and to certify accordingly." This subject has excited so much attention on the Continent as almost to produce a literature of its own.'

The *British Medical Journal* in 1877 added: 'A correspondent at Naples states that the Appeals Court has had before it a case not likely to inspire confidence in the minds of those who look forward with horror to the possibility of being buried alive. It appeared from the evidence that some time ago, a woman was interred with all the usual formalities, it being believed that she was dead, while she was only in a trance. Some days afterwards, when the grave in which she had been placed was opened for the reception of another body, it was found that the clothes which covered the unfortunate woman were torn to pieces, and that she had even broken her limbs in attempting to extricate herself from the living tomb. The Court, after hearing the case, sentenced the doctor who had signed the certificate of decease, and the Major who had authorized the interment each to three month's imprisonment for involuntary manslaughter.'

Such fears towards the end of the century were not helped by studies such as *Premature Burial* by Dr Franz Hartmann (1895), which gathered details of more than 700 known cases where this had almost or actually happened. One of his examples was of the famous French tragedienne, Mlle. Rachel, who on 3 January 1858 appeared to die near Cannes, but who suddenly revived during the embalming process. Unfortunately it had gone too far and she died of poisoning ten hours later. In a similar vein was *Death and Sudden Death* in 1902 by Paul Brouardel, a French pathologist and professor of forensics at the University of Paris. In it Brouardel suggested that the chances of a person being accidentally buried alive were very slim, provided a thorough examination had been performed by a qualified medical practitioner, but he did admit and give examples of occasions when even experts had got it wrong. One of these was the case of the Doctors Clarke, Ellis and Shaw who witnessed the hanging of a young man in 1858. The prisoner dropped seven or eight feet and after about fourteen minutes was pronounced dead by the three doctors. However, an hour and a half later they noticed a steady pulse of eighty beats per minute. The doctors then opened the man's chest to 'observe the heart directly' and timed its contractions at forty beats per minute. This went on until five hours after the hanging the heart finally stopped.

Adding to the general worry was *Premature Burial and How It May Be Prevented* by William Tebb (1905) which collected, from recent medical records alone, 219 cases of

Illustration for Edgar Allan Poe's story *The Premature Burial*
by Harry Clarke (1889-1931), published in 1919.

narrow escapes from premature burial, 149 where unfortunates seemed to have woken in the grave, ten instances of dissection while still alive, three cases of a narrow escape from this and two cases of people reviving whilst being embalmed. Regarding the danger of hasty burial during times of plague, Tebb quotes the tale of a solicitor living in Gloucester. He reported that many years before, his office caretaker had been an old woman who, with her husband, had been in charge of the Cholera wards during the epidemic of 1749 which had killed 119 people in Gloucester alone. She had told the young solicitor that when patients died, they were put in their coffins as soon as possible to ease crowding in the wards. 'Sometimes' she had said, 'they did come to afterwards, and we did hear them kicking in their coffins, but we never unscrewed them 'cause we knew they got to die.'

Medical science has come a long way in the last century but even now cases pop up regularly in the news of people waking in the mortuary or on the point of burial. Science has the means for testing thoroughly for lingering life, but they are not always applied when a death seems routine. It can easily be imagined then how troubled the Victorians became by the claustrophobic nightmare possibility of being buried alive. Edgar Allen Poe summed this fear up neatly in his 1844 short story *The Premature Burial*:

'To be buried while alive is, beyond question, the most terrific of these extremes which has ever fallen to the lot of mere mortality. That it has frequently, very frequently, so fallen will scarcely be denied by those who think. The boundaries which divide Life from Death are at best shadowy and vague. Who shall say where the one ends, and where the other begins? We know that there are diseases in which occur total cessations of all the apparent functions of vitality, and yet in which these cessations are merely suspensions, properly so called. They are only temporary pauses in the incomprehensible mechanism. A certain period elapses, and some unseen mysterious principle again sets in motion the magic pinions and the wizard wheels. The silver cord was not for ever loosed, nor the golden bowl irreparably broken. But where, meantime, was the soul?'

In the story Poe's narrator tells of his tendency to fall into cataleptic trances and consequent fear that if this happened among strangers they might bury him before learning the truth, a possibility he dwells upon in claustrophobic detail. As a result he avoids travel and has made other arrangements too, such as having his coffin and tomb designed to be opened from the inside, and having an alarm bell triggered by the slightest movement of the corpse.

All these precautions seem to have been in vain however when he surfaces into consciousness and finds himself seemingly trapped in his nightmare, in a bare, unyielding, coffin-like space with no means of escape or any alarm bell at hand . . .

The story has a surprising and rather unlikely optimistic ending but there was no such easy comfort for the many other Victorians who dreaded being buried alive. Instead many resorted to the practical precautions mentioned by Poe's narrator – ranging from simply being buried with a crowbar and shovel to quite elaborate alarm systems that could be triggered from within the coffin.

Dozens of such devices were patented but one of the first and most popular was the Bateson Revival Device invented in 1852 in Britain by George Bateson. This had an iron bell mounted on the coffin just above the deceased's head and activated by the slightest hand movement. It was advertised as: 'A most economical, ingenious, and trustworthy mechanism, superior to any other method, and promoting peace of mind amongst the bereaved in all stations of life. A device of proven efficacy, in countless instances in this country and abroad.' There is no record of it actually saving any lives but no doubt it calmed many fears and sold well enough to make Bateson rich. It failed to allay his own fears though – fears responsible for the invention in the first place. He remained so afraid of being buried alive that in 1886 he committed suicide by dousing himself in oil and setting himself alight.

Edgar Allan Poe's own death in October 1849 is somewhat shrouded in mystery. While in poor health he went missing on a trip to New York. He turned up in a derelict

state in Baltimore a few days later. He was disorientated, incoherent and not only had he apparently been drinking heavily – a recurring vice – but he was wearing the rags of someone else's clothing while somehow having managed to hold onto an elegant walking cane. A few days after that he died of disputed causes. His doctor friend Snodgrass, who was a temperance reformer, attributed it to alcohol poisoning, but others suggested pneumonia or simple exposure as a tramp to the winds and rain of Baltimore (one only hopes for Poe's sake that there was no doubt about the actuality of his death). For whatever reason, Poe was unconscious or delirious during his final days, believing his dead wife to be alive again and having conversations with people no-one else could see. He was buried in a pauper's grave because his friends were not given time enough to arrange a decent funeral. In 1875, after a collection by Baltimore schoolchildren, his remains were moved to a grander plot where he was reunited with his wife and beloved mother in law, whom he had called Muddy.

In 1949, the centenary of his death, a curious tradition began at the stone marking the original burial spot in the Westminster Hall and Burying Ground in Baltimore. Three roses and a half-drunk bottle of cognac were laid on the grave by a mystery visitor in the early hours of the morning, as has happened every year since. The significance of the items is unknown but reasonable speculation suggests the roses could represent the three persons buried below. As news of this unknown benefactor spread, Poe enthusiasts began lying in wait to see who the visitor might be. They were rewarded with glimpses of a caped, hatted and heavily scarfed individual carrying a silver-topped cane. He toasts the dead poet before leaving his gifts and melting into the shadows. Occasionally he leaves a note, such as the one in 1993 which said: 'The torch will be passed.' This was taken to suggest that the Poe Toaster, as he or she was nicknamed, was not after all immortal but preparing to hand over to a successor. In 1999 another note was left saying that the original Toaster had died the year before. This seems to have been borne out by a change in the Toaster's behaviour, more notes having been left with references to and comments on current affairs – although of course some other pranksters could be responsible for these. The identity of the Poe Toaster(s) remains a mystery, despite occasional attempts at unmasking. In 2007 almost sixty witnesses, including reporters, attended the ceremony, the most to date and from all over the world.

Poe's short story *The Premature Burial* was memorably (and very loosely) adapted for the cinema by Roger Corman in 1962 in a film of the same name starring Ray Milland.

PROPITIATING THE DEAD

One of the most terrifying things about vampires, in both fiction and folklore, is that their first victims are often those dearest to them in life. Also it is not just warlocks, suicides and evil people who became vampires after death. The virtuous may also become one either by being a vampire's victim, or through being possessed by an evil spirit able to make use of personality traces for its own ends. So any strong attachments, but particularly hate, bitterness or disappointment can be latched onto by the evil spirit, which has often been a great incentive for settling grievances with a dying person.

From the earliest times people have feared the dead, however much they may have loved them in life. For most of history people have gone to elaborate lengths to ensure that the dead rest peacefully in their graves. The more powerful the person in life, the more sumptuous the funeral and tomb; and the motive was never purely grief or the urge to celebrate a glorious life in the modern manner. Beneath lay the fear of that power turning to malice from beyond the grave. In less material ages than our own such malice was viewed with very real dread, leading to the ancestors often being paid more homage than even the gods who, being that much further removed from the mortal plane, were less likely to notice anyway.

Even in more deity-centred religions there is some, often a very large, recognition of the ability of the dead to influence the lives and fortunes of the living, even if only through intercession with higher powers. In the broad sweep of human history the idea that the dead simply blink out of existence is really quite an anomaly. It is not a peculiarly modern notion, because some ancient Greeks and others also held it, but it is almost certainly true that most humans who have ever existed have fervently believed the opposite; as do the majority alive on the planet today.

So elaborate funeral rites were often designed at least in part to prevent the spirit of the departed turning nasty, however benevolent they may have been in life. It goes beyond restless consciences and unburied hatchets. There is, or was, widespread fear that in the vulnerability of its newly disembodied state an evil spirit might possess the dead, if they were not sufficiently mourned by those left behind. In many cultures it is also common for mourners to spill their own blood on the grave as an offering to the departed, to sustain the spirit during its tricky transitional phase and pre-empt any vampiric urges which might prompt it to take such nourishment by force. With Australian aboriginals amongst many others it was once common for mourners to slash their faces and bodies to draw blood to feed and calm the newly deceased. More commonly, animal blood has been used to the same end, a beast being sacrificed for the funeral and its blood being poured onto the grave so that the dead could share the feast. On the island of Samos in Greece to this day it is a common custom to leave out a pitcher of water before going to bed at night, in the belief that if they fail to do this the house ghosts might strangle them in their sleep.

JG Frazer, whose *The Golden Bough* remains a classic of comparative mythology, also published in 1936 a three volume study called *The Fear of the Dead* in which he gathers hundreds of examples of   traditional rituals from around the world for pre-empting possible malice from the dead. Many are surprisingly consistent over wide geographical areas which in the past had little interaction. Such as, for example, among people dwelling in simple huts it is common for that of a dead person to be abandoned and left to fall into ruin, the dead person's family building a new one elsewhere. In Africa

and South America when a powerful king died it was common practice to abandon his entire village and build a new one elsewhere.

A less drastic measure for more substantial houses was making a hole in the wall for the removal of a corpse for burial, instead of simply carrying it out through the door. This was a common custom in Denmark until a little over a century ago, when the custom of using such 'corpse-doors' died out, but was still well remembered by older country folk. On many old Danish houses the outline of these 'doors' in the brickwork are still visible, often in the shape of a large keyhole. The assumption behind the practice is that spirits of the dead are able to retrace the path of their funerals but, being dim-witted in their freshly discorporate state, will be totally baffled if they find the way changed or blocked. Another cunning ruse is to bear the coffin out through the usual doorway, but then to block it off and open another one on the opposite side of the house before the mourners have returned from the funeral. Then the restless spirit will fail to recognise its own house and be forced to return to the graveyard.

Milder-still customs with similar intent that have survived to the present day include reluctance to speak ill of the dead and carrying a corpse out of the house feet first so it is facing away from its home and thus hopefully its soul will be less likely to remember the path home. Others were to fix charms (particularly of iron and often of garlic and hawthorn) around the threshold and doorway, scattering seeds in front of the threshold and along the way to the grave – identical to charms for keeping out vampires and other bogeys as it happens – or simply to replace the door with a new one to confuse the ghost.

* * *

Measures like the above were applied to all dead people because of the fear that any newly deceased person's soul or spirit might be hijacked by some passing demon and be turned against its nearest and dearest; but some kinds of death have almost universally been held to predispose its victim to malice towards the living, leading to additional precautions being taken. Possibly surprising to us now is that chief among these is a mother dying in childbirth, or soon after. The traditional explanation for this is was (and still is in places) that the mother's emotional bond with her baby is so strong that not even death can keep her away from it; and that grief and frustration will drive the ghost mad and liable to savage everyone close to her in life.

From the Pacific right through to Africa early travellers observed a popular ruse for placating the spirits of such unfortunate mothers, which was to bury them with their arms cradling the trunk of a banana tree, or a carved wooden doll, to convince the ghost that she and her child had not been separated.

Across India there is a widespread belief that mothers who die in childbirth or soon after will return as vengeful spirits to plague the living. The Indian ethnologist Sarat Chandra Roy in the late 1920s closely observed such fears and customs among the Oraon or Uraon people, a forest-dwelling people of central and eastern India and Bangladesh. There they called the ghost of a woman dying in or soon after childbirth a 'churil' or 'malech' which is said to carry a load of charcoal on its head, which it believes to be its baby. Any man who passes by its grave is liable to be attacked, being tickled mercilessly until he falls down senseless. He can escape this fate by calling out the ghost's name in life, or else by snatching its load of charcoal, either of which will render the spirit powerless. Its favourite victims though are drunken men wending their way home and too befuddled to notice or react to their peril. These often have to resort to a spirit-doctor to lift the churil's curse, which can lead to emaciation and even death.

To prevent such attacks, the feet of women dying in childbirth are broken and twisted backwards with long thorns inserted into the soles to discourage walking abroad. The unfortunate woman is also often buried face down in the grave so she cannot find her way out of it. A more brutal method of preventing the creation of a churil among neighbouring peoples is (or was) to drive nails into the corpse's head and eyes, though sometimes it is considered sufficient just to drive nails into the doorframe of their home.

Among the Kachin people of Burma (Myanmar) fear of women dying in childbirth is so great that traditionally her family would abandon the home. The eyes of the corpse would then be bound with her own hair to prevent her seeing anything, then the body would be wrapped in a mat and removed from the death chamber by way of a hole in the wall or floor and cremated far away from the village along with all her possessions, so that there is as little as possible to which the dead woman was attached to draw her back to the land of the living.

In Malaysia such ideas crystallised in the terrifying and bloodthirsty spectre of the penanggalaan, to which we'll return later.

* * *

Violent death of any kind is also widely believed to leave a spirit unable to rest in the grave and special precautions are often taken to encourage it to do so. The supposition is that being cut off in the midst of life, the ghost will seek to revenge itself on those who have caused this to happen, often threatening whole communities. Among the ancient Greeks it was recorded practice for anyone plagued and being driven to madness by the ghost of someone they have killed, to sacrifice a finger to it, which seems to have been enough to calm the vengeful spirits. The most famous example of this (in some versions of his tale) was Orestes. After killing his mother Clytemnestra in revenge for her murder of his father Agamemnon, Orestes was driven almost to insanity by the furies invoked by his mother despite having been commanded to do the deed by Apollo. So at a temple to the goddesses of madness – the maniae – on the road from Megalopolis to Messene, he bit off one of his own fingers and was duly cured.

Similar sacrifices of a finger by mourners or murderers have been recorded all over the world, as has the ancient Greek custom of expelling a murderer (even when the killing is justified) from the community for a time to allow the angry ghost to calm down and to perform cleansing rituals to pacify it. Among Guyanese Indians in South America there used to be a common belief that after a justified revenge killing, the murderer must drink some of his victim's blood to avoid being haunted by his ghost. This was usually done by digging up the grave on the third night and sucking the blood through a sharp-pointed straw.

Similar notions survive strongly today in many parts of the world and did not die out that long ago in places like Europe and America. In nineteenth century Scotland it was still widely believed that anyone who died prematurely through accident or murder was doomed to roam the earth as a ghost until their destined hour of death. Even in twentieth century Britain Air Chief Marshall Hugh Dowding, Commander of the RAF Fighter Command during the Battle of Britain claimed to be visited in dreams by the ghosts of his young pilots who had died in battle, saying that they found it hard to come to terms their condition. Admittedly though, this belief did not receive much sympathy from his peers and was among the factors that led to his removal from command even as the country was celebrating its victory in the Battle of Britain, over which Dowding had presided.

Relics of such beliefs still cling surprisingly to many people who are otherwise completely rational materialists who deny the reality of ghosts. Just ask any estate agent trying to sell a house where someone has recently been murdered or committed suicide.

* * *

Suicide has always aroused more fear than any other form of violent death. In almost every culture special measures have been taken for the disposal of a suicide's remains in order to protect the living. As mentioned earlier, the law in England requiring suicides (along with violent criminals) to be buried at a crossroads with a wooden stake through the heart was abolished by Act of Parliament on 4 July 1823. Opposition to it had been growing, along with increasing sympathy for suicides and this came to a head when King George IV's carriage was held up by a crowd of angry protestors at the burial of suicide

Abel Griffiths at the crossroads where Victoria Station now stands. This turned out to be the last such burial in London.

Twenty-two year old Abel was a law student who had killed himself in remorse after murdering his father. A professional friend had testified that he'd had a 'depression of the brain' and was of unsound mind (the only excuse in law for killing oneself without it being a criminal offence) but the jury found otherwise. Public feelings ran high against his crossroads burial and were seemingly shared by those who actually carried it out, because they dispensed with the usual rituals of coating the body in lime and impaling it with wooden stake and mallet. From 1823 suicides were for the first time allowed (though it did not always happen) to be buried in churchyards, though only between nine and midnight and without ceremony.

Excavations in Cambridgeshire have found evidence of criminal burial grounds at crossroads that had been in use from Anglo-Saxon times to the nineteenth century, most notably the one at Gallows Gate near Fowlmere, about ten miles south of Cambridge. Digging in the 1920s turned up about sixty skeletons in shallow, haphazard graves, many decapitated or with extended necks that suggest hanging. Also on the Cambridgeshire – Suffolk border there is a crossing on the Icknield Way near Euston called the Boy's Grave. This is supposed to be the tomb of a young shepherd who hanged himself because he thought he had lost one of his sheep. It turned out that he hadn't and sympathisers have been tending the grave ever since. He was still left buried at the crossroads though.

A similar sad tale is attached to Dead Maid's Cross at Thoulstone, Wiltshire, on the A36 between Bath and Warminster. The story goes that long ago there was a farmer's daughter living nearby who had two lovers. When they learned about each other they decided to settle the matter by a duel in Prickett's Wood. During the course of this, one of them killed the other. Then he was promptly killed by his rival's black dog. And then, when the girl heard that both her lovers were dead, she went and killed herself and thus

came to be buried at the crossroads. Her father's farm is now called Dead Maid's Farm while the woods became Black Dog Woods, and a neighbouring farm on the A36 is called Black Dog Farm in memory of the beast's fierce loyalty.

Elsewhere in the world: traditionally in Togo, West Africa, when someone hanged themselves from a tree, the tree was considered poisoned, or perhaps haunted by the suicide's unhappy and malevolent ghost. So the whole tree was chopped down, and the particular branch buried with the corpse in the place reserved for violent deaths (usually crossroads). Usually also only the person's immediate family will go looking for the body of a suicide because it is considered particularly unlucky to be the first to find one. This makes the family especially vulnerable to its attentions.

In East Africa by Mt Kilamanjaro the Wachagga traditionally allow the burial of a suicide with the rest of the tribe, but the place where they hanged themselves has to be purified with holy water and a goat is strangled with the same rope to appease the suicide's ghost.

* * *

One consequence of unquestioning belief in the capacity of the dead to harm the living is that it can be used as a threat, and there are many tales of the threat being carried out all over the world. In Madagascar it used to be a popular form of revenge among many tribes and the Mahafali tribe was particularly famous for the epidemics of revenge suicides that regularly possessed their young men.

In India ritual suicide was a way of life for the Charan tribe of Gujarat and Rajasthan in north-west India. The Charans traditionally were a high caste of bards and scholars who were rarely troubled by bandits on their travels because of their readiness to commit suicide, often in mass, to take revenge on anyone who offended them. If someone stole their cattle, the whole village used to descend on the robbers and if their beasts were not willingly returned, the Charans would behead several of their old men or women. Or else one or more of them would set themselves alight and dance their curse against the thieves until they dropped dead. This is called the ceremony of traga and its power is still widely dreaded, thanks to many tales of it apparently working spectacularly well.

R.V. Russell in *The Tribes and Castes of the Central Provinces of India* (first published in 1916 but still in print) tells of one such incident which must have done much to refresh people's awe of the Charans. The chief of Siela, a town in the Kathiawar region on the Arabian Sea, had a debt demanded of him by a Charan. When the chief refused to pay, the Charan marched on Siela with forty others intending to besiege the chief's house until the claim was settled. The chief, however, closed the town gates against them so the Charans began a vigil outside the walls. For three days the debtee fasted. Then he sacrificed the lives of several of his companions. Then he dressed in clothes padded with cotton steeped in oil and set them alight. As he died, he cried: 'Now I am dying but I will become a headless ghost in the palace, and will take the chief's life and cut off his prosperity.'

After this the Charans returned to their homes, leaving the curse to do its own work. Which indeed it seemed to do because three days after the debtee's suicide the chief's wife tripped and fell down the stairs, being seriously injured. Many witnesses reported a headless phantom around the palace and finally the malevolent ghost seemed to enter the chief's own head and drive him violently mad, lashing out at those around him and even killing a female servant in his rage, or tearing at his own flesh with his teeth. Everyone knew this was the work of the ghost and began avoiding the palace. Many exorcisms were tried but all failed until a foreign astronomer of great reputation arrived. He went around the palace tying charmed ribbons and sprinkling holy water and milk. Then he drove blessed iron nails into the ground at the four corners of the mansion and two by the doorway.

For the next forty-one days the astrologer chanted and prayed and made daily sacrifices at the suicide's grave to pacify his spirit. Finally the preparations were complete and the chief's exorcism began. He reacted violently but was thrashed into submission. Then the astrologer dug a sacrificial fire-pit and placed a lemon between it and the chief, commanding the spirit to enter the lemon. But it replied contemptuously through the chief's mouth: 'Who are you to command this? If one of your gods were to come, I would not quit this man for him'.

But the astrologer and his servants persevered for days with charms and incense till finally the ghost was forced into the lemon, upon which the lemon began to bounce about wildly and the chief came back to his senses. The bouncing lemon was driven out of town by a noisy procession with drums and horns, mustard seeds and salt being scattered on the lemon's path. Finally the lemon was buried with salt and mustard in a pit ten feet deep, the tomb being sealed with stones mortared with lead and with charmed two-foot iron nails hammered in at each corner. And that was the last that was heard of the vengeful Charan ghost.

THE SPIRITUALIST THEORY

Vampires tap into all the usual fears of the restless or vengeful dead, but with the added dimension that they have tangible, physical bodies. The question naturally arises though, if they are physical creatures how do they get out of an unopened grave? Many folktales do describe the vampire climbing out of its coffin, but far more often the grave is undisturbed till the vampire hunters dig it up to find the bloated and uncannily preserved corpse within, suggesting an ability to escape as a kind of vapour. This has carried through into fiction, with Count Dracula and others occasionally materialising out of dust or mist.

In Greece and neighbouring countries, this is exactly what they believed. Professional vampire hunters would look for holes leading down to the coffin, holes that need be no wider than a finger for the vampire to escape. The theory was that the corpse itself remained in the coffin while its semi-substantial body roamed the night.

Spiritualists who addressed the problem in all seriousness at the close of the nineteenth century explained the phenomenon in terms of astral projection. They suggested that the form a vampire adopts when hunting for blood is its 'etheric double'. This was said to be more substantial than a ghost but less than the entombed corpse, to which it is attached by a kind of etheric umbilical cord. Some vampires, they suggested, could result from the premature burial of people capable of astral projection, which is how they would be forced to sustain themselves in the grave. Blood was their only possible food because its partly spiritual composition (according to tradition) gives it a similar nature to the etheric double.

Montague Summers himself, writing in the 1920s when Spiritualism was still taken quite seriously, enthusiastically embraced its explanation of vampire physiology. This was taken even further by the Theosophists, who could almost be described as the Jesuits of the Spiritualist movement because they tried to establish a rigorous intellectual foundation for their beliefs.

Theosophy is now often dismissed as a passing intellectual craze of the late Victorians, but the mostly Indian philosophy on which it was based had been carefully honed over many centuries and so carries a certain weight. The belief system was undoubtedly medieval, but in the writings of Madame Blavatsky and others this was married to Victorian pragmatism and belief in science. The result was a clear and plausible world-view, if one is first prepared to accept the premise of spiritual dimensions being an integral and very real part of existence.

One leading Theosophist, C.W. Leadbeater, considered the place of vampires in the cosmic scheme of things in *The Astral Plane*, first published in 1895 and kept in print long afterwards by, ironically enough, Indian publishers. To put his views into perspective one has remember that to Leadbeater and his colleagues the dead were simply persons currently unattached to a material body. Death was considered just another phase of existence.

In a review of the various beings one is liable to meet on the Astral Plane, Leadbeater considers the shades of people who have died suddenly, whose attachment to life has not first been weakened by age or illness: 'In the case of an accidental death or suicide . . . the withdrawal of the principles from their physical encasement has been aptly compared to the tearing of the stone out of an unripe fruit. The personality will consequently be held in the seventh or lowest subdivision of the plane. This has been described as anything but a pleasant abiding-place, yet it is by no means the same for all those who are compelled for a time to inhabit it. Those victims of sudden death who have been pure and noble have no affinity for this plane, and so the time of their sojourn upon it is passed either in happy ignorance and full oblivion, or in a state of quiet slumber, a sleep full of rosy dreams.

'On the other hand, if men's earth-lives have been low and brutal, selfish and sensual, they will be conscious to the fullest extent in this undesirable region; and it is possible for them to develop into terribly evil entities. Inflamed by all kinds of horrible appetites which they can no longer satisfy directly, they gratify their passions vicariously through a medium or any sensitive person whom they can obsess; and they take a devilish delight in using all the arts of delusion which the astral plane puts in their power in order to lead others into the same excesses which have proved so fatal to themselves. It should be noted that this class may be called minor vampires; that is to say, whenever they have the opportunity they prolong their existence by draining away the vitality from human beings whom they find themselves able to influence.'

Moving on to vampires proper, Leadbeater continues:

'These creatures are commonly regarded as mere Medieval fables; yet there are examples to be found occasionally even now, though chiefly in countries such as Russia or Hungary. The popular legends about them are probably often considerably exaggerated, but there is nevertheless a terribly serious substratum of truth beneath the eerie stories which pass from mouth to mouth among the peasantry of Eastern Europe.

'It is just possible for a man to live a life so absolutely degraded and selfish, so utterly wicked and brutal, that the whole of his lower mind may become entirely enmeshed in his desires, and finally separate from its spiritual source in the higher self. But when we remember how often, even in the worst of villains, there is to be found something not wholly bad, we shall realise that the abandoned personalities

must always be a small minority. Still, comparatively few though they be, they do exist, and it is from their ranks that the still rarer vampire is drawn.

'The lost entity would very soon after death find himself unable to stay in the astral world, and would irresistibly be drawn in full consciousness into "his own place", the mysterious eighth sphere, there slowly to disintegrate after experiences best left undescribed. If, however, he perishes by suicide or sudden death, he may under certain circumstances, especially if he knows something of black magic, hold himself back from this appalling fate by a death in life scarcely less appalling – the ghastly existence of the vampire.

'Since the eighth sphere cannot claim him until after the death of the body, he preserves it in a kind of cataleptic trance by the horrible expedient of the transfusion into it of blood drawn from other human beings by his semi-materialised astral body. He thus postpones his final destiny by the commission of wholesale murder. As popular "superstition" again rightly supposes, the easiest and most effectual remedy in such a case is to exhume and burn the body, thus depriving the creature of his *point d'appui*. When the grave is opened the body usually appears quite fresh and healthy, and the coffin is not infrequently filled with blood. In countries where cremation is the custom, vampirism of this sort is naturally impossible.'

Few people in the West now accept the world view that allows such an explanation to carry much weight, but this was the cultural climate in which Bram Stoker wrote *Dracula*. It was then still quite possible for intellectuals to believe that vampires might be real without being totally ridiculed. Arthur Conan Doyle is just one of the most famous cultural heroes who cultivated interests in science and the 'occult' side by side. He did not go quite so far as to believe in vampires, but he famously found the notion of the Cottingley Fairies plausible enough. Stoker himself probably belonged to the mystical Order of the Golden Dawn where such currents of thought freely circulated, though it is unknown whether he shared their beliefs or was simply looking for raw material for his fiction.

Basically, the Theosophist explanation of vampires is simply a restatement of old folk beliefs within a more robust philosophical framework. This may no longer be acceptable as a scientific point of view but it does demonstrate the adaptability of vampires both in belief and fiction. Vampires have been less easy to dismiss from the imagination than many other monsters, which suggests that they embody some deeper or more subtle aspect of human nature.

CHAPTER III

BLOODLUST

I WAS NOT ALONE. The room was the same, unchanged in any way since I came into it; I could see along the floor, in the brilliant moonlight my own footsteps marked where I had disturbed the long accumulation of dust. In the moonlight opposite me were three young women, ladies by their dress and manner. I thought at the time that I must be dreaming, for though the moonlight was behind them, they threw no shadow on the floor. They came close to me and looked at me for some time and then whispered together. Two were dark and had high aquiline noses like the Count's, and great dark, piercing eyes that seemed almost red when contrasted with the pale yellow moon. The other was fair, fair as can be, with great wavy masses of golden hair and eyes like pale sapphires. All three had brilliant white teeth that shone like pearls against the ruby of their voluptuous lips. There was something about them that made me uneasy, some longing and at the same time some deadly fear. I felt in my heart a wicked, burning desire that they would kiss me with those red lips.

They whispered together, and then they all three laughed. The fair girl shook her head coquettishly, and the other two urged her on. One said: "Go on! You are first, and we shall follow; yours is the right to begin."

The other added: "He is young and strong; there are kisses for us all."

Jonathan Harker in
Bram Stoker's *Dracula*

Bloodlust is generally taken to mean a love of violence, the desire to kill and maim for revenge, greed or simple sadistic pleasure. Often that's just what it does mean, but there is a creepy level in considering vampires on which those things are secondary. It is blood itself that the vampire is after as the elixir of its unnatural vitality. The consequences for the victim are secondary. The vampire's victims are mere prey. Or where there is more than indifference it is a perverted and selfish kind of love, a wish to initiate the victim into the vampire's own sunless and outcast world.

Vampires not only promise forbidden and otherwise unknowable sensual pleasures, but there is a perverted mystical element to their fascination. The notion of vampirism taps into an ancient reverence for blood as the mystical bearer of life, if not the actual substance of life itself. As Renfield screams dementedly at one point in *Dracula* 'The blood is the life! The blood is the life!'

Just as atheists often turn to church ritual for the great rites of passage such as birth, marriage and death, for which their everyday beliefs feel inadequate, so this atavistic belief in the supernatural power of blood continues to shape the emotions of people who have otherwise slipped out of the embrace of organised religion. For all the blessings of rationalism, there are mysteries it fails to address. Love, death, sex and suffering often require a larger vocabulary — the language of symbols.

In the ancient world blood sacrifice was used to propitiate the gods just as much as to pacify the recently deceased. The annual ceremonies centred on the death and resurrection of the Greco-Roman god Attis are a good example. This god originated in Phrygia in what is now Turkey but by the time of the Roman Emperor Claudius his cult had reached Rome itself with a bloody ritual enacted each March designed to secure fertility for the coming agricultural year. Like some gory precursor of the Christian Easter, this began with the cutting and dressing of a sacred evergreen pine tree, this being the form in which Attis had been reincarnated. It was covered with violets, the flowers which were said to have sprung from the droplets of his blood, and then an effigy of the god was fixed to the tree trunk which was raised upon an altar. On the day of the spring equinox this was buried and then two days later came Sanguis, the Day of Blood. Amid an orgiastic frenzy of music and dancing the high priest started events by cutting himself deeply and making a generous offering of his own blood on the altar and tree, his example being followed by the lesser priests and then as many of the congregation as were moved to follow suit. The next day everyone celebrated the god's resurrection as a result of all this bloodletting and then everyone gradually calmed down and went back to their normal business.

Unsurprisingly, the Aztecs in Mexico had a much bloodier version of this ceremony to encourage the rebirth of their maize goddess Chicomecoatl, which means 'seven-serpent' in honour of the serpents that symbolized the crop-nourishing rain (or, some

Chicomecoatl

say 'seven guests' because she is the goddess of all food and drink, not just maize). According to Lewis Spence's *Myths of Mexico and Peru*, this began with a general fast for a week at the start of April, during which the people decorated their houses with bulrushes sprinkled with their own blood from cuts in their hands and feet. Then they went to the maize fields where they plucked stalks of the new maize which they laid in the village hall. A mock battle then took place before Chicomecoatl's altar after which bundles of maize from the previous harvest were offered to the goddess and then later saved for the next year's seed. Other food offerings were also made, especially including cooked frogs to encourage the rains.

Then later at the beginning of July another festival was held to celebrate the corn's ripening. For two weeks there was feasting and dancing and at the centre of the ceremonies was a female slave, usually a captive who had been carefully trained in the dancing-school but kept ignorant of how the dance would culminate. On the final night of the celebration all the village women danced in circles around her, chanting the deeds of Chicomecoatl, then at dawn they were joined by the village headmen who danced the final dance then led the slave to the pyramid of sacrifice. There she was stripped naked and without warning a flint knife was plunged into her chest and her still beating heart was offered up to the maize goddess. Other accounts say she was first decapitated; her blood was then collected for sprinkling in the fields and her body skinned by the high priest, who wrapped the skin around him in the renewed dancing. None of the new corn could be eaten before the virgin's sacrifice.

* * *

Blood has always been one of the most potent of all symbols. The ancient Hebrews were proscribed from drinking animal blood because, the prophets declared, the life of the animal resides in the blood, and that portion belongs to the Creator, whose partiality for blood sacrifices is well demonstrated in the Old Testament. His preference for blood over other offerings was clearly demonstrated early on when Cain's offerings of the fruits of agriculture were spurned in favour of Abel's blood offerings of the first-born of his flocks, leading to the famous jealousy that resulted in the first biblical murder.

In other cultures though, the drinking of blood was positively encouraged for recognisably similar though reversed mystical reasons. Norse saga tells of a cowardly prince who was transformed into a fearless warrior through drinking wolf's blood, and many other ancient warriors, including the Carthaginians, Gauls, the Sioux tribe of America and the Maori of New Zealand, all at some time used to toast victory with a cup of their fallen enemy's blood in order to steal their strength and also, perhaps, fend off the anger of the dead enemy's ghost by imbibing some of his essence and therefore in a way becoming one with him. The Hawaiians and young warriors of the Bering Straits would, after killing their first enemy in battle, drink some of his blood and eat a small part of his heart.

Nor was it only enemies who were eaten. Some Australian Aboriginal tribes used to eat their dead in order to guarantee their rebirth within the tribe and Herodotus (*History* I, 216) in the fifth century BC wrote of the Massagetes people in Armenia: 'Human life does not come to its natural close with this people; but when a man grows very old, all his kinsfolk collect together and offer him up in sacrifice; offering at the same time some cattle also. After the sacrifice they boil the flesh and feast on it; and those who thus end their days are reckoned the happiest. If a man dies of disease they do not eat him, but bury him in the ground, bewailing his ill-fortune that he did not come to be sacrificed.'

Eating human flesh and drinking blood has widely been imagined to strengthen the consumer in a more than practical way. The Christian communion service can itself be seen as a spiritualization of this practice, in which by eating the flesh and blood of their Saviour, followers hope to imbibe His immortality. As Jesus said in the synagogue at Capernaum: 'Except ye eat the flesh of the Son of man, and drink his blood, ye have no life in you. Whoso eateth my flesh, and drinketh my blood, hath eternal life; and I will raise him up at the last day. For my flesh is meat indeed, and my blood is drink indeed. He that eateth my flesh, and drinketh my blood, dwelleth in me, and I in him'. (John VI, 53-56)

In the days of Charlemagne at the end of the eighth and beginning of the ninth centuries, this doctrine led to an unfortunate misunderstanding among the newly Christianised Saxons in Germany who took it as encouragement for the ritual eating of human flesh. Strict laws had to be introduced to discourage the practice and anyone suspected of eating human flesh was put to death.

Blood could also be used to communicate with the dead, an example of which is given in Homer's *Odyssey*. When Odysseus wishes to consult the dead, he goes down to the gates of Hades and summons them by filling a pit with the blood of sacrificed sheep. This not only attracts the silent shades of the dead but gives them strength enough to speak.

Blood has also often been held to have miraculous healing properties. From ancient times till the Middle Ages drinking or bathing in human blood, particularly that of virgins, was prescribed by surprisingly eminent authorities as the cure for many serious illnesses. In ancient Rome the blood of executed criminals was used by doctors to treat the wealthy, while the blood needed to save many a mortally wounded Medieval knight was provided by maidens willing (or so one very much hopes) to sacrifice their own lives in return for going straight to Heaven.

The ancient reverence for blood has survived into the modern age better than many other superstitions. The breath or pneuma is no longer really seen as the spiritual essence of our being. We still say 'bless you' when people sneeze, but don't seriously believe they are in danger of losing their soul at such moments, if we still have any idea at all of why we say it. But blood is still seen as the carrier of life in a very real sense, thanks to medical transfusions – the first of which on record in Europe was given to Pope Innocent VIII on 25 July 1492. After a slight recovery he died anyway, as did the three boys whose blood he received. Their families were compensated with a ducat each.

Bram Stoker picks up on this in his novel where science, in the form of medical blood transfusion, tries to undo Dracula's depredations to save Lucy's life. Unsuccessfully in the end but, given that blood types had yet to be categorised, Stoker got the odds about right for surviving transfusion from random donors, as happens with Lucy Westenra.

Blood transfusions as performed in the novel were surprisingly common in Victorian times on the grounds that, although sometimes fatal, if a patient was going to die anyway the procedure was worth trying. The odds of surviving transfusion from four randomly selected donors have been reliably calculated as about six to one, assuming the recipient does not have a particularly rare blood group. Much of Stoker's medical knowledge about blood was probably gleaned from one of his brothers who wrote a major study on the subject. The existence of incompatible and identifiable blood groups was eventually established by Karl Landsteiner in 1901, an achievement which eventually won him the 1930 Nobel Prize in physiology or medicine.

Many people assume that as a staid Victorian Stoker was unconscious of the sexual implications of all this exchanging of bodily fluids but this is hardly likely as Lucy's fiancé Arthur feels he has 'made her truly his bride' as Van Helsing expresses it, by giving her his blood. What that implies about the other donors is of course left unexplored beyond her other, disappointed, suitor Dr Seward declaring: 'No man knows till he experiences it, what it is to feel his own life-blood drawn away into the veins of the woman he loves.'

We still have the greatest respect for the life-giving properties of blood but in ancient times the reverence was that much greater because the mechanics were so little understood, as were the ways in which its virtue might be conveyed from one being to another. It was obvious that if a wounded person lost too much blood they died but until science cracked the reasons why, imagination had to fill the gap.

Because of its seemingly mystical nature, blood was believed able to convey a much wider range of blessings than those we now recognise. Pliny recorded in his *Natural History* (26: 1,5) that the Egyptian pharaohs used to bathe in human blood to cure or stave off leprosy. Constantine the Great was advised by Greek doctors to bathe in freshly killed children's blood to cure his leprosy, but having converted to Christianity the pleas of their mothers and reluctance to spill so much innocent blood prevented him. Luckily he seems to have been cured by Pope Sylvester washing away his sins with Holy Water. The great Persian physician Avicenna, whose views on medicine were unchallenged till the sixteenth century, recommended the blood of various creatures, including humans, as potent medicine for many illnesses; while in ancient Rome the drinking of human blood was believed the only effective cure for dropsy.

The eighteenth century German historian Ludwig Gebhardi (1738-1809) noted in *The History of Hungary*: 'The drinking of the blood of human beings is not a mark of barbarity even in our time, for epileptics are often allowed to drink from the still warm blood of newly executed wrongdoers.' Elisabeth Bathory probably knew of this remedy and, given the 'epileptic' fits of her childhood it must have helped fuel her own blood mania. In Renaissance Italy noble ladies used to refresh their complexions by rubbing their faces with a freshly bisected pigeon while even in late nineteenth century Paris it was common in high society for revellers to visit the slaughterhouse at the Porte de la Villette for a quaff of fresh blood to repair the ravages of the night.

In the Middle Ages the physicians of Montpelier and Salerne prescribed virgins' blood as a cure for many diseases. A twelfth century manuscript *Der Arme Heinrich* by the celebrated German poet Hartmann von Aue tells in chilling detail of a case in Montpelier in which a maiden had offered her blood to help cure a knight of leprosy. Before going ahead the physician questioned the girl closely to ensure that her seemingly selfless offer was genuine, warning her that if it was the result of pressure from her parents or the knight himself, or from ignorance of the consequences, her sacrifice would be in vain. When she still professed her pure intentions, he pressed on:

'I will undress you, so that you stand naked, and your shame and hardship will be great, which you will suffer because you stand naked before me; I will then tie up your arms and legs, and if you don't feel pity for your own life and body think of this pain; I will cut to your heart and tear it out live from your breast.'

When despite all the discouragement the maid persisted in going ahead and stripped naked for the sacrifice, she was taken to a high table where she was tied down and then the surgeon 'took up a sharp knife which he was wont to use on such occasions. Its blade was long and wide . . . for he felt sorry for her and wanted to kill her quickly.'

Human nature being what it is, some tales suggest that other virgins were less eager donors and were sometimes even simply snatched and drained of the precious fluid in their veins without much compunction, especially if they were peasants; but in book seventeen of Malory's *Morte d'Arthur*, written in the late fifteenth century, only the noblest motives prevail. This tale is more romantic than historical of course, but it says much about what Malory and his audience believed at the time, and it's quite possible that in everyday life other maids than the one in Montpelier really were moved to similar altruistic self-sacrifice by the notion of thus attaining Heaven.

Behind such sacrifices the ancient pagan belief in the mystical properties of blood was reinforced not just by the Church's teachings about salvation through the drinking of Christ's divine blood, but by attitudes towards both virginity in general and the Virgin Mary in particular. For mystical reasons virgins' blood was believed far more potent than the blood of those who had tasted the pleasures of the flesh – while in the story that follows, the lady of the castle would be seen by medieval eyes as a kind of representative of the Virgin Mary on earth, a Christianised equivalent of the Celtic queens who represented the earth goddess for their realm and whose wellbeing was necessary for the fruitfulness of the land. Hence it is not as unreasonable as it may seem to our eyes for her to request the blood of passing virgin princesses to restore her health, even if it meant their death. The lady is not just a selfish tyrant sacrificing other lives for her own, but is seeking to restore the health of her lands through becoming healthy again herself.

BLOOD AND THE GRAIL QUEST

On their quest for the Holy Grail, the knights Galahad, Perceval and Bors, riding with Perceval's sister, happened to pass a certain castle from which an armed knight came galloping to meet them. He asked if Perceval's sister was still a virgin. When told that she was, he immediately took her mare's bridle and said she must stay to fulfil the custom of the castle, which was that every passing noble maiden had to fill a large bowl with blood from her right arm. A dozen knights then rode out to enforce this demand but Galahad and his friends drew their swords and soon despatched them to heaven. Then out came riding sixty more.

'Fair lords,' said Galahad, unimpressed, 'have pity on yourselves and let us pass in peace lest we have to slay you all.'

'Nay,' came the reply, 'we counsel you to surrender the maid. Plainly you are the best knights in the world and you have done enough hardy deeds this day. So we will let you go, but we must have the custom fulfilled and there are more of us to ensure that it is.'

Galahad just laughed.

'Then you wish to die?' asked the knights of the castle.

'It has not come to that yet,' said Galahad, and they fell to battle again. The Grail knights proved invincible and by nightfall they were all still standing unscathed after killing half the castle's champions. A truce was called and, in the true spirit of medieval chivalry, Galahad and his companions were invited to stay the night at the castle and learn the reason for the custom they were fighting over.

So they entered the castle and were graciously received. Then after bathing and feasting they heard this tale: 'There is here in this castle a gentlewoman who is our mistress, and the mistress of many other castles besides.

Return of Arthur by William Dyce (1806-1864)

Many years ago there fell upon her a malady and when she had lain a great while she fell into a fever which no leech could cure. But at last an old man said that if she might have a full dish of blood from a maid, a clean virgin in thought and deed and a king's daughter, that blood would restore her health. So it proved, and for this reason was the custom appointed.'

'Now,' said Perceval's sister, 'I see that but for my blood this gentle lady must die.'

'That may be so,' replied her brother, 'but if you give as much blood as they are asking, it may be you that dies in her place.'

'Perhaps, but if I die to heal her then I shall get me great worship and soul's health, and worship to my lineage. Better is one harm than two, so therefore let there be no more battle. In the morning I will yield to the custom of this place.'

There was great joy in the castle at these words and no matter what her companions said, Perceval's sister would not change her mind. In the morning they heard Mass and she met the lady of the castle who truly seemed ill and close to death. So Perceval's sister said: 'Who will let my blood?'

A physician stepped forward and drew her blood till the basin was full. Then she said faintly to the lady: 'Madam, I am come to my death to make you whole, for God's love pray for me.'

With that Perceval's sister fainted. Galahad and his friends caught her and tried to staunch the flow of blood, but she had given too much of it to live. After a while she revived a little and said 'Fair brother Perceval, I die for the healing of this lady. I ask that you bury me not in this country, but as soon as I am dead put me in a boat at the next haven and let me go as adventure will lead me. And as soon as you three come to the city of Sarras, there to achieve the Holy Grail, you shall find me arrived under a tower. There bury me in the spiritual place, for there Galahad shall be buried, and you also.'

Perceval heard her words and granted them, weeping, and her soul departed from the body. That same day was the lady of the castle healed when anointed with the virgin's blood. Perceval laid his sister in a barge and covered it with black silk. The wind rose and drove the vessel from the shore and beyond sight.

Note: Sarras is the holy island in the eastern Mediterranean where in some versions of the Grail legend the quest reaches its climax. In the Lancelot-Grail or Vulgate Cycle which inspired Malory, Joseph of Arimathea visited the island on his way to Britain and his son Josephus was initiated into the mysteries of the Grail by Christ Himself. From there the Grail was taken to Britain where it was eventually achieved by Galahad, Perceval and Bors. They took it back to Sarras in Solomon's ship and established a realm of the Grail which they ruled benevolently for a year till Galahad died in ecstasy when the Grail was taken up to Heaven. Perceval also died soon after, whereupon Bors returned to King Arthur's court to tell the tale of their adventures.

VAMPIRE COUSINS

Folklore and modern fiction speak more often of male than female vampires, but in ancient times almost the reverse was true. To the Romans and Greeks most, if not all, vampires were female — lamiae, striges, empusae or succubi who were demons able to adopt human form to prey upon humans.

In Greek mythology the original Lamia was a queen of Libya who was seduced by the ever-amorous Zeus. When his wife Hera learned about it she destroyed Lamia's children in revenge. This drove the queen mad with grief and thereafter she went around destroying human children through jealousy. Later the term lamia was applied to a whole class of demons who behaved this way and who also seduced men to feed on their flesh and blood. Ovid wrote that striges were vampires able to assume the shape of birds 'which fly about at night sucking the blood of children and devouring their bodies.'

In Greek mythology the empusae were originally daughters of Hecate sent to frighten or eat travellers on lonely roads at night. They are often described as having the hind quarters of donkeys and brazen hoofs, but they could also appear as beautiful young women to seduce their prey. There is some confusion in the naming and attributes of the various demonic females but on one thing the various classical writers all agree, that the lamiae sacrificed to Hecate, the goddess of death who in the Middle Ages was seen as the Queen of the Witches. In ancient Rome there was a college of priests dedicated to fighting lamiae and the legal code known as the *Jus Pontificum* specifically forbade Romans 'to leave the dead exposed to the claws of Strygae or Lamiae.'

Louis Lavater, a sixteenth century theologian who studied the vampire phenomenon in the classical world, wrote: 'Mormo is a female form of hideous appearance, a Lamia . . . thought by ancient writers to be women who had the horrid power of removing their eyes, or else a kind of demon or ghost. These would appear under the guise of lovely courtesans who, by their enticing wiles, would draw some plump, rosy-cheeked youth into their embraces and then devour him wholemeal. Lamiae are also called Striges.'

Collin de Plancy in his *Dictionnaire Infernal* 1918 defined lamiae as: 'demons found in the desert in the shape of women, with dragons' heads at the end of their feet. Lamias haunt cemeteries, disinter corpses, eat them and leave nothing of the dead except their bones . . . Lamias are found in Libya who are extremely skilful runners; to more easily deceive those whom they wish to devour they show them their more beautiful parts

without speaking, for their voice is the hissing of a serpent. It is pretended that such demons still exist in Africa . . . Similar to witches, and the vulgarly named *strygae*, these demons are greedy for the blood of children. But not all demonomanes agree on the form of these lamias, Torquemada for instance stating in his *Hexameron* that they have a woman's figure and horse's legs, and that they are called *chevesches* (a kind of hawk) because of their cry and the greed these birds show for children's flesh. According to others, they are like sirens, while still others compare them to the ghouls of Arabia.'

Early Jewish and Christian tradition labelled such demons as the daughters of Lilith, Adam's rebellious first wife. When not appearing as humans the lamiae were often said to fly around in the form of screech owls, a belief which is echoed as far afield as Malaysia and Pre-Columbian South America. This is just one of several remarkable coincidences of belief around the world about this kind of glamorous female demon. The details vary about their origins and habits but some traits consistently stand out — such as that their originals are often women who have either died in childbirth or had their children violently torn from them and their own violence is revenge for this. On the other hand, sometimes no real explanation is given for their origins; the glamorous demons simply exist to lure men to their destruction and as such can be understood as projections of male anxieties about assertive women. This has led to Lilith in particular becoming a feminist icon — a symbol of the repressed female side of the Old Testament narrative.

In the classical world the distinction between lamiae and vampires as we think of them — dead people rising from their graves — was often blurred and usually the risen dead were seen as hostile; but not always. The Roman historian Phlegon of Tralles writing in the second century AD told the curious story he had heard of a girl called Philinnion who had died young. However, six months later her old nanny heard a disturbance in the bedroom of Machates, a young man who was lodging with the girl's parents. Peering through a crack in the door, the nanny was astonished to see her former charge making vigorous love to the young man. Night after night this happened until finally the nanny told the girl's mother what was happening. Of course it was not believed at first but under questioning young Machates confessed that he had indeed been receiving nightly visits from an amorous stranger, and that she had given him a ring and a ribbon as tokens of her love. The parents recognised them immediately as having been buried with Philinnion.

The following night they lay in wait and when Philinnion visited her lover again, they burst in and threw their arms around their beloved daughter. She however was far from happy. 'Oh, my dear parents,' she said, 'cruel indeed have you been in begrudging me visiting a guest in my own home and doing harm to no-one. But you will grieve sorely on account of your curiosity, for now I must return again to my appointed place. And trust me, it was not contrary to the will of God that I came here.'

Having said which, she fell dead onto the bed. When her tomb was searched it was found empty, but there in the coffin was a ring that young Machates had given her. When news of these strange events reached the city elders, they ordered that Philinnion's body be cremated outside the city walls and she was not seen again.

APOLLONIUS AND THE LAMIA

Philostratus, in his life of Apollonius of Tyana, renowned philosopher and mystic of the early Christian era (whose authority often challenged that of Christianity itself), tells this tale concerning one of the Master's pupils, a young man named Menippus. Philostratus explained that he was telling the story in such detail because: 'many people are aware of it and know that the incident occurred in the centre of Hellas; but they have only heard in a general and vague manner that he once caught and overcame a lamia in Corinth.'

Menippus was a young Lycian (from what is now south-west Turkey) who was as handsome as he was clever, having a face like Apollo and the grace and strength of an athlete. Menippus had an admirer, a beautiful foreign lady, a Phoenecian it was rumoured, who lived in a wealthy suburb of Corinth. They met one evening when Menippus was out walking alone. Immediately she declared that she had long loved him from afar and begged him to visit her later that night, saying: 'When you come, you will know the place by my singing, and you shall have wine sweeter than you have ever tasted before. There will be no rival to trouble you, and together we two beautiful beings shall dwell in perfect happiness.'

Menippus was a skilled philosopher and an ardent student, but he was also young and passionate and it was an invitation he could hardly refuse. So that night he visited the lady as arranged and the evening passed as wonderfully as she had promised. In fact Menippus felt his wildest dreams had come true and fell passionately in love with the mysterious stranger. He began to spend every spare moment with her, and many that were not spare, so that his studies soon began to suffer. Apollonius noticed the change in his pupil but said nothing for a while, merely observing the infatuation with interest and curiosity. But finally he said:

'Menippus, you are the finest of youths and could take your pick from all the women in this city, so why have you chosen instead to cherish a serpent in your breast?' Menippus was astonished and furious but Apollonius continued: 'This female is of a kind you cannot marry. And why should you want to, do you really believe she loves you?'

'How can I not believe it,' Menippus replied angrily, 'since in every possible way she has shown that she loves no-one better in all the world?'

'And would you then marry her?'

'With all my heart I can think of no greater delight. In fact we intend to be married tomorrow because I can wait no longer.'

Apollonius, who no doubt was already well aware of this, said no more. But the following day he presented himself at the wedding breakfast where all the guests were assembled and, approaching the bridegroom, asked: 'So where is this dainty lady you mean to wed?'

Blushing slightly, Menippus introduced her.

'And to which of you belongs the silver and gold and all the other furnishings of this fine banqueting hall?'

'To the lady,' Menippus replied, 'for as you well know this is all I have of my own,' indicating his philosopher's cloak which was all he or any of his fellow students possessed.

Then Apollonius said: 'Have you read in Homer of the Gardens of Tantalus, how they exist and yet do not exist? Such is the nature of all this finery, it has but the semblance of reality. And this fine bride of yours is but one of the vampires that people call lamiae. These creatures fall in love and are devoted to the pleasures of Aphrodite, but their main love is for the flesh and blood of gullible humans whom they decoy with voluptuous delights only so they might then devour them at their feasts.'

'What nonsense!' exclaimed the bride, laughing. 'If this is all the fruit of your philosophy it is little wonder my lover is losing his taste for it. You are simply jealous, Apollonius, that he prefers my teachings to yours.'

However, Apollonius's wisdom consisted in more than just words. With a clap of his hands all the gold and silver on the tables rose like bubbles into the air and vanished. And at his command all the wine-bearers and cooks and most of the guests likewise disappeared. And when the lady herself tried to escape she found herself pinned by the pure force of his will. She began pleading for mercy but Apollonius would not free her till she admitted the truth. Then she confessed that she was indeed a lamia who had been fattening Menippus up for this feast at which he had been intended as the main course. And she admitted that she had done this many times before.

Then Apollonius released her and she too vanished, leaving behind one of the best known legends about Apollonius, and one which was famous even during his lifetime. Much later it was given fresh life by Keats who made it the basis for his famous poem *Lamia* in 1819, which in turn inspired some notable Romantic paintings.

THE PRINCE AND THE
ENVIOUS VIZIER

In Arabic folklore vampires are also usually, though not always, female and have much in common with the lamiae, often using their physical charms to secure dinner. Also called ghouls, they are as interested in eating firm young flesh as in drinking blood. When fresh meat is not available they gather in cemeteries and feast on recent corpses. The ghoul will be familiar to readers of *The Arabian Nights* in which, on the fifth night, Scheherezade tells the tale of The Prince and the Envious Vizier:

At one time there lived in Persia a rich and powerful king called Yunan who had a son who was passionately fond of hunting. The king also had a Vizier, who had to accompany the son always to see that he came to no harm. But it so happened that, as was often the way in fairytales, the Vizier hated the Prince. He could not stop thinking how with each year the Prince's power grew as much as his own diminished. So one day when they were out hunting and an antelope passed by, the Vizier cried: 'Go Prince! Chase that creature for if we do not feast on him tonight we cannot call ourselves hunters!'

Away galloped the Prince with no thought for his companions, who were soon left far behind. At last the antelope vanished into the desert and the Prince realised he had no idea where he was or how to get home. He guessed also that this was probably no accident, for he knew of the Vizier's jealousy. As he rode aimlessly along, searching for some road or familiar landmark, the Prince came upon a damsel who was weeping bitterly.

In reply to his kind queries she told him: 'I am an Indian princess. I was on a journey through this desert when sleep overcame me and I must have fallen from my horse.

When I woke, the caravan and all my servants were gone and I have no idea how to find them again.'

The Prince naturally enough took pity and mounted the princess up behind him. After a while, still lost, they happened to pass some ruins and the lady, pleading the call of nature, asked to be set down awhile. The Prince waited patiently, but when she did not soon return he followed to investigate. Within the ruins he heard her saying: 'Patience a little longer, my children, for I have brought you today a plump and juicy meal.' To which young voices replied in a piping chorus: 'Bring him quickly, Mother, that we may fill our bellies with his sweet flesh!'

The Prince was terrified, knowing he had fallen among ghouls. He retreated but before he could reach his horse, the lady emerged from the ruins. Seeing his alarm, she asked what the matter was. 'Oh,' he replied, half-truthfully, 'I have been thinking of an enemy of mine who this day has tried to kill me, and who may yet perhaps succeed.'

'Are you not a King's son?' she replied, getting ever nearer and cutting him off from his horse. 'Can you not give money to this enemy and so appease him?'

The Prince replied: 'He will not be appeased with money or anything less than my life. That is why I fear him. I am a wronged man.'

'If you be wronged, as you say, why do you not call upon God to save you from your oppressor?'

Having little choice, as she was now almost upon him, the Prince raised his eyes and voice to heaven, calling, 'O Thou who answers the prayers of the oppressed and can banish all evil, help me and cause my enemy to depart from me; for Thou art able to do whatsoever Thou wilt!'

THE VAMPIRE OF BAGHDAD

A Dominican exorcist, Mathias de Giraldo in his *Histoire Curieuse et Pittoresque des Sorciers* (1846), recorded the following tale which he heard from some Arabs, and which has very similar elements to the tale of Sidi-Nouman in the fuller editions of *The Arabian Nights*:

In the fifteenth century a rich merchant lived in a suburb of Baghdad. His one great disappointment in life was that his only son and heir, Abdul Hassan, showed no signs of wanting to marry and have children to secure his fortune against the future. At last the merchant decided to take matters into his own hands and find a wife for the boy. He chose the daughter of an old friend whom he loved like a brother. This girl may have been very rich and beautiful enough but the son couldn't stand her and asked for time to consider the matter. This he tried in all seriousness to do, because he loved his father dearly and wanted to put his mind at rest. But no matter how hard he tried, Abdul just could not bring himself to accept the proposed marriage, nor could he even suggest any other bride because there happened to be no-one just then that he wanted to marry.

One moonlit night as Abdul Hassan was wandering alone in the country beyond Baghdad, pondering his problem, he heard marvellous singing from a nearby grove. Following it, he came to a lonely house where a maid stood on a balcony serenading the night. More beautiful did she seem than the nymphs of paradise and her song was so sweet that it shamed the nightingales. Instantly stricken with love, Abdul fell to his knees praying for just a glance from her to ease his sudden need. But after a while she turned and went in with no sign of having noticed him.

The following day he returned to the area to make enquiries. He learned from the neighbours that the maid was seventeen years old, unmarried and the daughter of an old philosopher who, for all his wisdom, had no dowry to give her, but had tutored her well in all the noble arts and sciences. All of which only inflamed the young man's passion further. Hurrying to his father he said: 'Father, you know that I have always put your wishes before my own; but now I ask you to let me follow my own heart. Let me choose my own bride.'

Then he told his father about the maid he had found and fallen in love with. The old merchant had not become rich by accident and was not at all pleased to learn about the penniless object of his son's affections. For a while he argued but then, seeing Abdul's determination, he relented and consoled himself that at least he could be sure of grandchildren.

Soon enough it was all arranged and, as in a dream, Abdul Hassan met and married the lovely Nadilla. She proved everything he could have hoped for; more lovely than the moon, more gifted than the stars. Most of all, she seemed to love Abdul as much as he loved her and for three months all was rapture and bliss. Then one night Abdul woke in the small hours to find the bed empty beside him. At first he thought little of it but as time passed without her return he began to worry. Then an hour before dawn Nadilla returned stealthily and slipped back into bed. Abdul pretended to be asleep and said nothing, but he resolved to uncover the mystery.

The following night when they had gone to bed and kissed goodnight, Abdul Hassan again feigned sleep and soon felt Nadilla slip quietly away. Quickly dressing, he followed her into the streets of the sleeping city where, after many detours in which he nearly lost her, Nadilla finally entered a cemetery. With growing dread, Abdul saw her descend into a large and lamp-lit tomb. Creeping closer, he peeped in and to his horror saw his beautiful young wife feasting with what seemed a company of beggars. At first he could not tell what they were eating, and did not dare guess because ghastly suspicions were forming in his mind.

Only now did it strike him that in the three months of their marriage he had never before seen Nadilla eat anything beyond a few grains of rice or crumbs of bread. Always there had been some excuse that he had not thought to question. Then there was no avoiding the awful truth of the feast in the tomb because there was carried into the centre a fresh corpse which the dreadful crowd fell upon in frenzy, chanting and howling in ravenous delight, the lovely Nadilla as much as than the others.

Sick to his soul, Abdul Hassan crept away home but still he said nothing to his wife when she crept in just before dawn. All that day he kept his tongue, but that evening he pressed Nadilla to share his supper. She excused herself as usual, saying she was not hungry. Abdul insisted and when she still refused he finally lost his temper and cried: 'No, you have no appetite because you prefer instead to feast upon the dead with ghouls and vampires!'

She made no reply, nor indeed did she say a word for the rest of the evening but was so silently furious and so seemingly untroubled by shame that her husband seriously wondered if he had dreamed the scene in the cemetery. When the time came to go to bed, she lay apart from him, rigid with fury. But in the middle of the night, when she thought Abdul asleep, she suddenly hissed: 'Now you pay the price for your blasphemous curiosity!' And she sprang upon him before he could move, pinning him to the bed and fastening her teeth upon his throat to drink his blood. Luckily Abdul had thought to take a dagger to bed with him and, striking out in terror, he killed her.

The fair Nadilla was duly buried with as little fuss as possible, but three nights later she again came to her husband in her winding-sheet and tried to strangle him. The dagger proved useless this time and it was only with the greatest luck that Abdul managed to break free and escape.

The following day her tomb was opened and Nadilla's body was found slightly breathing, seemingly but asleep. Going to her father, Abdul Hassan demanded an explanation. With great reluctance the old philosopher told him that, two years before, Nadilla had married one of the Caliph's officers but he had caught her, so he claimed, in the greatest debaucheries and had killed her. But she had then returned to her father's house in good health, denying all the tales about her, and he had kept her in seclusion refusing also to believe them. She was after all his own flesh and blood, how could he not believe her? And how could he not believe the evidence of his own senses that she was still alive?

Returning to Nadilla's tomb, Abdul Hassam built a great pyre of scented wood and burned the vampire to ashes which he scattered on the Tigris, and she was never seen again.

And no sooner were these words spoken than the ghoul was convulsed and vanished with a wail. The Prince eventually found his way home and when he told his father all that had happened, the Vizier was made to pay with his life for having goaded the Prince into such danger.

LILITH

In Hebrew and Christian legend Adam's first wife, Lilith, is generally seen as a lamia or vampire. The Babylonians knew her as Lilitu, a name that seems derived from their terms for lechery, lasciviousness and luxury. In her milder moods Lilith and her band of demonic daughters were believed to seduce single men in their sleep so they often kept charms by the bedside to frighten the lamiae away and prevent 'wet dreams'. The lamiae were also partial to the blood of babies.

Nowhere does the Bible mention Lilith by name, though there is a passage in Isaiah 34.14 containing a word translated as either 'lamia' or 'screech owl' and which some have claimed is a reference to Lilith : 'And demons and monsters shall meet, and the hairy ones shall cry out to one another. There hath the lamia lain down and found rest for herself.' (Douay version.)

Other Judaic and apocryphal Christian scriptures have preserved her tale in greater detail and Lilith was a lively source of speculation during the Middle Ages. According to these legends God originally moulded both Adam and Lilith from the mud of creation, intending them to be equals. However problems soon arose, particularly because Adam always liked to be on top when making love. Finally after one argument Lilith uttered the secret name of God, clapped her hands and flew away in the form of an owl. At Adam's request God sent angels to try and persuade her to return. When this failed she was cast into the Outer Darkness and the more compliant Eve created in her place.

Lilith, however, refused to disappear quietly. She found ways back into our world and in the Outer Darkness she met other banished powers, demons and fallen angels with whom she mated and so gave birth to hosts of lesser demons, evil spirits and djinns. She became queen of the succubi with a burning grievance against Adam and Eve and all their offspring, whom she tormented at every chance. So the story goes anyway, there is undoubtedly another side to the tale. It is rumoured that in the form of a half-serpent (human from the waist up, snake below), it was Lilith who tempted Eve in the Garden of Eden, thus bringing about the Fall.

The screech-owl is Lilith's special creature, whose form she often adopts when out hunting for blood. She especially loves the blood of newborn babies, offspring of the usurper Eve. She also seduces lone men in their sleep in order both to drink their blood and steal their semen for the creation of new demons. In this guise she is a liliot or succubus. Often after seducing some man she and other succubi transform themselves into males and as lilin or incubi they seduce lonely females to impregnate them with the stolen sperm, whereby they give birth to monsters. In either guise Lilith is said to ravish her victims so thoroughly that they are never afterward satisfied with human partners.

The Christian Church took these and similar legends very seriously and in the thirteenth century Rome decreed that the incubus and succubus were real creatures, incarnate demons, to whose wiles priests and nuns were particularly susceptible. Many modern evangelical Christians still believe in the everyday reality of these demons as completely as they believe in Heaven, Hell and eternal life.

SUCCUBI AND INCUBI

The Fiend that goeth a-night
Women full oft to guile,
Incubus is named by right;
And guileth other men while
Succubus is that wight.

Description of Wales from Caxton's *Chronicle*

Where vampires were given legitimacy in the east through their recognition by Orthodox Christian dogma, in the west a similar recognition was given by the Roman Church to succubi and incubi, the female and male aspects of demons who plagued the virtuous with lascivious fancies. The succubus is a direct descendant of Lilith and the lamia, only her goal is not the flesh or blood of her victims, but their semen. After stealing this she transforms herself into an incubus, equally ravishing to the opposite sex, and uses the stolen semen to impregnate women, especially nuns. This at least was the accepted Church doctrine by the thirteenth century after hundreds of years of debate. Being demons, the succubi and incubi did not have real bodies, but through some dispensation of God they were able to assume bodies that felt real to their victims. The semen was real enough but somehow transformed so it often resulted in the birth of monsters or, if not a monster, to a child peculiarly susceptible to evil – a warlock or witch. One of the most famous legendary characters said to have been conceived this way was Merlin.

Rossell Hope Robbins in his *Encyclopaedia of Witchcraft and Demonology* (1970) quotes a Dominican source for the following description: 'What incubi introduce into the womb is not any ordinary human semen in normal quantity, but abundant, very thick, very warm, rich in spirits and free-form serisity. This, moreover, is an easy thing for them, since they merely have to choose ardent, robust men, whose semen is naturally copious, and with whom the succubus has relations and then the incubus copulates with women of a like constitution, taking care that both shall enjoy a more than normal orgasm, for the greater the venereal excitement the more abundant is the semen.'

The extreme eroticism mentioned above was a crucial feature of these demons, as with Lilith. In the fifteenth century Pico della Mirandola mentions a man who had apparently been consorting with a succubus for forty years and who would rather die in prison than give her up.

In particular the demons took great delight in spreading mischief by disguising themselves as eminent clerics for the purposes of debauchery and thus creating the most outrageous scandals. So the bishops and cardinals declared anyway. Very, very earnestly. Their victims were very often nuns who seem to have succumbed to their charms with alarming regularity. Ludovico Sinistrari in the seventeenth century mentions a case he knew where a nun was spied cavorting with a naked youth by several of her sisters. Under threat of torture she confessed to having regularly been 'indecently intimate with a comely youth' who was assumed to be an incubus.

The sixteenth and seventeenth centuries were particularly rife with succubi and incubi, according to the records of the Inquisition; then in 1725 Louis XV's personal physician suggested that the demons were simply the result of overheated imaginations, or an excuse for immoral behaviour. This was not the final word on the matter but seems to have marked the beginning of the end of succubi and incubi being taken seriously by most people.

RUSSIAN VAMPIRES

Russia is a particularly fertile ground for vampire stories, and from Russia comes the belief that a wooden stake must be driven through the heart of the vampire with a single blow if you wish to do more than simply aggravate the monster. This idea does surface elsewhere, such as in the *Arabian Nights*, but did not seem such common knowledge outside Russia, which perhaps accounts for some tales of the stake not working. As in the case of the Indian vampire, or Strigon, said to have been rampant near Larbach in 1672. When impaled with a thorn stake, it merely plucked the thing from its chest and flung it scornfully back at its tormentors.

From Russia and Poland also comes the belief that vampires can walk abroad between noon and midnight rather than the more common sunset and sunrise, but otherwise we are plainly dealing with the same creature that plagued Transylvania, Wallachia and the Balkans. Incidentally, in some parts of that region it is believed that a vampire can only call you by name once and you will be safe if you do not answer. For which reason people often to this day won't answer to their name at night unless it is called at least twice.

The finer details of East European vampires vary from region to region. In Bulgaria they are said to have just one nostril and hairy palms to their hands. Also in Bulgaria it was once a common practice for vampire hunters to bottle them. They would chase the vampires with a fragment of some holy icon, corner them till they had no escape but to hide in a bottle, then seal it with a cork to which the icon was affixed. Then the bottle would be buried in some out-of-the-way place in the hope that no-one would find it and set the demon free again.

In Poland and parts of Greece vampires might be met during the day whereas in Russia they are immobilised or destroyed by dawn. In Baron von Haxthausen's description of Transcaucasia (as recounted by Montague Summers) he tells the tale of a vampire called Dakhanavar who lived in the mountains of Ulmish Altotem, and who would let no strangers into the area to count its valleys. Anyone who tried was attacked in the night and had the blood sucked from the soles of his feet till they died.

Despite this, two bold adventurers came to try their luck and when night came they curled up together to sleep, each using the other's feet for a pillow. During the night the vampire came as usual and, feeling about in the dark, found a head. Running his cold hands down the body, eager to reach the feet, he found to his surprise another head.

'Strange,' exclaimed the vampire aloud. 'In all the three hundred and sixty-six valleys of these mountains I have sucked the blood of people without number, but never did I meet one with two heads and no feet!'

Saying which, Dakhanavar wandered off in bemusement and was never again encountered in that country. And ever since it has been known that there are three hundred and sixty-six valleys in the Ulmesh Altotem mountains, as many as there are days in the year with a spare one for leap years.

* * *

In parts of Russia the vampire is called Upierczi and besides the usual mischief it is held responsible for drought. Suicides, witches, warlocks and those who have suffered violent death are liable to rise from their graves as Upierczi. The surest way of disposing of them is to drown them in a lake or river, but the usual methods also apply. If nailed to its coffin, the nails must be driven in with single blows or the creature will revive.

In other regions it is called a Mjertovjec and has a purple face. It is active from midnight till cockcrow in the morning. People afraid that one of their family might become a Mjertovjec sprinkle poppy seeds along the path home from the grave, because like most vampires it has no choice but to count them and will not have time enough to trouble their relations.

In neighbouring Poland and Bulgaria the vampire is called Oupire, has a harelip and a tongue pointed like a bee's sting. Besides the usual causes, a child born with teeth will grow into an Oupire. Its speciality is tolling a bell at night and calling out the names of people who then die soon afterwards. Among the suggested cures are reburying the vampire face downwards and/or with a willow crucifix. Another precaution is to place some earth from the threshold of the Oupire's former home into its grave. This will confuse the vampire and discourage it from trying to get home.

THE COFFIN LID

Here, mildly edited, are a couple of the many similar vampire folk-tales collected by W.R.S Ralston in his *Russian Folk Tales* published in 1873.

Long ago in Russia a peasant, or moujik, was driving along a country road with a cartload of pots when he was overtaken by night. For a while he pressed on, hoping to find shelter, but his horse went slower and slower till finally it stopped beside a graveyard. No amount of pleading, cursing or beating would drive it another step, so there was nothing for it but to make the best of things. The moujik set the horse to graze, gathered some rugs and went to try and get some sleep on one of the graves.

Just as he was drifting off, he felt the tombstone move beneath him. Scrambling away, he watched the grave open and a corpse climb out, wrapped in a pale shroud and carrying its coffin lid. Laying the lid by the church door, the vampire strode rather stiffly off into the night. With courage bordering on madness, the peasant removed the coffin lid to his cart and, arming himself with an axe, waited to see what would follow.

Towards dawn the vampire returned and, after hunting vainly around for the coffin lid, finally spied it in the cart beside the moujik. Approaching, the vampire hissed menacingly: 'Give me back my coffin lid or I'll tear you limb from limb!'

'What about my axe?' replied the bold peasant, holding it up for inspection. 'It seems more likely to me that I might chop you into little pieces.'

Then the vampire began to beg instead, saying he could not get back into his grave without the lid, and would perish if dawn caught him in the open.

'I'll return it perhaps,' said the moujik, 'if you tell me what you've been up to tonight.'

So the vampire told how he had visited a nearby village and there drained the blood of two young men until they had died.

'Well then, tell me how they can be brought back to life and you can have your coffin lid.'

Eyeing the sharp axe and glancing also at the brightening sky, the vampire said reluctantly: 'Cut off the left skirt of my shroud and take it to the house where the young men lie dead. Pour some live coals into a pot and put the piece of shroud in too, then lock the door behind you and the smoke will bring them back to life.'

So, with great care, the moujik cut off the left skirt of the shroud and returned the coffin lid. The vampire scurried back into its grave but just as it was settling in a cock crowed nearby and the sepulchre was left slightly open, with one end of the coffin lid still sticking out. Noting this, the moujik set off for the village and by the sounds of weeping soon found the house where the murders had happened. 'Stop your wailing,' he told the relations, 'I can bring them back to life for you.'

'If you can do that,' they replied, 'we'll give you half of all we own.'

So the moujik did just as the vampire had told him. He called for a pot and some live coals. Then, clearing the room of spectators, he carefully placed the piece of shroud on the coals and sealed the death-chamber behind him so that it could fill with smoke. In next to no time there came the sound of coughing and, when the door was opened, they found the two young men as alive and well as ever.

Amid the celebrations, the moujik gently reminded their relations of the reward he had been promised, but their mood was strangely altered. 'Since you knew how to bring them back to life,' they accused him, 'perhaps it was you who killed them in the first place!' Then they seized and bound the moujik so he could be handed over to the authorities.

Now it was the moujik's turn to plead and tell the strange tale of how he had learned what to do. Soon the story spread through the whole village and everyone marched on the graveyard to test the truth of it. They found the grave slightly open, just as described. Within they found the coffin, and within that a corpse with no visible sign of decay. A great fire was kindled and an aspen stake driven through the vampire's heart before it was consigned to the flames, after which the moujik received a rich reward after all and the village was no longer troubled by its night-stalker.

THE SOLDIER AND THE VAMPIRE

A soldier of the Russian Imperial Army on leave once set off on foot for home. Approaching his village at last, he came to a mill that stood apart from it. He and the miller had once been great friends, so he called in and received a warm welcome. Soon vodka and ale were flowing and they lost themselves in talk of the past and all that had happened since they had last seen each other. Almost before they realised it, night had fallen and the trooper's thoughts turned to his beloved family. But as he rose to leave, the miller said anxiously: 'No, no, my old friend, you can't go now. Night has fallen; you may never reach the village.'

'How so?' asked the soldier. 'The moon is bright and the village not far. What could possibly happen between here and there?'

All cheer drained from the miller's face. 'A terrible warlock has died amongst us, my friend, and by night he rises from the grave and wanders through the village committing such terrible crimes I cannot even bring myself to describe them. Not even the bailiffs dare stand against this monster, so what hope have you alone?'

The soldier however had seen battle and the wide world and was not about to be scared by peasant superstition. 'As a soldier I belong to the Crown,' he declared boldly. 'And no Crown soldier is afraid of phantoms of the night. I will be off; I cannot wait any longer to see my dear family for whom I have journeyed so far.'

So, full of patriotic courage, not to mention vodka, he set off into the night and it so happened that his path took him right past a cemetery where he saw a great fire blazing on one of the graves. Curiously he approached and found a strange-looking man mending boots there by the light of the fire.

'Hail, brother!' greeted the soldier.

The warlock, for of course it was he, looked up and asked what the soldier was about.

'Why, I've come to see what you are doing,' he replied.

The warlock seemed pleased by this reply and, throwing aside his work, cried: 'Come along, brother, let's enjoy ourselves. There's a wedding on in the village tonight; let's you and me go and join the party.'

'That sounds a good idea,' replied the soldier, who had guessed who he was talking to and was determined to prove his boast to the miller.

So they went off to the wedding feast and were freely welcomed. The warlock drank and drank, then danced on the tables and drank some more, all in the highest spirits. Then suddenly his mood turned ugly and he chased all the relations and guests from the house before casting a spell on the bride and groom so that they fell asleep. Producing two phials and an awl, he pierced their hands and drew off a quantity of blood into each phial. 'Now let's be off,' he said to the soldier.

On the way back to the graveyard the soldier asked why he had taken the blood.

'Why, so the couple will die. In the morning no-one will be able to wake them. I alone know how to return them to life.'

'And how is that?'

'They must have cuts made in their heels and their own blood poured back into the wounds. See, I have the groom's blood here in my right pocket and the bride's in my left. I have the power of life over them, but my pleasure is to withhold it.'

The soldier made no comment and soon the warlock began boasting further: 'Whatever I wish to do,' he said, 'that I can do.'

'Then it is impossible for anyone to get the better of you?'

'Impossible? Not quite. If someone were to build a fire of aspen boughs, a hundred loads of them, and were to burn me on that pyre, then he would get the better of me. Only he'd have to be sharp, for snakes and worms and all kinds of reptiles would crawl out of my insides; and crows and magpies and jackdaws would come flying from the flames. And if any one of them should escape, then I would survive. If so much as a single maggot were to escape, in that maggot I would slip away and become whole again.'

Again the soldier made no comment, and he and the warlock walked and talked of other things till at last they came back to the graveyard, where the fire had burned out.

'Well brother,' said the warlock, 'you've been good company tonight but now I'm going to have to tear you to pieces or you'll be telling the world all my secrets.'

'That may not be so easy,' replied the soldier bravely, 'you're talking to a soldier of God and the Tsar.'

The warlock howled and sprang upon him, but the soldier drew his sword and fought back stoutly. Back and forth across the graveyard the battle raged and for a long time neither had the upper hand. Then at last the soldier began to tire and fear for his life, realising he had met his match. Both God and the Tsar seemed very far away, but just as he despaired, a cock crowed for the dawn. The warlock struggled free and raced back to his grave. He reached it, but not before the soldier managed to snatch the two phials from his pockets.

Going to the village, he found his family and heard all about the couple who had perished at the warlock's hands on their wedding night.

'Take me to them,' said the soldier, and when they reached the place he asked the mourners what they would give him if he brought the couple back to life.

'Take what you will,' they replied, 'even if it is half of all we have.'

So the soldier proceeded to do as the warlock had instructed him. He made incisions and poured blood into the wounds, taking the greatest care to give each their own blood. Soon the couple woke to great rejoicing and the soldier was fêted by the whole community. Then off he marched to tell his tale to the authorities. Soon a hundred loads of aspen wood were rumbling towards the cemetery, followed by a great crowd of villagers. The warlock was dragged from his grave and thrown onto a great pyre that was set alight. Then as he began to burn there crawled from his body snakes, worms and all kinds of reptiles; and there flew out of the flames crows, magpies and jackdaws, just as the warlock had foretold. But the peasants were ready and with sling, stone and arrow they knocked all the flying things out of the sky and back into the flames, and of the creeping creatures not so much as a maggot was allowed to escape the furnace.

And so the warlock was consumed to ashes that were scattered on the wind; and from that moment there was peace at night in the village and the soldier had only to ask for anything and it was given to him.

RUSALKI

In Slavic folklore the rusalki are nymphs who live in rivers and pools, living underwater during the winter but emerging during spring and summer to sport on the shore or even wander the neighbouring woods and fields. In daylight they are usually invisible and their passage through the fields can only be traced by the rippling of the crops; but in the dusk or at night they appear as beautiful young women clad only in mist or their own flowing hair. They have enchanting voices which they use to attract passing young men, often to their doom by luring them down into the watery depths.

In parts of southern Russia this was once deemed an unfortunate consequence of falling in love with a rusalka. There the rusalki were traditionally viewed as fundamentally benign nature spirits whose favour was courted with ribbons and garlands of flowers to benefit the crops. More commonly though, in northern Russia and elsewhere, they were seen as malign creatures whose sport was luring young men to their death by drowning and the same offerings were made but to avert their malice rather than court their favour.

Rusalki are fond of riddles and in the south this was one way to win their favours; but in the north the riddling was in deadly earnest because failure to solve or come up with a good riddle meant almost certain death, like Bilbo playing the riddling game with Gollum. Rusalki are commonly said to be the souls or even the re-animated corpses of suicides, maidens who have drowned themselves after being jilted by a lover, which is why they revenge themselves on other young men. Other explanations are that they are unbaptised, often unwanted babies who have been drowned by their mothers, or sinners who have died without absolution. Rusalki are believed to be most active and dangerous in the first week of June, when children in the Slavic lands were once commonly forbidden to swim.

The folk legend of the rusalka has been immortalised in art many times, most notably in Pushkin's 1819 unfinished dramatic poem *Rusalka* and the similarly titled operas by Alexander Dargomyzhsky (1856) and Antonín Dvořák (1901). Gogol also used the legend for his 1831 short story *May Night or the Drowned Maiden*, which inspired Rimsky-Korsakov's 1879 opera of the same name.

MALAYSIAN VAMPIRES

Remarkably similar to Lilith's brood and the classical lamia is the Malaysian Langsuir, who often hunts in the guise of an owl. The first Langsuir (or Pontianak, the terms are often interchanged) is said to have been an extraordinarily beautiful woman whose child was still-born and had the appearance of an owl. Seeing this, the mother screeched with grief, clapped her hands and flew away in the form of an owl herself, with hideous claws with which she perches on the rooftop hooting in a sad and ominous way. Driven mad with grief, she preys on humans, particularly men and babies.

When not in owl form the Langsuir appears as a terribly beautiful woman wearing an exquisite and perfumed robe of jade green. Her fingernails are as long and sharp as talons and often poisonous. Her shining, jet-black hair falls to her ankles and hides the hole in the back of her neck through which she drinks blood. Curiously enough it is supposed to be possible to tame this creature by cutting her hair and nails short, and stuffing them into the unnatural hole in her neck. After this she might lead a contented and quiet life for many years and make a very good wife, but something usually breaks the spell in the end and she flies off again into the wild.

If a woman dies in childbirth, or within forty days of it, the following precautions were once recommended to prevent her becoming a Langsuir. Her mouth is filled with glass beads to prevent her shrieking; needles are placed in the palm of her hands to stop her clapping them together; and a hen's egg is placed in each armpit so she cannot flap them like wings. It still happens that a woman who dies in childbirth has verses from the Koran inscribed on her fingernails to prevent her becoming a Langsuir. The male counterpart of this creature is the Bajang whose origins are more obscure. Both are liable to attach themselves to sorcerers and do their bidding, often being passed from one generation of shamans to the next like a bizarre heirloom. Even in colonial times anyone proven by a native court, or even just believed to have used one of these creatures to harm his neighbours, was banished or killed.

The closest thing in the Malay Peninsula to the Western vampire is the Penanggalan which has the appearance of a severed human head with a mane of tangled hair, penetrating bloodshot eyes and a long protruding tongue which it uses (given the chance) to suck the blood of women giving birth. This apparition flies through the night seeking victims with its entrails dangling behind it. Like the Langsuir it delights most in killing children by sucking their blood but will also feed on the blood of women in childbirth. One legend says that the first Penanggalan came into existence through a bizarre accident:

Long ago a woman was meditating in penance for some crime in one of the large wooden vats the Malays use for storing palm vinegar. One presumes it was empty and chosen so she could contemplate her sins without distraction. But along came a man who was curious and asked what she was doing. Startled out of her trance, she leaped up and somehow managed to kick her own chin with such force that her head flew right off, dragging the intestines behind it, and ended up perched in a nearby tree. Ever after it lingered near that house as a demon, screeching like an owl at the birth of every child and trying to force its way in to drain its blood, or that of the mother.

Other versions of the tale say that the Penanggalan was originally a woman who died giving birth to a stillborn child. Her grieving husband held a funeral attended by the whole village, but when he returned sadly to his home on the edge of the village he was startled by a shriek of laughter. Looking up, he saw his dead wife squatting on the roof devouring their dead child, after which she continued to prey on other newborn babies.

Yet another tale tells that the first Penanggalan was a woman who took service with a demon in order to become a witch and learn how to fly. She smeared a magic ointment around her neck that enabled her head to detach itself (apart from the entrails) and fly away from the rest of her body in search of blood. Later she could return and re-enter her body and go about her normal business. Any witch with the power to become a Penanggalan is sure to have a large vat of vinegar somewhere in her house, because the entrails swell up after leaving the body and must be soaked awhile in vinegar before squeezing back into it.

Ways to guard against the Penanggalan include hanging thistles around doors and windows and spreading thorns of the pineapple or pandan plant wherever blood is spilt, because the creature is afraid of getting its intestines caught up in these. Steel pins, nails and knives also scare the creature

Whatever its exact origins, belief in the Penanggalan and Langsuir was profound until modern times and persists in many areas, especially in the countryside, where motorists still think twice before picking up glamorous stray females on lonely roads at night in case they turn into vampires; and they still hang briars and thorns around houses where a child is to be born. The traditions are also shared by neighbouring countries like Burma, Thailand and the Philippines, where the local equivalent is known as the Manananggal, which means 'self-remover' in Tagalog, the widest-spoken tongue in the Philippines. It is very similar in nature and appearance but instead of being just a disembodied head, the Manananggal usually retains its upper torso and long dangling breasts. Eyewitnesses describe it as having tangled hair, long arms, talon-like fingernails and sharp teeth. Almost its only weakness is that for some reason the Manananggal in normal everyday guise cannot bring itself to touch a stingray's tail.

In 1992 in the Phillippines there was a curious outbreak of Manananggal hysteria and for a while all the popular papers and TV newscasts were filled with accounts of sightings and even struggles with this vampire. An elderly woman suspect was even interviewed on nationwide TV by Cesar Soriano amid raging controversy over her claims of innocence. The matter was resolved only when the reporter produced the dried tail of a stingray for her to touch under the beady eye of the camera and millions of viewers. When she managed it without flinching the suspicion passed elsewhere.

Later, in September 2001 a spiritual healer or bomoh appeared on prime time TV news on Channel TV3, claiming to have captured a shape-shifting vampire in a jar. As later reported in the Straits Times he said it had taken about an hour to catch the creature, which he happily displayed to the news cameras. It resembled a wad of cotton, possibly because it had been caught near a cotton tree, about the size of two tennis balls and with a small face. Closer inspection was impossible for fear that the 'langsuir' might escape. The plan was to throw the jar and its vampire into the sea.

In Thailand the local equivalent of the Penanggalan is called the Phi kraseau, meaning 'fifth ghost'. In addition to being a hideous flying head dangling its entrails behind it, this variant has an internally flashing red or green light. Its staple diet is human blood, excrement, and the foetuses and birth organs of pregnant women. Besides enjoying wide credence in the countryside the Phi kraseau is a staple monster in the thriving Thai horror movie business.

Vampire Bats

'When I saw him four days ago down at his own place he looked queer. I have not seen anything pulled down so quick since I was on the pampas and had a mare that I was fond of go to grass all in a night. One of those big bats that they call vampires had got at her in the night, and, what with his gorge and the vein left open, there wasn't enough blood in her to let her stand up, and I had to put a bullet through her as she lay.'

Quincy in Bram Stoker's *Dracula*

When the Spanish conquistadors arrived in South America in the fifteenth and sixteenth centuries they discovered the vampire bat, whose fame swiftly spread back to

Europe and attached itself to the vampire tradition there. There are suggestions of vampires and bats being linked before this in Europe, but only to the same extent as other liminal creatures like rats, owls and wolves, and only to about the same extent that bats are associated with ghosts, witches and the like.

Quincy in the quote above is completely wrong in his description of the vampire bat of course. The three known species are all small creatures completely incapable of draining enough blood from a horse to kill it. Moreover, they just lap at the blood from small, anaesthetised incisions rather than sucking it in true vampire fashion, but the element in their saliva that prevents blood-clotting has been named draculin anyway. Vampire bats only kill their hosts through sometimes spreading diseases, especially rabies, which can cause epidemics and create real problems. In fact thousands of livestock die every year in Brazil from rabies spread by vampire bats, and they often infect people too; but that is incidental to their purpose, as with other bloodsuckers like ticks, fleas and mosquitoes. Normally a few spoonfuls of blood are enough to glut a vampire bat so much that it is unable to fly and has to waddle off to a quiet corner to recuperate; and if it is not carrying anything like rabies its host is none the worse for the encounter.

However, in world mythology there are a number of other bat-like monsters that probably pre-date knowledge of the vampire bat. In India there is the baital made famous by Sir Richard Burton's 1870 translation of Hindu folk tales *Vikram and the Vampire*. Burton's wife Isabel, who edited the book believed the stories to be the seed of *The Arabian Nights*. Like that collection it is a set of stories within a story, beginning with the capture of a baital or vampire by the legendary Raja Vikram; then the vampire tells a series of tales which make up the body of the book. The baital or vetala is described in the tale a large creature hanging in a glowing tree at a crematorium, from which position it was in the habit of entering and re-animating the corpses brought for disposal: 'Its eyes, which were wide open, were of a greenish-brown, and never twinkled; its hair also was brown, and brown was its face — three several shades which, notwithstanding, approached one another in an unpleasant way, as in an over-dried cocoa-nut. Its body was thin and ribbed like a skeleton or a bamboo framework, and as it held on to a bough, like a flying fox [fruit-bat] by the toe-tips, its drawn muscles stood out as if they were ropes of coin. Blood it appeared to have none, or there would have been a decided determination of that curious juice to the head; and as the Raja handled its skin it felt icy cold and clammy as might a snake. The only sign of life was the whisking of a ragged little tail much resembling a goat's.'

On the island of Seram in Indonesia they tell of the Orang Bati, a large human/bat hybrid that flies around at night trying to snatch children to carry back to the extinct volcano they inhabit during the day. They are described as red-skinned people with black bat-wings and a long tail. Similar creatures are reported on other islands but they do not harm people. The creature has reportedly been spotted by Western visitors and there have been suggestions that it could be a real creature – a giant monkey-eating bat in fact, that attacks children on Seram because the island has no monkeys, unlike the others; but no reliable specimens have yet been found,

In the Philippines their local vampire, the aswang, is often said to travel in the form of a bat, though it can also take the shape of a dog, pig or even a human – usually a horrible old woman with bloodshot eyes, long black tongue and holes in her armpits containing magical oil. Like many other vampires, the aswang's favoured prey is children, though it has been suggested that this is just claimed by parents to keep their children in at night. Ways of guarding against intrusion of an aswang into the house include hanging magical and religious amulets above the doors and windows and sprinkling salt on the frames, and drawing crosses in the ground outside the house with a piece of iron. Also known as 'tik-tik' from the sound they make, aswangs are said to be particularly dangerous in Holy Week.

NATIVE AMERICAN VAMPIRES

What the Spanish found in Mexico along with vampire bats was a thriving, if rigid, empire ruled by a god-king. He oversaw a religion in which human sacrifice famously played a major part even when worshipping such seemingly benevolent deities as Flower Feather (Xochiqetzal), a counterpart of Venus, or Five Flower (Macuilxochitl) the patroness of music and games.

Unsurprisingly, the Mexican night was populated by a host of other bloodthirsty sprites, not least of them the witches known placatingly as The Ladies, or Ciuateteo, who liked to gather at crossroads. They were said to be women who had died in their first labour and were presided over by a Mexican Lilith known as Tlazolteotl, goddess of sorcery, lust and evil whose totem creatures were the snake and screech owl. The Ladies were very pale-skinned and said to fly through the air on broomsticks. They were liable to attack anyone they met during the hours of darkness, but their special taste was for the blood of children. Any child visited by one of these vampires would afterwards waste away and die. To guard against this, Mexicans carefully sealed their houses at night with charms and thorns, and left offerings of tasty food at crossroads to keep the witches from wandering. In addition, many Mexican sorcerers had a taste for human blood, at least so the Spanish missionaries said.

In Guyana and some neighbouring Latin American countries there is still widespread belief in 'Ole Higue', a vampiress who seems a hybrid of African, Native

American and European beliefs. By day she seems normal, usually an old woman who keeps to herself; but at night she removes her skin, stores it carefully in a calabash and travels around as a ball of fire seeking victims whose blood she sucks while they are asleep, her favourites being young children. She is said to enter houses through the keyhole and for this reason many Guyanese still leave keys in a horizontal position after locking the door at night. Their hope is that they will hear the key rattle as Ole Higue tries to squeeze through. Then if they are quick enough they can crush her by turning the key and in the morning will find a pile of bones on the threshold.

Another way of defeating Ole Higue is to find the calabash where she has stored her skin and fill it with hot peppers. Then when she tries to put it back on she will scream with pain and thus reveal herself. A third weakness which she shares with other vampires across the world is that if you scatter grains of rice on the threshold she will feel obliged to count and collect them before entering, and if there are more than she can easily hold in her hand this should keep her occupied all night and she will be found still on the doorstep in the morning, whereupon she can be beaten to death with the special broom some Guyanese keep for just this purpose.

This may seem like no more than an colourful folk legend except that it is still sometimes taken very seriously. In April 2007 an old woman was beaten to death in the village of Bare Root, fifteen miles east of the Guyana capital, Georgetown, by villagers convinced that she was an Ole Higue. A baby was said to have been attacked and some witnesses said that before dawn the woman had seemed to be a dark ball with flickering flames and had assumed human shape as the sun rose. A quantity of rice was found scattered around the body, along with a broom made from manicole palm fronds. Two arrests were made.

The Ashanti people of Ghana in West Africa tell of a very similar witch they call the Obayifo, who lives unrecognised in the community and can leave her body at night as a ball of light and attack people. Like Ole Higue she is especially fond of the blood of children but will attack anyone at need. Under other names this kind of witch was feared throughout the Bantu tribes of Africa, which is probably how the idea reached Guyana through the slave trade.

North America has its vampires too, the most famous of which is the Wendigo

(Windigo, Windago, Windiga, Witiko and other variants). This is a cannibalistic demon, possibly more like a werewolf than a vampire in fact, that can possess people and drive them to eat human flesh. The fear of becoming a Wendigo was once very common in the Algonquin and related tribes but is apparently fading as Native Americans become urbanised. In appearance the Wendigo is gaunt and grey, looking almost like a walking corpse well on the road of decay. It gives off a terrible but sweet stench and its thin lips are usually torn and bloody. Its hunger can never be satisfied and in some tribes Wendigos are said to grow into giants – the more they eat, the bigger and hungrier they get. Simple greed can be enough to turn a person into a Wendigo (or make them vulnerable to possession by one) but more commonly it is supposed to be the result of eating human flesh. This was taboo even in times of famine, when the proper response was considered to be patient resignation or suicide.

Up to the twentieth century, so great was the fear of becoming a Wendigo among the Algonquin that when they felt or imagined the symptoms coming on, they would ask to be executed, and occasionally this happened when all other remedies failed. More commonly, when an individual became unstable and violent, others would diagnose the cause and carry out the execution. In Canada the authorities largely turned a blind eye to such incidents until a landmark case in 1907 when an Oji-Cree chief and shaman known as Jack Fiddler, famous for his power in defeating Wendigos, was arrested for the alleged murder of one, his own niece in fact whom he believed to have become one. Fiddler committed suicide before the trial and this marked the end of legal autonomy for the aboriginal Canadians.

The Wendigo has entered popular culture through comics, films and horror stories, beginning with Algernon Blackwood whose 1910 story *The Wendigo* introduced the legend to a wide audience for the first time. In it he has a character, Dr Cathcart, say: 'the Wendigo is simply the Call of the Wild personified, which some natures hear to their own destruction'.

CHINESE VAMPIRES

Given that for most of their histories China and Europe have only known of each other as dim rumours, it is odd how similar their ideas about vampires are. Most probably these notions were passed back and forth along the Silk Route or brought west by the Mongolian hordes, but early researchers can be forgiven for simply assuming vampirism was a real curse common to both regions. Similar tales are told in Tibet, though the Tibetans themselves have never suffered much from vampires because, they claim, of their practice of sky-burial, of dismembering the dead and feeding them to vultures.

In China the vampire is known as a Jiangshi (literally 'stiff corpse') and is generally regarded as a demon that has taken possession of a human corpse, which it nourishes by feeding on other corpses or living humans. Alternatively, it is the person's own lower soul that revives the cadaver. This idea springs from the Chinese belief that each person has two souls – the Hun, or superior soul, which strives for heaven; and the Po, or inferior soul which is inherently malign, the shadow side of even the most saintly dispositions. Where the Po is strong enough, even the smallest portion of the body such as a toe or finger is enough for it to build up from into a vampire, particularly if exposed to the light of the moon.

Chinese vampires are said to have red, staring eyes and claw-tipped fingers. They are immensely strong and can fly through the air. Like western vampires they suffer from appalling halitosis which is often enough in itself to kill their victims. A good way of distracting vampires in China, as almost everywhere else, is to scatter grains of rice in their path because they feel obliged to stop and count almost any kind of seed (there must be some symbolic explanation of this habit of vampires but for the moment it escapes me). The only sure way of destroying the Jiangshi is cremation, though often beheading and impaling it with a stake will do the trick.

Most descriptions of Chinese vampires are so similar to European ones that they are clearly talking about the same creature. One novelty is that Chinese vampires are often described as being covered in long white or pale green hair, which is probably due to the prevalence of grave mould in parts of China. It is also less apparent that the Jiangshi's victims in turn become vampires themselves, or that the vampire's main interest is to drink its victim's blood. That has crept into modern movies but is largely due to the influence of Western films. In Chinese translations Dracula is often described as 'a blood-sucking Jiangshi', as if that was an additional characteristic. But these are relatively minor points that are outweighed by what the monsters have in common. Here are a few good examples of Chinese vampire folk tales adapted from Gerald Willoughby-Meade's *Chinese Ghouls and Goblins*. This was first published in 1928 but is still probably the best source for such tales outside of China itself, which he never actually visited, his studies being pursued in the libraries, museums and Anglo-Chinese societies of London.

No Room at the Inn

At Ts'ai Tien in Shan Tung province, south of Peking, four travellers arrived late one night at a tavern. Weary and famished, they gratefully warmed themselves by the fire and tucked into a welcome meal, but when they asked for lodgings they were told that every bed in the place was taken. They were in no mood to be thrown out into the night again so they begged the landlord to find some corner for them, no matter how uncomfortable. At last the innkeeper gave way. Leading them outside, he took them to an outbuilding where, he said, his daughter-in-law lay awaiting burial, having recently died. If they did not mind sharing a room with her corpse, the travellers were welcome to stay there, otherwise they must make shift for themselves.

Well, they were past caring about corpses. Accepting his offer, the four were shown into a dim room where, behind a filmy curtain in one corner, the dead girl lay on a bed as if asleep. They took little notice as mattresses and bedding were laid out and soon three of the travellers were happily snoring. The fourth, however, felt uneasy and it was a while before he too began to drift into slumber. Then he heard a soft but ominous rustling. Half opening his eyes, he saw the curtains in the far corner parting and the young woman gazing upon her guests with a hungry light in her eyes. Softly she approached and stooped in turn over each of the three sleepers, enclosing their heads in the veil of her raven hair. And each in turn stopped snoring.

The fourth, faint with terror, buried his head under the blankets and prayed furiously to every god he could think of as he felt the soft pressure of the girl bending at last over him. Either the prayers worked or the vampire was too sated to bother winkling him out from under the covers. Whichever, after what seemed an age he felt the pressure lift and when at last he dared peep out he saw the dead girl again lying on her bed.

Gathering his courage and his clothes, the traveller tried to wake his companions but got no response, nor did they seem to be breathing. Something else did stir though and, looking up, the traveller found that the vampire was awake again. With a shriek he rushed for the door and just managed to bolt it behind him before racing away barefoot under the waning moon, looking for the inn and hearing the door behind him being pounded and shaken with terrifying force.

In the confusion and dark he lost his way and found himself running through a wood with no house in sight. Glancing back, he found the vampire hot on his heels and gaining with every step. When it was almost upon him, the man caught in desperation at a passing willow tree, swung himself around it and doubled back the way he had come, but the trick only gained him seconds before the vampire was clawing again at his back. In desperation he dived into the trees, then tripped and fell. His last glimpse as he tumbled into a ditch and oblivion was of the vampire swooping upon him with its eyes blazing like fire.

The next morning he was found by some passers-by. To his own complete astonishment he had no more than lacerated feet and a few bruises to show for his adventure. Nearby they found the corpse of the vampire withered by the sun and with its talons deeply embedded in a tree-trunk. Plainly it had mistaken the tree for its victim and tried to strangle it so fiercely it had been unable to pull free. The traveller's three companions were found back at the little house completely drained of life.

THE HAUNTED TEMPLE

There was once a Chinese shepherd who took to grazing his flock near a deserted temple. At least, it was deserted apart from the great festivals of Spring and Autumn. Then priests and worshippers came from all over the district and the place came alive with light and bustle and music. But at all other times it was shunned and the elements were steadily reducing it to a ruin.

The shepherd was new to the area and was puzzled by this waste of so grand a place. It also occurred to him that in bad weather it would provide perfect shelter for him and his sheep. However, he was a cautious and law-abiding fellow so before moving in he first checked with the local authorities if permission was needed. Thus he learned that the temple was haunted and not even priests dared spend the night there outside of the two festivals. The shepherd, however, was used to spending nights alone in wild places and had no fear of ghosts. So when no objection was raised, he resolved to put the matter to the test. Arming himself with a big leather whip and a lantern, he gathered his sheep and herded them into the temple at dusk. Then he settled down for the night but resolved to keep awake in case anything should happen.

The temple was dedicated to three great warriors of antiquity who had been elevated to gods for their part in calming their troubled times. In the fitful light of his lantern, the statues looked rather menacing and the shepherd could see how easily one might imagine that their eyes were watching him, and their limbs twitching as if about to come suddenly to life. But he personally was not the imaginative kind and he concluded that perhaps this was why people were afraid of the place. They just let their imaginations run away with them. Then he was about to nod off despite his resolve when he heard something stirring in the direction of the statues.

A tall, gaunt and hideous figure seemed to rise from the floor below the statues, vaguely human in aspect but covered in long pale hair. Its eyes glowed like burning red coals and soon fastened themselves upon the shepherd. Then it darted towards him with an eager hiss, clawed hands outstretched and seeming to fly across the stone floor with its long hair trailing behind. The shepherd was momentarily stunned with amazement, but he had faced wolves and tigers alone before and he recovered in time to throw himself aside. He lashed out with his whip and it connected with a sharp crack, but the apparition merely grinned, baring sharp white fangs. It snatched the whip from his hands and the shepherd turned and fled in terror for the door, just slamming it behind him as the thing crashed against it like a thunderbolt. There came a howl of fury and the door was wrenched from his grasp. The shepherd ran for his life, climbing the nearest tree in the courtyard like a monkey with its tail on fire.

He immediately regretted this, thinking himself trapped, but when he could climb no further and dared look back, he saw that the nightmarish creature seemed unable to cross the temple threshold.

With dawn the apparition vanished, and soon afterwards some villagers came along to see what had happened. They were less surprised to find the shepherd up a tree than they were to find him still alive, and listened with great interest to his tale. Then, emboldened by their numbers and the daylight, they went to investigate the temple and found a curious black vapour issuing from cracks beneath the pedestal of the triple statue. This was enough to quench their curiosity for the moment, but they took their tale to the local magistrate who ordered an investigation.

The pedestal was broken and the flagstones removed. As they dug down, the workmen came to the body of a very tall man, gaunt and hideous and covered in greenish hair just as the shepherd had described. The body was carried out into the courtyard and a pyre built around it, and when it was lit the vampire screamed and writhed amid the flames like a living being, the blood pouring from it in hissing streams. The ashes were scattered on a nearby river and from that day the haunting ended, though it was long before anyone, including the shepherd, dared spend a night in the temple alone.

A characteristic of Chinese vampires that seems at first sight unique to them is a terror of bronze bells which seem to have had much the same effect on them as crucifixes and sacred Christian symbols had on Dracula and his kin. This is not as peculiar as it may seem though, because the bronze bell was to Taoism in China what the crucifix and consecrated host are to Christianity. Also it is worth recalling that when bells were introduced to Ireland by the first Christian missionaries they were said to have the power of banishing demons and fairies by their mere chiming, a sound that had never been heard in that country before. Some of those early saints' bells have survived to this day in jewelled reliquaries. Modern fictional vampires seem to have overcome their fear of or vulnerability to such things however, possibly in proportion to the declining weight of faith behind them in an increasingly agnostic age. The same is probably true in China regarding bronze bells, but Willoughby-Meade unearthed this tale from Chihli province (now Hebei, the north-eastern province surrounding Beijing) from a time when religion still carried weight.

It seems that long ago one of the mountain villages was plagued by a Jiangshi that terrorized it every night, attacking anyone it could find, but particularly children. The villagers sought the aid of a powerful Taoist priest living nearby and finally he agreed to come to their aid. He arrived armed with nets and snares and other magic paraphernalia for trapping a vampire. But, said the priest, for his plan to succeed he needed a brave volunteer from the village to close his trap. Well, no-one was too eager to put themselves in the front line but eventually a young man stepped forward and had his part in the plan explained.

Towards evening the priest and villagers closed in on a cave believed to be the vampire's daytime resting place. The priest laid his traps all round the entrance to the cave with the villagers in a semicircle at a safe distance behind that; all but for the priest himself who had set up an altar facing the cave and the brave volunteer who was crouched right beside the cave mouth itself with two little copper or bronze bells. These, he had been assured were protection enough from the vampire because, the priest had explained: 'the sound of copper instruments renders spectres powerless.'

When night fell the vampire rushed out of his cave for his usual nightly depredations but stopped short when faced with the priest and his altar. Realising he was no match for the saint, the vampire darted left and right to get past him and found the ways blocked by the priest's magic nets and incantations. Finally he turned to flee back into his cave but there stood the brave volunteer shaking the bells for all he was worth. The vampire glared at him with eyes like lightning but could not approach because of the bells. And thus the whole night passed with the Jiangshi trapped in a magic circle. Then finally the first rays of dawn brightened the sky and the vampire fell dead. The villagers burned the body to ashes amid a great celebration and the village was never troubled by its like again; but the brave young volunteer ever afterwards could not stop shaking his hands as if frantically ringing two bells; and when people asked why he did this, he told them this tale.

CHAPTER IV

DRACULA, THE BLOOD COUNTESS AND BLUEBEARD

I HAVE ASKED MY FRIEND ARMINUS, of Buda-Pesth University, to make his record; and he must, indeed, have been that Voivode Dracula who won his fame against the Turk, over the great river on the very frontier of Turkey. If it be so, then he was no common man; for in that time and for centuries after he was spoken of as the cleverest and most cunning as well as the bravest of the sons of the "land beyond the forest." That mighty brain and that iron resolution went with him to the grave. The Draculas were, says Arminus, a great and noble race, though now and again were scions who were held by their coevals to have had dealings with the Evil One. They learned his secrets in the Scholomance, amongst the mountains over Lake Hermanstadt, where the devil claims the tenth scholar as his due. In the records are such words as "stregoica" — witch; "ordog" and "pokol" —

Satan and hell; and in one manuscript this very Dracula is spoken of as "wampyr", which we all understand too well. There have been from the loins of this one great men and good women, and their graves make sacred the earth where alone this foulness can dwell. For it is not the least of its terrors that this evil thing is rooted deep in all good; in soil barren of holy memories it cannot rest.

Dr Abraham Van Helsing
in Bram Stoker's *Dracula*

IN THE ANNALS OF VAMPIRISM three real life monsters of sadism are inescapable, even though none has ever seriously been accused of being an actual vampire in the sense of having risen from the grave to feed upon the blood of the living. They are the original Vlad Dracula, Elisabeth Bathory and Gilles de Laval, more famous as Bluebeard.

All three were demonic in their behaviour and at least two dabbled in black magic, but there was nothing else supernatural about them. They were mortal humans like you or me, though their behaviour was monstrous on a scale that almost defies belief and this is why they stand out so sharply. The horrors they inflicted for amusement on those in their power exceed almost any nightmare or work of fiction so they stand as both warnings and examples of a certain wild extreme of human behaviour that has come to be personified in the fictional vampire.

Here they are presented in order of their relevance to the vampire mythos rather than chronologically. Bluebeard came first, dying in France while Vlad Dracula was still a child; while Elisabeth Bathory was born about 84 years after her distant cousin Vlad's death.

VLAD DRACULA: THE IMPALER

Bram Stoker based his fictional Dracula partly on the historical one but it is noteworthy that in the novel he describes him only in heroic terms, leaving the reader to guess how the evil crept in later. Yet Stoker must have known about the real Vlad the Impaler's fearsome reputation, even though it was glossed over in the Romanian and Russian accounts which concentrate on his very real achievements as guardian of the gateway of Europe against the Turks.

Perhaps he did this for dramatic effect, to make some point about how easily virtue can change into vice. All characters in the book are equally liable to become monsters once infected with the taint of vampirism. Virtue alone is no defence; it takes either physical means like garlic or a wooden stake through the heart, or sacramental ones like the crucifix, the Communion wafer or Holy Water to keep Dracula at bay. Even going to war with Dracula has its contagion, as we see in Van Helsing's increasingly manic and ruthless behaviour during the chase, which at times almost mirror the actions of his quarry.

In the film *Bram Stoker's Dracula*, along with many other loose ends of the plot that Coppola ties up is his suggestion for why Dracula changed. Taking up Stoker's position, the film portrays Dracula at the beginning as a hero embittered in his moment of triumph against the Turks by first a trick which drives his beloved wife to suicide, then her rejection by the Church because of that suicide. This is what turns him to evil in the film. Coppola juggles with the facts but it makes great dramatic sense and probes deeper into the same good/evil question that Stoker was playing with. While he remains a monster, we are drawn to sympathise with Dracula by seeing things from his point of view. He becomes more a tragic figure like Macbeth than a simple psychopathic demon, and a whole new dimension is added to his pursuit of Mina Harker.

It also puts a finger on one attraction of vampires. We can relate to them because most of us recognise that at some stage we too have shifted into monstrous behaviour through justifiable rage at some injustice or other. Or we at least know people who have. Lurking here is an insight into the nature of evil – that grinning, murderous psychopaths who delight in evil for its own sake are in fact few and far between. Most of the great wrongs in the world are perpetrated by people who genuinely believe themselves to be on the side of the angels, putting right some injustice or ridding the world of what they perceive to be wrong. The original Dracula was a great example of this, even if his story was not quite as portrayed in the film.

The historical Dracula, known also as Vlad Tepes or the Impaler, Prince of Wallachia, was born around 1430 in the ancient German fortress town of Schassburg. Now called Sighisoara in Romania, it lies some hundred kilometres southward of Bistrita (where Bram Stoker's novel opens) and between the converging Transylvanian Alps and Carpathian Mountains. His birthplace survives as the house of a modestly rich burgher. Its only distinction from the rest in the street is a plaque declaring it to have been the home in 1431 of Vlad Dracul, Dracula's father.

By a strange coincidence 'dracul' in Romanian means either dragon or devil, so Dracula means the son of whichever you wish. Many had every reason to consider Dracula the son of Satan in his day, though few dared even whisper this. In the uncertain spelling of the time, Dracula's name also appeared on official documents as Dragulya, Dragkwlya, Dragwyla or, in Hungary, as Dracole; some of which survive as surnames today. His father received his name as an honour from the Holy Roman Emperor who bestowed on him the Order of the Dragon in 1431. This bound him to defend Christianity against the Turks who were then determinedly trying to invade, and who for a while seriously threatened to colonise half of Europe.

Dracul was also given two duchies in Transylvania as his power base and crowned Voivode or Prince of Wallachia, modern Romania's southern province running from the Transylvanian Alps down to the Danube. This last gift, however, only meant that the Emperor gave his blessing for Dracul to seize the principality by force from his half-brother, which he succeeded in doing five years later. Once on the throne, Dracul began playing one side off against the other, signing a pact with the Turkish Sultan and even at one point joining the Turks for a murderous raid into Transylvania, overlooking that the victims were his own subjects. The Turkish Sultan Murad (Mohammed or Mehmet II) still had his suspicions though and forced Dracul to hand over his two younger sons, Dracula and Radu, as hostages for good behaviour.

Vlad Dracula remained a prisoner in Asia Minor for four years until he was about eighteen. His conditions seem to have been comfortable enough, but his father's political machinations meant that life for the hostages often hung by a thread. It has been suggested that this is what led to Dracula's legendary sadism later, and it certainly can't have helped, but it had no such effect on his brother Radu. He happily accepted the Turkish yoke and customs, particularly the pleasure-loving ones, became a favourite with the Sultan and later a willing pawn in his power games.

Dracul's balancing act could not last forever and in 1447 the Christian Emperor's Balkan crusaders, helped by many Wallachian nobles, assassinated him along with his eldest son Mircea. Dracula then briefly became Prince of Wallachia, being released by the Turks who thought he might be more trustworthy than his father; but Dracula trusted no-one around him and after a couple of months fled to Moldavia. There he made a lasting friend and ally in his cousin, Prince Steven, and they agreed that whichever first came to power would help the other.

Gradually Vlad Dracula picked his way through the tangled politics of his inheritance until his father's old duchies were restored to him and he became the official Imperial candidate for the Wallachian throne. This again meant that the Holy Roman Emperor simply sanctioned him taking it by force, which he did with Prince Steven's aid. After deposing and executing the incumbent prince (another relation) in 1456, Dracula gave a clear signal of how he intended to rule.

He summoned all the bishops and nobles, or boyars, to his palace at Targoviste. They came, curious and unsuspecting, confident that they were the real power in the land. They believed that Dracula, as with his many short-lived predecessors, could only rule with their blessing. But Dracula had no intention of being their pawn and had neither forgiven nor forgotten his father's murder. He knew that many of his guests that day had helped or approved of it, and would dispose of him in the same way without a second thought if it suited them. So he asked each noble how many Princes of Wallachia they had seen come and go. They were puzzled but replied openly enough, and even some of the younger ones could boast of having seen seven reigns.

Only those who could not possibly have had a hand in Vlad Dracul's assassination were spared. The rest, some five hundred in all, were dragged from the palace by Dracula's troops and impaled live on wooden stakes prepared for the purpose. The stakes were deliberately blunted and oiled to prolong the agony as they slowly worked their way through the bodies of their luckless and squirming victims. Never again did anyone unlucky enough to be questioned by Vlad the Impaler answer without thinking very hard indeed. He left in his trail neatly arranged forests of stakes topped by writhing or rotting bodies, applying his favoured form of justice on an ever grander scale to both Turk and Christian with equal enthusiasm. In his Bulgarian campaign alone he is said to have impaled twenty-five thousand people, besides those that were simply burned.

The most famous of Vlad Dracula's massacres took place in the city of Brasov, when in the course of one grisly April day thousands of Saxon burghers, his supposed subjects, were impaled on a hill around the chapel of St Jacob, which Dracula looted and burned. He also set fire to the city. There were other massacres less famous but just as bad, such as that at Sibiu a year later in 1460. Then 10,000 of the mostly German citizens, men women and children, are said to have perished. Also at Fagaras and many smaller towns named in the German pamphlets, fore-runners of today's newspapers, which were the chief means of spreading Dracula's infamy abroad, at least one of which was probably studied by Bram Stoker in the British Museum Library. It's impossible to know how factual these pamphlets were and, since they were often written from his victims' point of view, they may well have exaggerated Dracula's infamy, but the broad picture they paint is generally accepted as true.

One of the main authors of the tales about Dracula was Michael Beheim, a travelling minstrel who sang at most of the courts of Central and Eastern Europe. In a poem running to over a thousand lines he outlined many of Dracula's most famous outrages, his source being Brother Jacob, a monk who had fled from Dracula's court to the monastery at Wiener-Neustadt, home of the court of Emperor Friedrich of Austria:

> I myself, Michael Beheim
> Visited this brother
> Who told me much of the horror
> Committed by the Voivode Dracula
> A part of which I put into verse

These verses and other records made by the monks at Wiener-Neustadt were the basis of most of the news-sheets that chilled and thrilled audiences across Central Europe even long after Vlad's death. For a while in the late fifteenth century copies even outsold the Bible (which was the bestseller of the century thanks to the invention of the printing press around 1439) and printers seized upon it as a quick money-spinner alongside their more sober publications. In sixteenth century Russia some twenty-two versions of the story – *Slovo o Mutyanskom Voyevode Drakule* – were in circulation, usually presenting Dracula in a positive light as an indirect way of justifying the excesses of Ivan the Terrible, the first Tsar, who fiercely forged the template of modern Russia and extended its reach eastward as far as the Pacific Ocean.

A particularly nauseating custom which Dracula practised at Brasov and elsewhere, and which is celebrated in many woodcuts of the time, was to feast with his retinue in the midst of the carnage he had created, calmly enjoying the spectacle of his victims' agonised struggles as he dined. There is a tale too of how once when a dinner guest complained about the stench, Dracula had him impaled on a stake tall enough to raise him above it.

There is also a tale of how Dracula was once entertaining an envoy from King Mathias Corvinus of Hungary, the most powerful monarch of Central Europe at the time and Dracula's supposed overlord. All went as it might in any other court till at the end of the feast a golden stake was brought in and mounted upright in the midst of the hall in front of the ambassador. He, knowing Dracula's reputation, eyed it nervously, feeling suddenly very sober. Dracula watched with a sardonic smile, and then asked if the man could guess why the spear had been set there.

'My lord,' the envoy replied carefully, 'I imagine that some nobleman here has wronged you, and the spear is golden to make his death more honourable.'

'Indeed,' Dracula replied, still smiling, 'your guess is true. You are the most noble ambassador of the most noble King Mathias and I have had this stake prepared for you.'

'My lord,' the envoy said, calling on all his diplomacy, 'if I have committed any crime worthy of death, punish me as you choose for you are a just and lawful ruler and therefore cannot be held guilty of my death. I alone bear that blame.'

Dracula laughed and said: 'Any other answer and I would truly have impaled you, my friend. King Mathias chose you well for you know how to address a great ruler.' And he showered the man with gifts before sending him on his way.

Less nimble-witted envoys ended up on the stake, and as they were impaled Dracula was fond of saying things like: 'I am not guilty of your death but your own master is. If he knows you are dull-witted and unversed in the ways of court, then he has killed you by sending you here. And if somehow you came of your own choice, then you have committed suicide.'

And to their masters he would send the message: 'Do not waste the time of a great prince again by sending one of such little intelligence and culture.'

There is a story too of how Dracula was once visited by two Hungarian monks seeking alms. He had them brought to him separately in a courtyard full of the dead and dying on stakes and wheels and asked: 'How do you judge these people on the stakes?'

The first replied 'Lord, you punish without mercy. A judge should be merciful and in my view all these unfortunates are martyrs.'

The second monk said: 'Lord, God has empowered you to punish the wicked and reward the good, so surely these people must have committed great crimes to deserve such a terrible fate.'

'You are a wise man,' Dracula said before rewarding him with fifty gold ducats and ordering a coach to take him to the Hungarian border. But the first monk was recalled and told: 'Why have you left your cell and your monastery to visit the courts of great rulers when you know nothing? Just now you told me these people are martyrs. Well I wish to make you too a martyr so like them you can go straight to Heaven.' And he was impaled with the rest.

Curiously enough, in some Russian versions of this story, in which Dracula is presented as a model of the harsh but fair ruler, his verdict is reversed. The critical monk is rewarded for his honesty and the other impaled for his craven obsequiousness.

Not content with impaling his victims, Dracula also devised many other ingenious tortures. He had a vast copper cauldron fashioned with a lid having head-sized holes. Then his victims were put in the water-filled container with just their heads showing and it was brought to the boil. He was fond of impaling mothers and children simultaneously in each others' arms, or impaling people sideways so they tore themselves apart in their struggles. He forced mothers to eat their children and husbands to eat their wives. He was also fond of feeding the heads of suspect noblemen to crabs and then serving up the crabs at a feast where he entertained their friends and relations.

Dracula relished all these tortures openly and shamelessly, and justified his actions with a paranoid logic that demanded nimble thinking from those who would escape his attentions. So how did he get away with such monstrous behaviour? And why, after he was deposed and imprisoned in 1462 by the Hungarian king was he later allowed to marry Mathias's sister and return briefly to power? Why is he now chiefly remembered in Romania as a national hero rather than a monstrous tyrant?

There were reasons, as with other successful tyrants before and since. One was that his main targets within his own country were not particularly popular with the bulk of the people anyway. When Dracula massacred the nobility, the common folk hardly cared because they had little to thank them for anyway. And the rich middle-class Germans who controlled most of the trade and wealth in Romania were envied and resented by the natives, much in the way that Jews were later resented in Germany itself.

Sometimes Dracula was totally indiscriminate in his savagery, but usually those who happened not to be his victims could find some excuse for his harshness. For many common folk there were even benefits to his rule. For one thing, crime (apart from Dracula's own excesses of course) became almost non-existent because of the ferocious penalties dealt out for even the tiniest misdemeanour.

Much stress is laid on this in the Romanian tradition. One story tells of a Florentine merchant passing through the country on his way home with a carriage laden with rich goods. Arriving at Targoviste, Dracula's Wallachian capital, he asked the prince for a guard to be set over his goods and money for the night. Dracula replied that there was no need, the Florentine could sleep in the palace leaving his carriage unattended in the city square, safe in the knowledge that no thief would dare touch it.

The merchant had no choice but to accept this. However, when he checked his goods the next morning he found 160 golden ducats missing. Dracula was furious, but assured him the money would be returned. Privately he ordered his servants to replace the money and add one extra ducat. Then he warned the people of Targoviste that if the thief were not immediately produced, he would raze the city to the ground and impale everyone in it. The thief, or most likely some unlucky scapegoat, was promptly handed over and received due punishment. The merchant meanwhile, returned to his carriage and was impressed to find the money restored. Going to Dracula he said: 'Lord, I have found all my money, but there is one ducat more than before.'

Dracula replied: 'It is good you told me this, you may go in peace. If you had not confessed to that extra coin I would have impaled you beside the thief.'

It is also said that Dracula once placed a golden cup by a fountain for the use of travellers and it remained there safely for years.

Besides the lack of crime there were also very few beggars or tramps in Dracula's fief once he had applied his mind to the problem. Deciding one day that they were a drain on the gainfully employed, besides making the place look untidy, Dracula invited all the old, sick, homeless and poor in the land to a great feast in Targoviste. They came in their hundreds. Any qualms they felt were dispelled by the great banquet laid out for them. No expense had been spared. They had the finest wines, the choicest fruits, the most tender flesh of fowl and four-footed beast. Soon they were all singing and laughing and toasting their prince's benevolence.

At the height of the revelry Dracula himself appeared and asked his guests if there was anything they still lacked. 'No, no!' they all cried (or so it was reported). 'Our good lord is generous above all others and surely understands the will of God.' Then Dracula asked if they wished to be relieved of all further cares in life, never again tasting need or poverty. They should have thought twice but yelled to the effect that they would like nothing better. So Dracula had the doors and windows sealed and the hall burned to the ground with all that were inside.

As with all the Dracula tales, the slant depended on who was telling it. In German versions this is left as a bare example of Dracula's mercilessness. In Romanian and Russian traditions, he justifies his act by saying: 'It is written that man should earn his living by the sweat of his brow, yet these people live by the work of others. This means they are useless to mankind. It is worse than robbery. Forest brigands may demand your purse but if you are stronger than them you can escape. But the poor take your goods stealthily and steadily, and play on your pity. It means they are worse than thieves.'

In his treatment of the poor, Dracula was not totally out of tune with his times. Other Medieval potentates are supposed to have done much the same. The most famous instance is probably that of Archbishop Hatto of Mainz in Germany. During a great famine in the year 913 he is said to have grown so tired of the starving crowds clamouring round his well-stocked granaries that he invited them all to a feast in a great barn and then, in the words of an old English ditty:

> When he saw that it could hold no more,
> Bishop Hatto he made fast the door,
> And while for mercy on Christ they did call,
> He fired the barn and burnt them all.

> 'Faith, 'tis an excellent bonfire,' quoth he,
> 'And the country is greatly obliged to me,
> For ridding it in these times so forlorn,
> Of rats that only consume the corn.'

However, Providence was obviously paying closer attention to Bishop Hatto than to Dracula later on, because the next day he learned that rats had broken into his granaries and eaten all the corn. What is more, an army of rats was advancing on the Episcopal palace. The Bishop fled to the nearby Rhine and was rowed out to a tower built on a rock in midstream as a refuge for just such emergencies. But the rats somehow managed to swim across and eat him alive. So the tale goes anyway. A mid-river tower near Bingen is still pointed out as the place where this happened.

Gypsies fared little better in Dracula's principality. On one occasion when three hundred of them migrated into Wallachia they were rounded up and the three finest were roasted (no doubt alive). The rest were forced to eat this flesh, after which Dracula declared: 'Thus must you continue till none are left, unless you choose to go and fight the Turks' which in the circumstances they did most willingly. On other occasions though, he simply had Gypsies massacred.

Foreign merchants passing through the country could also not be sure of their reception. We have seen how one survived coming to Dracula's notice, but in 1461 six hundred others who crossed the Danube to escape the turmoil of war ended up on the stake and had their goods confiscated.

Not the least alarming feature of Dracula's behaviour is his apparent complete certainty of his own righteousness. Before settling down to enjoy the spectacle of someone's torture he generally took care to extract some kind of admission of guilt or incompetence from his victims.

Dracula still has his apologists, who blame his excesses on the violent times in which he lived and the propagandist slant of the German pamphlets which recounted them, and which were naturally partial to the Saxon settlers and merchants he treated so harshly. And it is true that many of his cruelties were learned from the Turks as a youthful hostage when often it was only a whim that saved him from impalement himself. Also his general principles were shared by other rulers and politicians of the time. Machiavelli in *The Prince* written not long after, advised that any commander of a large army should 'not mind being thought cruel; for without this reputation he could not keep an army united or disposed to any duty.' Also: 'One ought to be both feared and loved, but as it is difficult for the two to go together, it is much safer to be feared than loved.' However, Vlad's enthusiasm for inflicting extreme suffering on the defence-less seems to go well beyond such excuses and even contemporary tyrants were awed and disgusted by his excesses.

Dracula's excuses for cruelty were also often very thin, even in those anecdotes that are on his side. One tale famous throughout Eastern and Central Europe, and which Romanian parents still tell their children today, tells of how the prince was one day offended by the sight of a peasant wearing a badly made tunic. Feeling that this reflected badly on the orderliness of his realm, Dracula had him hauled before his court for judgement.

'Have you no wife that you wear such rags as these?' he demanded.

'Indeed, lord, I have a wife,' replied the hapless peasant.

'Then is she old and crippled?'

'No, my lord, she is young and healthy.'

'Then she must be very lazy to make a tunic like this that does not even cover the calf of your leg,' declared the tyrant; and the poor woman herself was summoned.

'Tell me,' said Dracula, 'does your husband not work hard in the fields, sowing and reaping to feed you and keep a roof over your head?'

'He does indeed, my lord.'

'Then it is a pity for you. If he does his work well, why can you not do yours and keep him clothed decently as a wife should? You are too lazy for such a man.'

With that he had her impaled and provided the peasant with a new wife who was warned to work harder than the first.

Many factors combined to place a homicidal maniac like Dracula on the Wallachian throne, but the main one was that he was seen by more civilized rulers to the west as their chief bulwark against the Turks who were then a very real threat to the whole of Europe. Three years before Dracula came to power the Turks had captured Constantinople and overrun much of the Balkans. Wallachia and Transylvania blocked their way to the European heartland and Dracula's main virtue in the eyes of his nominally Christian allies was that he was no more afraid of the Turks than of anyone else.

He kicked off his campaign in typical style. When envoys came from Sultan Mohammed II in 1461 seeking diplomatic concessions, Dracula received them coolly in the throne room at Targoviste. When they bowed to him without removing their turbans, Dracula asked why they insulted him so.

'Lord,' they replied, 'this is our custom. We do not remove our turbans even in the presence of the Sultan.'

'Very well,' Dracula said, 'then I would like to strengthen you in your custom.'

And he ordered that their headgear be fastened to their heads with iron nails just long enough to do the job without killing them (a trick later emulated by Ivan the Terrible). Afterwards he said: 'Now go and tell your master that he may be used to such insults from his servants but we are not. In future let him not try and impose his customs on the civilised rulers of other countries, but keep them in his own.'

The Sultan naturally took this as a declaration of war and determined to destroy Dracula, but to begin with he was devious. Pretending no great offence, he invited Dracula to discuss their differences at the fortress of Giurgiu on the River Danube, the border between their countries. The aim was to assassinate him there, but Dracula arrived with his army, seized the fortress through a trick of his own, destroyed it and marched the garrison of about 20,000 back to Targoviste where all were impaled on a forest of stakes outside the city.

Open warfare followed and the Turks launched a vast army of perhaps a quarter of a million across the Bosphorus. The Romanians appealed to their allies for troops but while everyone applauded their nerve, that was about all the support they got.

Dracula was left facing the might of the Turkish Empire with about 30,000 mainly Wallachian followers. He resorted to guerrilla tactics and a scorched earth policy. Retreating north to the Transylvanian Alps and Targoviste, he emptied the country as he went, burning and poisoning anything that could help his enemies, then doubling back occasionally and savaging them with a daring and ferocity that stunned the Turks.

Advancing across the blackened wasteland of what had been Wallachia, Sultan Mohammed and his army came at last to Targoviste only to find it too abandoned and stripped of its treasures. Outside they found the rotting remains of the Giurgiu garrison. Although terror was one of the Turks' own favoured weapons, the Sultan was sickened. 'What can one do against a man like this?' he is reported to have said, and turned for home with the bulk of his army, leaving a remnant to hunt down Dracula and establish his brother Radu on the Wallachian throne.

Dracula was besieged for a while in Poenari Castle high in the Carpathian Mountains but managed to escape, leaving his wife to throw herself from a tower into the river far below rather than face capture. But when Dracula approached the Hungarian king for fresh troops he was carted back to Budapest and thrown into prison. For the moment he had served his purpose and opened the way for a negotiated settlement with the Turks.

Little is known of the twelve years of Dracula's imprisonment save that it grew progressively lenient, leading at last to his betrothal to King Mathias's sister and reinstatement as the official candidate for the Wallachian throne. The Russian ambassador to Hungary, however, reported that in the early days of his confinement Dracula continued his habits of cruelty. Lacking human subjects to practise them on, he procured all kinds of small animals from his gaolers and tortured them to death in an inventive variety of ways strongly reminiscent of the behaviour of Renfield, the lunatic in Stoker's novel who becomes the slave of the fictional Dracula.

His egomania likewise remained intact. Shortly after his release, and while still living in Budapest, some guards chasing a criminal burst into Dracula's courtyard. Drawing his sword, Dracula immediately beheaded the captain of the guard and in the confusion that followed the criminal escaped. When in due course an enquiry came from the king as to why he had committed this crime, Dracula sent back the reply: 'I committed no crime, the captain committed suicide. Anyone who invades the house of a great ruler should perish thus. If he had come to me and explained the situation, I myself would have delivered the criminal into his hands.'

As usual, he got away with it.

Dracula's return to power followed much the same course as before. The Transylvanian duchies of Fagaras and Almas were restored to him and he moved to Sibiu where he planned his campaign with Prince Bathory of Transylvania, his commander-in-chief, and gathered support from the ever-fickle boyars. In 1476 he advanced into Wallachia and recaptured Targoviste before advancing to the new capital of Bucharest, a town Dracula himself had founded and which had been chosen, it was said, by his usurping brother Radu for its closeness to his Turkish masters. In November Dracula captured Bucharest and was once again crowned Prince of Wallachia; whereupon his allies from Hungary and Moldavia mostly packed up and went home, seeing their job as done.

This left Dracula in a perilous position and he had no time to secure his power base before the Turks attacked. In this, his third reign was almost a repeat of the first, and like the first it lasted a mere couple of months. Then, realising the hollowness of his title, he had fled until he could return in strength. This time he had no choice but to go to war, and it was a fatal decision.

There are two versions of how Dracula met his end. One tells how, his army having put the Turks to flight, Dracula climbed a hill to watch the slaughter. Being closer to the enemy line than his own, he disguised himself as a Turk and was attacked and killed by his own men, dragging five of them into the afterlife with him. The other version says he was attacked during battle by traitors from his own ranks, which somehow seems more likely and perfectly laudable. Perhaps they dressed him up as a Turk afterwards and claimed not to have recognized him.

Either way, Vlad the Impaler finally perished in 1476 at the age of forty-five. He is estimated to have personally ordered the death by torture of some 100,000 people, quite apart from the normal casualties of war, and his name inspired awe and terror in the hearts of millions more of his contemporaries. Undoubtedly some people mourned his passing, for the reasons that combined to bring him to power, but on a wider scale the news must have been greeted with a huge sigh of relief.

* * *

If anyone was qualified to become a vampire after death, particularly in that part of the world, it would seem to be Vlad Dracula the Impaler, but there is little or no evidence to suggest this was ever believed in his native country despite the thriving vampire traditions. When Stoker has Van Helsing mention a manuscript in which the connection had been made, it was almost certainly an invention. It was Stoker's own idea to weave together the two great strands of Romanian legend and then transplant them plausibly to Victorian England.

Possibly his book would have worked just as well had Count Dracula been a totally fictional creation, since despite his enormous fame throughout Europe in the fifteenth century, the real Dracula had become almost forgotten outside Romania by the nineteenth. Transylvania too could, for most readers, just as easily have been a totally fictional place. Indeed, many believed it was and some still do, though in decreasing numbers since the opening up of Eastern Europe to the wider world. Yet Stoker's research undoubtedly paid off and gave the book many of the strengths that see it still in print today. He also gave Romania a lucrative tourist attraction that otherwise would mean nothing to the outside world, although reconciling the fictional Dracula with their national hero is an ongoing conundrum for the Romanian National Tourist Office.

Many if not most Romanians had not even heard of Bram Stoker's vampire Count before the collapse of communism in 1989, or the dictator Ceausescu might have hesitated before likening himself to his country's other great tyrant of yore, boasting to his Health Minister in 1970 that great rulers such as himself only came along every 500 years (ironically he was executed by firing squad in sight of Vlad's palace in Targoviste). So when the Iron Curtain came down ordinary Romanians were somewhat bemused by the often exotically dressed Western tourists who flocked to their country asking if this castle or that was where Count Dracula had lived. The novel was only translated into Romanian in the early 1990s, which at least let the natives know what all the fuss was about, without solving the problem of how to tap into a lucrative new source of revenue without letting a national hero be turned into a monster.

Vlad's cruelty had not been forgotten in his homeland. Until at least the recent past country children were still told tales like that of the lazy wife he impaled to set an example to her successor; but Romanian folklore had largely come to agree with Vlad's own estimation of himself as a harsh but wise ruler bringing order to his unruly fief

and championing civilisation against the barbarous Turk. Even today serious Romanian historians are inclined to dismiss the generally accepted scale of his atrocities as German exaggerations of the time, putting the number of his victims as perhaps a few hundred rather than the many thousands usually attributed to him. Perhaps time will show who is right but in a way that's not the immediate problem the Romanians face, which is how to distinguish the real Dracula from Bram Stoker's fictional vampire while at the same time pleasing all parties.

The dilemma is neatly summed up by the motto on Dracula's Spirit vodka sold in Romania:

> The history has borne the sacred hero
> The myth has borne a bloody vampire
> The hero and the fiend bear one name:
> DRACULA

In his novel Bram Stoker made a connection that others had not, and turned a real life monster (or merely fierce but fair ruler of course, for any Romanian reading this) into a vampire and one of the greatest blood-curdlers of fiction. So why did it take a Victorian novelist to do this when Eastern Europe was rife with legends of vampires in the fifteenth century and even the most positive reading of Vlad Dracula's actions make him a prime candidate for becoming one?

There is perhaps a simple explanation. Dracula's body was supposedly buried in the island monastery of Snagov near Bucharest, but his head was taken back to Constantinople by the Turks to be put on public display as proof of the death of their legendary foe. And as everyone knows, beheading is one of the surest ways of destroying a vampire, or preventing one coming into being.

* * *

The clash between Stoker's Dracula and their own has not led the Romanian tourist authorities to discourage vampire tourism. However distasteful it may be to their patriots and historians, most Romanians have learned to tolerate the Dracula enthusiasts with humour. Arriving at the capital Bucharest in the south, as most visitors do, you can dine at the Count Dracula Club restaurant in a setting that Hammer Films might be proud of. Twenty-five miles north of Bucharest you can visit Vlad the Impaler's supposed tomb (there are rumours that in the 1930s his grave was opened and found to be full of animal bones). About the same distance again brings you to

Targoviste, Vlad's main seat of power, with the remains of Poenari Castle in the mountains to the north perched a thousand feet above the tangled Arges valley and at the top of about 1,400 steps. This should really be labelled Dracula's Castle but that title usually goes to Bran Castle about twenty miles south-west of Brasov in Transylvania proper. Admittedly Bran does look much more the part though it is unlikely that the historical Dracula spent much time there. North of Brasov one can visit Dracula's birthplace in Sighisoara, a house on main square marked with a blue plaque. Besides this, Sighisoara is generally rated the most perfectly preserved medieval town in Europe.

The Borgo Pass east of Bistrita on the main road through the Carpathian Mountains to Moldavia generally comes as a bit of disappointment to Stoker fans because here he did let his imagination go and it is far less forbidding than in the book. There was also no castle anywhere near there until the 1980s when a theme-park style one was erected by the government for tourists in the general area described in the novel; but beyond these reservations most visitors report getting a genuine and spooky insight at some point when visiting the Borgo Pass into why vampires have been taken so seriously in this part of the world. The Hotel Castle Dracula also has in its favour that one can ham it up there as much as you like without offending any local sensibilities. In Bistrita likewise you can spend the night in The Golden Crown Inn, named in the 1970s after the one in the book where Jonathan Harker lodges on his Transylvanian journey. The menu is even the same and bears a greeting from the Count assuring the visitor of a warm welcome at his castle.

THE BLOOD COUNTESS

High on any list of human monsters has to come Countess Elisabeth Bathory who was distantly related to Dracula and born almost a century after his death. Her atrocities were not on quite the same scale and yet in some ways she chills the blood even more, because she bothered even less with excuses for her tortures. Her tale also illuminates how powerless most people were in those times against the whims of their rulers, how great those rulers' excesses had to become before their peers moved against them, and even then how lightly they escaped retribution. Although not strictly speaking a vampire she comes close enough to it, and has influenced vampire fiction so much, that her life almost demands a brief review here.

The Countess was born Erzsébet Báthory in August 1560 in a part of Hungary bordering Transylvania, where her family was based, after having migrated from Germany and changing their name from Gutkeled to Bathory, meaning 'brave' in

Hungarian. This was a clear reference to their success on the battlefields of Eastern Europe but more particularly they claimed it as a tribute for having killed the last dragon in the region. To flaunt this claim, three dragon claws appear on the shield of their coat of arms, encircled by a winged dragon biting its own tail. Elisabeth was in fact born into one of the richest and most powerful clans in that part of the world, which included cardinals, counts and princes in its ranks, including King Steven of Poland who reigned from 1575-86. In her childhood Elisabeth suffered from occasional seizures that may have been epileptic fits, but seems to have grown out of them.

She was groomed for high office from the beginning. She spoke several languages including Hungarian, German and Latin, and was engaged at the age of eleven to Count Ferencz Nadasdy, the 'Black Hero of Hungary', whom she married at fifteen in one of the most lavish ceremonies of the time in Central Europe. As she was richer than him, Nadasdy added her surname to his own and they took up residence in Csejthe Castle in northern Hungary (or Cachtice, now in Slovakia).

With her husband mostly away fighting the Turks with the Hungarian army, in which he rose to be the most powerful general, Elisabeth is believed to have had many affairs with partners of both sexes. She attended lesbian orgies at her notorious aunt Klara Bathory's mansion in Vienna and apparently consorted quite openly with her manservant Istvan Jezorlay at home in the early years of her marriage while her husband was away. Despite this and her atrocities she was reckoned to have been a good mother to her own children. In a typical letter she wrote:

'My much beloved Husband, I am writing to offer my service to my beloved Lord and master. As to the children, Grace be to God, they are all right. But Orsika has trouble with her eyes and Kato suffers with her teeth. I myself, thanks be to God, am all right, although I have pain in my eyes. May God guard you and be with you. Sarvar, Anno Domini 1596, 8th day in the month of July.'

She also took to dabbling in black magic, guided by the professed witches Anna Darvulia and Dorottya 'Dorka' Szentes, and amused herself by inflicting harsh and ingenious punishments on her servants, having them beaten with sticks or horse-whipped for the slightest offence. One was smeared all over with honey and left naked out in the open for twenty four hours at the mercy of insects. In these tortures she was aided by her children's nanny Iloona Jo and other accomplices, including her major domo Johannes Ujvary, nicknamed Ficzko the Dwarf, who vied with each other for

inventiveness in their tortures. Elisabeth's favourite subjects for her games were large-bosomed girls under eighteen. She is not known to have tortured any males.

Her husband occasionally disapproved of Elisabeth's excesses but more often fed her imagination with tales of torture on the battlefront, where his Turkish foes called him 'the Black Bey' and one habit after battle was to juggle with the heads of his enemies. For 'disciplining' her servants he taught Elisabeth a novel form of torture called 'star kicking' which involved stuffing paper between a maid's toes and setting it alight – the girl kicked and screamed and the pain made her see stars. Also, when not exchanging marital pieties in their letters they sometimes swapped black magic recipes, such as this in one of Elisabeth's letters: 'Dorka has taught me a lovely new one. Catch a little black hen and beat it to death with a white cane. Keep the blood and smear some on your enemy. If you get no chance to smear it on his body, obtain one of his garments and smear it.'

Elisabeth was a famous beauty according to the tastes of the time, with a fair skin from her northern ancestors, and was said to spend over half her day tending to her appearance. Her manservant Ficzko at the trial said: 'Her Ladyship had a little black box in which she kept a mirror in a pretzel-shaped frame. She would make incantations before it for up to two hours a day.' In doing this she was probably tapping into an ancient vein of superstition regarding mirrors which led to the habit in Transylvania of covering mirrors in the presence of a dead person for fear that their reflection might become a spectre that would haunt the living. Tied up with this is the belief that vampires have no reflection in mirrors because they have no souls, with echoes of Sleeping Beauty's wicked stepmother consulting her mirror and Oscar Wilde's story of Dorian Gray. The last admittedly involves a painting rather than a mirror but it taps into the same superstition about a reflection being the soul of the person rather than a simple copy.

The superstition lives on in the fear that breaking a mirror brings bad luck for seven years and the rare but well documented modern condition called negative autoscopy in which people are unable to see themselves in mirrors. Elisabeth Bathory seems to have been completely in the grip of all such ideas and to have believed that blood sacrifices would in some magical way propitiate the spirit within her mirror and restore her youth. When her vanity became tangled with black magic and innate sadism she entered a whole new dimension of cruelty. After her husband's death in 1604 when Elisabeth was forty-three the prospect of middle age led to a phenomenal escalation of her torturing of young servant girls. With her husband dead and her children grown, she lost all control and began a ten year reign of almost unimaginable terror.

The legend goes that it all began one day when a maid snagged her hair while brushing it. Or some say Elisabeth merely spotted a fault with her headdress. Whichever, the Countess was so furious she lashed out and blood spurted from the unfortunate girl's nose onto her mistress' face. When she wiped it off, it seemed to Elisabeth that where the blood had spilled her skin had become as clear and transparent as in youth.

Believing she had discovered the secret of prolonged, if not eternal youth that she had been seeking, the Countess determined to bathe in the girl's blood. Summoning Ujvary and Thorko, she had them strip the servant, beat her and then drain all her blood into a vat in which the Countess then bathed her entire body. This soon became her regular habit at the magic hour of four in the morning when the night wanes and the new day invisibly begins.

Over the next decade Elisabeth's accomplices provided her with hundreds more such victims, luring peasant girls to the castle with the promise of employment, after which they were thrown into the dungeons on the slightest excuse. At the trial the Countess's manservant Ficzco said 'Mostly Dorka and other women went in search of the girls. They spoke to them about the good conditions of service [at the castle] . . . But women in all the villages were eager to get serving girls for her Ladyship. The daughter of one of them was killed and then she refused to recruit other girls. I myself went six times in search of girls with Dorka. Mrs Jan Barsony went to engage girls for the castle at Taplanfalva . . . Mrs Istvan Szabo, too, brought girls, among them her own daughter. She was killed and Mrs Szabo knew that she would be; yet she continued to engage many, many more.' And so on, in a dreadful litany of procurement for slaughter wherever they went, the Countess growing ever more reckless as her mania span out of control.

Not content with stealing their lifeblood, the Countess devised ever more elaborate tortures for her victims, whose wretched lives were often prolonged for days and weeks as she first inflicted agony and then drained their blood by slashing their bodies with razors. When Elisabeth grew exhausted by the exertion of her tortures, her trusted servants took over while she looked on, later rewarding them for their ingenuity. Sometimes her clothes became so soaked in blood she had to go and change before carrying on and if the victims died too easily she wrote a peevish comment on it in her journal.

All her victims were young females whom she often humiliated by parading them naked before the young men of the castle before being led to their awful deaths. On one famous occasion immortalised by the Hungarian artist István Csók, a group of them were soaked with water while out in the snow so that they froze solid. The flesh of these girls was often later fed in disguise to the young men who showed too much interest in the Countess's girls. Elisabeth was also said to have possessed the statue of a beautiful naked girl with real hair and teeth that was cunningly made for her by a German clock-smith. When touched, the clockwork statue would seize the person in a tight embrace and impale them with spikes that sprang from its breasts. Their blood ran into a channel where it could be collected for bathing and it was one of the Countess's amusements to order a servant girl to polish the thing while she watched.

This may just be a legend grown up around her famous Iron Maiden, the spike-lined coffin that was much later to inspire Bram Stoker to write a short story, but no doubt the Countess would certainly have had such a statue made if possible. Another of her torture devices was a spike-lined cage beneath which she would shower in the blood of her victim. Most of the torture was carried out in the privacy of the dungeons at Castle Csejthe, but she also built torture chambers in her other residences around the country,

including a mansion in Vienna where monks in the neighbouring monastery complained of screams that kept them awake at night and threw pots at the walls in protest. At the trial Bathory's manservant Ficzco told the court that 'at Nagy-Bittse castle girls were tortured in a pantry, at Sarvar castle in the castle keep that no-one was allowed to enter, at Csejthe castle in the dungeons and in a washroom, at Keresztur castle in the closet, at Lezeticze in the castle dungeons.' Even when visiting friends and relations she usually managed to find some dungeon or out of the way place to exercise her compulsions.

Rumours of what she was up to naturally did circulate, but to little effect. The families of her victims, being peasants, counted for little among the company of Elisabeth's peers. A neighbouring preacher, Pastor Ponikenusz, finally rebelled against having to bury so many of her victims and spoke out against the Countess from the pulpit, but to little avail at first beyond being attacked by a horde of cats which it was believed Elisabeth had conjured against him by witchcraft. A letter he wrote to a superior was intercepted by Elisabeth's spies.

But as Elisabeth's madness progressed the weight of evidence against her became impossible to ignore. What is more, as she continued despite her atrocities to age inevitably, the Countess was persuaded by one of her resident witches that what she needed was the blood of noble-born virgins. So Elisabeth began recruiting as maids the daughters of lesser nobility whose following disappearance was harder to explain.

Several of their deaths were passed off with excuses, but when the number rose to about fifty, questions finally began to be asked in the highest circles and the net began to close.

The tipping point was when the naked bodies of four girls were simply thrown from the castle ramparts to be eaten by wolves. This drove the Csethje villagers to make a complaint to King Mathias II of Hungary, and along with rumours he had already heard from other quarters he was finally moved to act.

The investigation was entrusted to Count Gyorgy Thurzo de Bethlenfalva, who was governor of the province and Elisabeth Bathory's son in law. On the night of December 30 1610 he led a raid on Castle Csejthe and walked into a nightmare. Entering the labyrinthine dungeons, he and his men first came upon the carelessly discarded body of a dead girl mutilated and burned so that 'her own mother would not recognise her,' as one witness expressed it, and completely drained of blood. Further on they found two others in a similar state but still barely alive. Deeper in the dungeons they found more girls hanging naked in chains whose bodies had been pierced in many places and who seemed to have been used as living milch-cows for blood. They finally caught the Countess herself literally red-handed in the very act of torturing another victim. Beneath the castle they found the remains of at least fifty other bodies for whom no other means of disposal had yet been found.

The official report of 7 January 1611, which was carefully filed away in the Vienna Imperial Archives, describes what followed: 'On seeing the signs of her terrible and beastly cruelties, his Highness became most indignant. At one with the counsel of his retinue, he ordered that the widow of Count Nadasdy, as befitting a bloodthirsty and bloodsucking Godless woman caught in the act, should be arrested, and he sentenced her to lifelong imprisonment in Csejthe Castle. He also ordered that Janos Ficzko, Ilona, Dorottya and Kata, her accomplices and helpers in the terrifying butcherings, which they themselves had admitted, should be put on trial, and for their horrifying deeds the hardest punishment be meted out on them so that justice should be done and others be deterred from similar wickedness.'

Elisabeth Bathory was not brought to trial because, as the Lord Palatine of Hungary wrote: 'The families which have won in the eyes of the nation such high honours on the battlefields shall not be disgraced by the murky shadow of this bestial female . . . In the interest of future generations of Nadasdys everything is to be done in secret. For if a court were to try her the whole of Hungary would learn of her murders, and it would seem to contravene our laws to spare her life. But having seen her crimes with my own eyes, I have to abandon my plan to put her in a convent for the rest of her life.' Later, and to her face he continued: 'You, Elisabeth, are like a wild animal. You are in the last months of your life. You do not deserve to breathe the air on earth, nor to see the light of the Lord. You shall disappear from this world and shall never reappear in it again. The shadows will envelop you and you will find time to repent your bestial life. I condemn you, Lady of Csejthe, to lifelong imprisonment in your own castle.'

So the Blood Countess was never formally either charged or convicted for her crimes. She was simply walled permanently into her bedchamber with only a small aperture left through which food could be passed; and died four years later in August 1614. Her chief aides were sentenced to death, the witches Ilona Jo and Dorottya being burned alive after having all their fingers torn off with red-hot pincers. Janos Ficzko was deemed less culpable and merely decapitated before cremation.

The trial confessions along with witness statements and all other records relating to the event were immediately hidden away and did not surface until found in a poor condition in the attic at Bicse castle (one of Bathory's residences) in the 1720s by a Jesuit priest, Fr Laszlo Turoczy, who published a partial account in Latin of what they contained. A fuller study appeared in 1796 by the German anthropologist Michael Wagener (*Beiträge zur Philosophischen Anthropologie*) who also studied the letters to his superiors of the Lutheran pastor of Csejthe, from which many of the tales above were taken.

Elisabeth Bathory's own record which she kept in her bedchamber was said by witnesses to have put the number of her victims at 650, but if true (the actual list has not survived) the chances are there were many more she found no time to write down. Her own name was kept out of all official records for a hundred years and even in the eighteenth century accounts of her misdeeds she was generally only referred to as Elisabeth. Some of her diaries are believed still to be in existence in the State Archives in Bucharest, access to which has been limited to a few determined scholars; but they have yet to be published or translated out of Hungarian.

That at least is the popular legend of Elisabeth Bathory, backed by the trial records, but an increasing number of scholarly and other voices (particularly in Hungary over the past century, where there is some eagerness to brighten the national record) have claimed that it is a complete fabrication and that the Blood Countess was in fact an early feminist martyr, the victim of patriarchal enemies jealous of her wealth, power and independence of mind. According to these revisionists the horror tales were simply invented by her enemies during the trial to break the Countess and steal her wealth, and the evidence in the trial records is no more reliable than the torture-induced 'confessions' of the infamous European witch trials. This is the argument of the 2007 film *Bathory* written and directed by Juraj Jakubisko, starring Anna Friel as Elisabeth.

It seems unlikely though that such a horrific legend could have grown from nothing, however exaggerated it may have become. There quite probably were political undercurrents at play, and Elisabeth's disgrace relieved the King of a considerable financial debt towards her, but the damage to the Bathory name alone would have discouraged her enemies and prosecutors (many of whom were related) from taking this drastic course if it had no foundation in fact. Nor would they have suppressed the trial records for a century.

The Blood Countess's story has been retold in many films over the years with varying degrees of realism. Notable among them are *Daughters of Darkness* (1970), *Countess Dracula* (1971), *Blood Castle* (1972), *Ceremonia Sangrienta* (1972), *La Noche de Walpurgis* (1972) and *Elizabeth Bathory: The Blood Countess* (1998) starring Lorelei Lanford.

The year 2007 also saw the filming in Eastern Europe of yet another version of the tale, *The Countess*, directed by and starring Julie Delpy with Radha Mitchell, Ethan Hawke and Vincent Gallo. Also, work continued on an opera, *Erzsébet*, a work in progress by composer Dennis Báthory-Kitsz, an indirect descendant who at the time of writing is hoping for a premiere performance in 2008 after having spent some twenty years on the project.

BLUEBEARD

The fairytale of Bluebeard was first written 1697 by Charles Perrault (the author who under the title *Mother Goose Tales* also gave us *Little Red Riding Hood, Sleeping Beauty, Cinderella* and *Puss in Boots*), though like most of Perrault's stories it was based on an existing folktale.

In the fable Bluebeard was a rich man with mansions and castles and more gold and silver than he knew what to do with. He also had, though, a beard that was so black it seemed blue, which frightened off any young woman he wanted to marry – that and the worrying fact that he had been married several times before to wives who had disappeared without satisfactory explanation.

Bluebeard's neighbour was a noble lady with two beautiful daughters. One day he went and asked the hand of one of them in marriage, leaving them to choose which was to be the lucky bride. Both girls were terrified of him but Bluebeard threw a magnificent party lasting eight days at one of his chateaux, and by the end of it the younger sister had been so seduced by the glory and extravagance of the entertainment that she agreed to marry him after all, which was done right away.

All went well for a month or so but then Bluebeard was called away on business. In leaving he gave his new wife the keys to his castle and told her to amuse herself all she liked in his absence – with friends and parties and anything else that took her fancy – save one thing only. The smallest key on the ring belonged to a little door at the end of a long corridor at the bottom of the mansion, and she must not use it. Any other lock

she could open save that one, and he would not answer for the dreadful consequences if she did.

She promised faithfully and Bluebeard rode off. Soon his wife filled the house with all her friends who went from room to room marvelling at all the treasures and wonders they found. The wife however could think of nothing but the little key on her ring and the forbidden room with the locked door at the bottom of the castle. So finally she slipped away quietly and went there alone. On the threshold she hesitated, thinking of her husband's terrible warnings, but there was no stopping now so she turned the key and stepped in. At first she could see nothing for the dimness, but gradually her eyes made out a dark, clotted pool covering the floor, in whose reflection she gradually made out the bodies of several women strung along the wall with their throats slit – Bluebeard's former wives.

In terror his newest wife dropped the key into the blood on the floor. She rescued it and, gathering her wits, locked the door again and fled to her chambers. But there she found the little key was stained with blood and though she washed and scrubbed it with sand and grit, nothing could remove the stain, because the key was of course enchanted.

Bluebeard unexpectedly returned home that very evening, having met news on the way that his trip was not needed after all. His wife tried her best to seem pleased, but she struggled and inevitably the moment came to return the keys. When Bluebeard saw the stain on the smallest one he knew immediately what she had done. His wife would have joined the others in the cellar, his cutlass was drawn and her throat lay bare to the blade, when luckily her sturdy brothers showed up just in time to save her life and slay the monstrous Bluebeard. After which they all lived happily ever after.

* * *

Bluebeard's tale is increasingly unfamiliar to young people because it has largely been dropped from the canon of fairytales deemed suitable for shaping infant minds. Which is not very surprising really. Frankly, it's hard to find any redeeming moral in it beyond the dubious one that Perrault himself attached to his tale – that wives should bridle their curiosity and unquestioningly obey their husbands or they could come to a sticky end. Unless perhaps it is that anyone marrying a rich man of dubious reputation should take care to have a couple of strapping brothers on call:

> Ladies, you should never pry,
> You'll repent it by and by!
> 'Tis the silliest of sins;
> Trouble in a trice begins.

There are, surely — more's the woe
Lots of things you need not know.
Come, forswear it now and here
Joy so brief that costs so dear!

This is hardly a fashionable sentiment, glossing over as it does the husband's much greater infamy, but it was probably more the bloodiness of the tale that led to its declining favour (at least as a moral tale cautioning against curiosity) from the 1950s on. Previously it had been adapted by Bela Bartok as his only opera *Bluebeard's Castle*, acclaimed as his first masterpiece after its premiere in 1918.

Angela Carter also reworked the tale in a feminist light in 1979 in *The Bloody Chamber*, a collection of updated fairytales including *Beauty and the Beast*, *Puss in Boots* and *Little Red Riding Hood*. Carter sets her Bluebeard fable at Mont St Michel in the early twentieth century but otherwise sticks quite closely to Perrault's storyline, with the notable exception that it is the heroine's feisty mother who comes dashing to her rescue at the end. Finally (though there have been many other adaptations of the tale) Jane Campion made memorable use of the Bluebeard theme in her 1993 film *The Piano*, which she wrote and directed. In it, not only do the main characters reflect the Bluebeard tale in their actions but they stage it as an amateur play within the film.

Not all scholars agree, but the existing folk story which Perrault drew upon is generally believed to have evolved from the true and even more blood-chilling tale of Gilles de Laval, Maréchal de Retz (or Rais), champion of the French Dauphin (later Charles VII) against the English and their Burgundian allies who sought to deny him the throne in the fifteenth century. Sabine Baring-Gould's *Book of the Werewolf* in 1865 was the first source to reveal to the general English-speaking public the full infamy of the original Bluebeard. Baring-Gould's sources included an abstract of the records of his trial commissioned by Ann of Brittany — a stroke of luck as it happens because the court records in the library at Nantes were largely destroyed during the French Revolution and the abstract helped a detailed scholarly reconstruction of the surviving records in the nineteenth century that Baring-Gould was able to draw upon.

There was nothing in his early life to suggest that Gilles de Laval would go down in history as one of humanity's greatest monsters. He was born in the autumn of 1404 at Machecoul, on the southern border of Brittany with Anjou. His wealthy father died at the tusks of a wild boar he was hunting when Gilles was only about eleven and his mother immediately remarried, abandoning Gilles and his brother René to the care of their powerful and wily grandfather, Jean de Craon, one of the richest and most ruthless men in France, who perhaps encouraged the pitiless streak in the boy and certainly let him run wild.

Gilles de Laval, Maréchal de Retz

In 1420 Gilles joined the court of the aspiring king Charles VII where his grandfather tried to further improve the family fortunes through a good marriage. After several failed attempts, possibly due to the untimely deaths of some of the brides, he secured for Gilles the hand and fortune of sixteen year old Catherine de Thouars of Brittany, whose lands adjoined his own — this despite Gilles's brusque manner of courting, which involved kidnapping the girl (who was also his cousin) and holding her by force at his grandfather's Champtoce mansion, where her uncle and two other hostages languished in the dungeons. By the time the ecclesiastical courts recognised the marriage and the hostages were released, their health was broken and the uncle died soon after.

The political situation at the time was that King Charles VI in his madness (he is believed to have suffered periodic fits of schizophrenia or porphyria from his mid twenties onward, during which he sometimes roamed his palaces howling like a wolf) had disinherited his son the Dauphin and signed the Treaty of Troyes by which Henry V of England, in alliance with the Duke of Burgundy and others, was to inherit the throne of France when Charles VI died. This was towards the end of the Hundred Years War between England and France. Many French were unhappy with the Troyes agreement but things were not looking very hopeful for the Dauphin until Joan of Arc famously burst upon the scene, raised the siege of Orleans and, after several other major battles which brought the Hundred Years War to a close, secured Rheims, traditional coronation site for the Kings of France, where the Dauphin assumed the crown as Charles VII.

By her side through all these adventures was her general Gilles de Laval, nicknamed Bluebeard on account of the deep black of his beard contrasting with the lighter hair on his head. To Bluebeard was given the honour of bearing the sacred Oriflamme at the 1429 coronation and he was appointed one of only three Maréchals de France in reward for his major part in Charles VII's triumph. As marshal, counsellor and chamberlain of the king, Gilles de Laval proved himself as able a politician as he had been a warrior but then, quite suddenly in 1433 after seven years of active service, he retired to his estates where he lived in a grand style, his fortune swelled by an inheritance from his grandfather who had died the year before.

His court at Tiffauges on the Loire was like that of a king, as described by J.K. Huysmans in La Bas, his fictionalised history of Gilles de Laval (or Gilles de Rais as Huysmans calls him):

'He had a guard of two hundred men, knights, captains, squires, pages, and all these people had personal attendants who were magnificently equipped at Gilles's expense. The luxury of his chapel and collegium was madly extravagant. There was in residence at Tiffauges a complete metropolitan clergy, deans, vicars, treasurers, canons, clerks, deacons, scholasters, and choir boys. There is an inventory extant of the surplices, stoles, and amices, and the fur choir hats with crowns of squirrel and linings of vair [squirrel fur]. There are countless sacerdotal ornaments. We find vermilion altar cloths, curtains of emerald silk, a cope of velvet, crimson and violet with orpheys [embroidery] of cloth of gold, another of rose damask, satin dalmatics [gowns] for the deacons, baldachins [canopies] figured with hawks and falcons of Cyprus gold. We find plate, hammered chalices and ciboria crusted with uncut jewels. There are reliquaries, among them a silver head of Saint Honoré. A mass of sparkling jewelleries which an artist, installed in the château, cuts to order.

'And anyone who came along was welcome. From all corners of France caravans journeyed toward this château where the artist, the poet, the scholar, found princely hospitality, cordial goodfellowship, gifts of welcome and largesse at departure.'

The religious festivals and other entertainments Gilles staged were famous for their extravagance. So lavish were they in fact that within a couple of years his vast fortune began feeling the strain and the marshal began selling off some of his estates to the Duke of Brittany, his cousin, and others to fund his sumptuous lifestyle.

In the wake of all this magnificence however, dark rumours began to spread about the children who went missing wherever the marshal went, in particular from the region around Machecoul, his favourite residence a day's ride to the south-west of Nantes on the Loire. This was a gloomy, fortress-like chateau with a deep moat and tall towers. In the colourful description of Baring-Gould:

'This fortress was always in a condition to resist a siege: the drawbridge was raised, the portcullis down, the gates closed, the men under arms, the culverins on the bastion always loaded. No one, except the servants, had penetrated into this mysterious asylum and had come forth alive. In the surrounding country strange tales of horror and devilry circulated in whispers, and yet it was observed that the chapel of the castle was gorgeously decked with tapestries of silk and cloth of gold, that the sacred vessels were encrusted with gems, and that the vestments of the priests were of the most sumptuous character. The excessive devotion of the marshal was also noticed; he was said to hear mass thrice daily, and to be passionately fond of ecclesiastical music. He was said to have asked permission of the pope, that a crucifer should precede him in processions. But when dusk settled down over the forest, and one by one the windows of the castle became illumined, peasants would point to one casement high up in an isolated tower, from which a clear light streamed through the gloom of night; they spoke of a fierce red glare which irradiated the chamber at times, and of sharp cries ringing out of it, through the hushed woods, to be answered only by the howl of the wolf as it rose from its lair to begin its nocturnal rambles.'

The ways by which the children disappeared were various but one was that on certain days the drawbridge at Machecoul was lowered and alms distributed to the poor by the marshal's servants. Often, it was said, children among the mendicants would be sent to the kitchens with the promise of some special treat, but were never seen again. Or some child would be sent to the chateau with a message by one of Gilles's cronies, and likewise disappear. Many children were recruited into the Sire de Retz's service with the promise of being trained as a page or chorister or even a soldier, only to disappear; and when their families enquired after them they would be airily assured that the individual had been sent to one of the marshal's other residences for training.

J.K. Huysmans in *La Bas* describes how news of these dark doings spread: 'At first the frantic people tell themselves that evil fairies and malicious genii are dispersing the generation, but little by little terrible suspicions are aroused. As soon as the Marshal quits a place, as he goes from the château de Tiffauges to the château de Champtocé, and from there to the castle of La Suze or to Nantes, he leaves behind him a wake of tears. He traverses a countryside and in the morning children are missing. Trembling, the peasant realizes also that wherever Prelati, Roger de Bricqueville, Gilles de Sillé, any of the Marshal's intimates, have shown themselves, little boys have disappeared. Finally, the peasant learns to look with horror upon an old woman, Perrine Martin, who wanders around, clad in grey, her face covered – as is that of Gilles de Sillé with a black stamin [scarf]. She accosts children, and her speech is so seductive, her face, when she raises her veil, so benign, that all follow her to the edge of a wood, where men carry them off, gagged, in sacks. And the frightened people call this purveyor of flesh, this ogress, "La Mefrraye," from the name of a bird of prey.'

Finally in 1440 the people's complaints were carried to John V, Duke of Brittany. He was inclined to dismiss them, reluctant to believe such charges against his illustrious kinsman and champion of France, but pressure came from other quarters, including the Bishop of Nantes and the highly-revered grand-seneschal of Brittany, Pierre de l'Hôpital. Finally the Duke gave way and despatched a sergeant-at-arms, Jean Labbé, and twenty troops to arrest the Sire de Retz. By a curious

chance he had been told by an astrologer years before that he would eventually pass into the hands of an abbé, which he had taken to mean that he would end his days as a monk; but when he heard the name of the sergeant who had come to arrest him, Gilles de Laval is said to have turned pale and then surrendered himself meekly, commenting that it was impossible to resist fate.

Several of the marshal's chief accomplices (including Gilles de Sillé and Roger de Briqueville) escaped, but two of his most trusted servants, Pontou and his treasurer Henriet, submitted to arrest with him, which was to prove his undoing. They were taken to Nantes where the investigation began on 18 September. To begin with the tribunal heard witness accounts from the families of children who, one way or another, had fallen into Bluebeard's hands by means of his servants and friends and never been seen again. These gave substance and detail to the rumours that had been circulating in the countryside, but without any solid evidence for what had become of the lost children, though one witness said he had been told by Roger de Briqueville's valet that he knew of a cask hidden in Machecoul castle full of children's bodies. He added that he had often heard tales of children being enticed to the castle and murdered, but that he had never believed it, or that the marshal himself had any hand in the murders. Another witness said she had entered the castle with the arresting sergeant Jean Labbé and in a stable had found a heap of ashes and powder that had a 'sickly and peculiar smell'. In a trough she had also found a child's shirt covered in blood.

When dozens of such testimonies had been gathered under oath, the evidence was presented to the Duke of Brittany. While he hesitated about whether to take the case to a full trial, a letter came from his jailed cousin in which Gilles de Retz repented his crimes and offered to give all his worldly goods to charity if only he were allowed to retire to a monastery for the rest of his life.

This letter apparently galvanised the Bishop of Nantes and Pierre de l'Hôpital, who had been denied a full search for evidence at Machecoul and could see their target slipping away, just as Elisabeth Bathory was to do in Hungary two centuries later. All possible pressure was brought to bear on the Duke till finally he authorised a full civil trial to begin on 11 October, presided over by Pierre de l'Hôpital.

The defendant appeared before the court in magnificent array. Baring-Gould again: 'He was adorned with all his military insignia, as though to impose on his judges; he had around his neck massive chains of gold, and several collars of knightly orders. His costume, with the exception of his purpoint [quilted doublet], was white, in token of his repentance. His purpoint was of pearl-grey silk, studded with gold stars, and girded around his waist by a scarlet belt, from which dangled a poignard in scarlet velvet sheath. His collar, cuffs, and the edging of his purpoint were of white ermine, his little round cap or chapel was white, surrounded with a belt of ermine – a fur which only the great feudal lords of Brittany had a right to wear. All the rest of his dress, to the shoes which were long and pointed, was white.'

Gilles de Laval seemed calm and confident and he greeted his judges with a request to speed along the trial as much as possible: 'for I am peculiarly anxious to consecrate myself to the service of God, who has pardoned my great sins. I shall not fail, I assure you, to endow several of the churches in Nantes, and I shall distribute the greater portion of my goods among the poor, to secure the salvation of my soul.'

Pierre de l'Hôpital congratulated him on his concern for his soul but reminded him that their immediate concern was for the fate of his body. To which the marshal replied tranquilly: 'I have confessed to the father superior of the Carmelites, and through his absolution I have been able to communicate: I am, therefore, guiltless and purified.'

However, the court was unmoved and pressed on. Under the threat of torture the marshal replied to various other charges laid against him at the same time, relating to disputes with other nobles, but completely denied all knowledge of the missing children. The court therefore called his two servants as witnesses. Faced with torture and eternal damnation the treasurer Henriet's nerve broke and he said that he would tell all he know. The other, Pontou, tried to stifle him and said that any testimony he gave would be the ravings of a madman; but he was silenced.

Then: 'I will speak out,' said Henriet, according to the court record, 'and yet I dare not speak of the horrors which I know have taken place, before that image of my Lord Christ,' and he pointed to a large crucifix above the judge's seat.

This was duly covered and he began the tale of his initiation into Bluebeard's terrible secret life. On leaving the university at Angers, Henriet had taken the position of Reader in the Maréchal de Retz's household. The marshal took a liking to him, made him a chamberlain and took him into his confidence, though to begin with Henriet learned nothing of the dark side of his master's life. After his master's brother the Sire de la Suze took over the castle of Chantoncé as part of a financial deal, one of his servants told Henriet that in the cellars of a tower they had found the horribly mutilated bodies of dead children, some of which were headless.

Henriet had not believed him but a while later when Gilles de Retz had retaken Chantoncé and was about to cede it to the Duke of Brittany, he summoned Henriet and two other faithful servants, Pontou and Petit Robin. First he made Henriet swear a solemn oath that he would never reveal what he was about to learn. Then he told the three of a task they must do before the castle could be handed over. They were to empty a certain well in one of the towers of children's corpses which were to be put into boxes and transported to Machecoul for disposal. It took half the night to carry out this grisly task with ropes and hooks, and the remains filled three large boxes which were shipped away down the Loire. Henriet had counted thirty-six heads but said there were more bodies than heads. Afterwards he was plagued by nightmares of these heads 'rolling as in a game of skittles and clashing with a mournful wail.'

Baring-Gould: 'Henriet soon began to collect children for his master, and was present whilst he massacred them. They were murdered invariably in one room at Machecoul. The marshal used to bathe in their blood; he was fond of making Gilles de Sillé, Pontou, or Henriet torture them, and he experienced intense pleasure in seeing them in their agonies. But his great passion was to welter in their blood. His servants would stab a child in the jugular vein, and let the blood squirt over him. The room was often steeped in blood. When the horrible deed was done, and the child was dead, the marshal would be filled with grief for what he had done, and would toss weeping and praying on a bed, or recite fervent prayers and litanies on his knees, whilst his servants washed the floor, and burned in the huge fireplace the bodies of the murdered children. With the bodies were burned the clothes and everything that had belonged to the little victims.'

Henriet said he had seen about forty children tortured and killed this way and was able to identify several that matched the descriptions of missing children given in earlier testimony, including the two sons of Guillaume and Isabeau Hamelin who had gone to Machecoul to buy some bread and never returned. Henriet said that while one of these boys was being tortured, the other was on his knees sobbing and praying to God for deliverance until his own turn came.

At this point the marshal's defence lawyer protested that the accusations were unbelievable fabrications because such monstrous behaviour was unknown except perhaps with some old Roman Caesars. To which Henriet replied:

'Messire, it was the acts of these Caesars that my Lord of Retz desired to imitate. I used to read to him the chronicles of Suetonius, and Tacitus, in which their cruelties are recorded. He used to delight in hearing of them, and he said that it gave him greater pleasure to hack off a child's head than to assist at a banquet. Sometimes he would seat himself on the breast of a little one, and with a knife sever the head from the body at a single blow; sometimes he cut the throat half through very gently, that the child might languish, and he would wash his hands and his beard in its blood. Sometimes he had all the limbs chopped off at once from the trunk; at other times he ordered us to hang the infants till they were nearly dead, and then take them down and cut their throats. I remember having brought to him three little girls who were asking charity at the castle gates. He bade me cut their throats whilst he looked on. André Bricket found another little girl crying on the steps of the house at Vannes because she had lost her mother. He brought the little thing – it was but a babe – in his arms to my lord, and it was killed before him. Pontou and I had to make away with the body. We threw it down a privy in one of the towers, but the corpse caught on a nail in the outer wall, so that it would be visible to all who passed. Pontou was let down by a rope, and he disengaged it with great difficulty.'

Last minute attempts by de Retz's defence to discredit this and similar testimony was undermined when Pontou (though admittedly under threat of torture) finally confessed that all his friend had said was true and then added other facts in the same vein known only to him.

All this evidence had been given in de Laval's absence. When he was summoned to hear the charges against him he arrived this time in a Carmelite habit and knelt to pray with every appearance of piety. Then first he asked permission to appeal for clemency to the King of France. When this was refused, he asked to appeal to the Duke of Brittany to be allowed to retire to a Carmelite convent to repent his sins at leisure. This too was brushed aside and the accusations of Henriet and Pontou were read out.

The Maréchal de Retz seemed stunned by what he heard and when invited by his counsel to deny the charges completely, he instead said: 'Alas, no, Henriet and Pontou have spoken the truth. God has loosened their tongues.'

After gathering his thoughts a moment he continued: 'Messires! It is quite true that I have robbed mothers of their little ones; and that I have killed their children, or caused them to be killed, either by cutting their throats with daggers or knives, or by chopping off their heads with cleavers; or else I have had their skulls broken by hammers or sticks; sometimes I had their limbs hewn off one after another; at other times I have ripped them open, that I might examine their entrails and hearts; I have occasionally strangled them or put them to a slow death; and when the children were dead I had their bodies burned and reduced to ashes.'

When Pierre de l'Hôpital asked if he had been possessed by the devil the marshal replied: 'It came to me from myself – no doubt at the instigation of the devil: but still these acts of cruelty afforded me incomparable delight. The desire to commit these atrocities came upon me eight years ago. I left court to go to Chantoncé, that I might claim the property of my grandfather, deceased. In the library of the castle I found a Latin book – Suetonius, I believe – full of accounts of the cruelties of the Roman Emperors. I read the charming history of Tiberius, Caracalla, and other Cæsars, and the pleasure they took in watching the agonies of tortured children. Thereupon I resolved to imitate and surpass these same Cæsars, and that very night I began to do so. For some while I confided my secret to no one, but afterwards I communicated it to my cousin, Gilles de Sillé, then to Master Roger de Briqueville, next in succession to Henriet, Pontou, Rossignol, and Robin.'

He then confirmed all the accounts given by his two servants and confessed to about one hundred and twenty murders in a single year. It was rumoured that apart from the writings of the more decadent Caesars the idea of drawing children's blood for alchemical purposes was first suggested to de Retz by the defrocked priest and

197

alchemist Francesco Prelati Montecatini, one of many charlatans entertained by the Marshal in the hopes of boosting his ever-strained fortune. In the delight of his new hobby though, he soon lost sight of its original purpose. Other alchemists had suggested blood as the key to the Philosopher's Stone, or even that it is the Stone itself; and Paracelsus in his alchemistic Fountain of Youth has blood give youth back to the old, though he was probably speaking symbolically.

No mention is made in Baring-Gould's account of de Retz drinking his victims' blood but there were many details of his atrocities that he glossed over, and many in turn had been glossed over by his sources, who had been equally sickened by the surviving court records. Others who have had access to the original records have mentioned him drinking blood, though even if so the marshal was not strictly speaking a vampire any more than Elisabeth Bathory. His delight seemed more in bathing in the blood and guts of his dying victims and rapturously inhaling their last breaths as he slowly cut their throats. Often after this he and his cronies would line the severed heads up for a macabre and bizarre beauty contest and the winner's head would be placed in honour on the mantelpiece.

Another of de Retz's delights was to have his accomplices torture a child for a while until it was sure it was about to die. Then he would enter, appear shocked and release the child. Then he would ask for a kiss in payment and as the tearfully relieved child eagerly gave it, he would cut its throat. Another of the Marshal's delights was to combine his love of church music with his love of causing pain, by having his choirboys sing in counterpart to the ones he was torturing.

From the civil court he was taken to the ecclesiastical court of the Bishop of Nantes which, in the light of his confession, took just a few hours to condemn him to death, refusing his repeated pleas to be allowed to retire to the Carmelite monastery at Nantes in return for surrendering all his wealth to the Church. The civil court then condemned the marshal and his two servants to be hanged the next day, 26 October 1440 and their bodies burned. In the case of the servants they were burned to ashes which were scattered on the wind; but the Maréchal de Retz was removed from the fire before it had taken hold and carried ceremonially to the Carmelite monastery where he had hoped to find asylum, but had to settle instead for a grand funeral in honour of his more glorious accomplishments as a champion of France.

* * *

Satisfying though the trial and its outcome were, several oddities about it and the case in general stand out to the modern eye. Firstly, that Bluebeard got away with his ghastly hobby as long as he did and found willing and apparently sane accomplices to share it with; and then when finally brought to trial his massacre of innocent peasant children was not considered enough in itself but was bundled with other relatively minor crimes against his peers, almost as if they were equivalent or even more important.

Then there is the casual threat of torture when the defendant and witnesses show reluctance to speak up. As shown by the lurid confessions arising from torture during the witch trials of the seventeenth century, people will confess to anything if tortured enough; and if their death is certain anyway, they might well confess to anything to avoid additional suffering. In Bluebeard's case there seems little doubt, even from this distance in time, that he was guilty of most or all of the crimes he was accused of; but a case could be made, as his defence tried, that Henriet was a fantasist and that Pontou and even de Retz himself went along with his story simply to avoid the rack, seeing how the court seemed set against them. This would be strengthened by the Duke of Brittany's apparent reluctance to order a thorough investigation for proof of the confessions, or even to track down de Laval's other accomplices who had escaped. Probably this was for fear of stirring up even more scandal, as with Elisabeth Bathory, but still, it leaves an uncomfortable lack of the kind of solid proof that would be required in court today while at the same time opening a window onto uncomfortable aspects of the past.

Gilles de Retz, Elisabeth Bathory and Vlad the Impaler were not technically vampires in the sense of having risen from the grave in search of fresh human blood to sustain their unnatural existence; but they were vampires in the very real sense that their souls fed on the agonies they inflicted on others, more so than the 'psychic vampires' that Conan Doyle, Montague Summers and others were fond of discussing – those people we meet in everyday life who quietly feed off the good spirits of those around them leaving them drained, depressed and unsure of themselves. Elisabeth Bathory is often said to have drunk the blood of her victims, but bathing in it was her chief recreation and the suffering she caused her victims. She and the other two were arch-sadists, that was their form of vampirism, and the world has seen many like them before and since, though few have managed satisfy their dark lusts to such a spectacular degree.

Chapter V

The Un-Living Legend

WE THREW OURSELVES against the door; with a crash it burst open, and we almost fell headlong into the room. The Professor did actually fall, and I saw across him as he gathered himself up from his hands and knees. What I saw appalled me. I felt the hair rise like bristles on the back of my neck, and my heart seemed to stand still.

The moonlight was so bright that through the thick yellow blind the room was light enough to see. On the bed beside the window lay Jonathan Harker, his face flushed and breathing heavily as though in a stupor. Kneeling on the near edge of the bed facing outwards was the white-clad figure of his wife. By her side stood a tall, thin man clad in black. His face was turned from us, but the instant we saw it we all recognized the Count - in every way, even to the scar on his forehead. With his left hand he held both Mrs Harker's hands, keeping them *away with her arms at full tension; his right hand gripped her by the back of the neck, forcing her face down on his bosom. Her white nightdress was smeared with blood, and a thin stream trickled down the man's bare breast, which was shown by his torn-open dress. The attitude of the two had a terrible resemblance to a child forcing a kitte's nose into a saucer of milk to compel it to drink. As we burst into the room, the Count turned his face and the hellish look I had heard described seemed to leap into it. His eyes flamed red with devilish passion; the great nostrils of the white aquiline nose opened wide and quivered at the edges; and the white sharp teeth, behind the full lips of the blood-dripping mouth, champed together like those of a wild beast. With a wrench, which threw his victim back upon the bed as though hurled from a height, he turned and sprang at us.*

Dr Seward's Diary in
Bram Stoker's *Dracula*

The Un-Living Legend

FOR MOST PEOPLE VAMPIRES ARE A FICTION that exists at a safe remove in books and films or, at worst, in nightmares that can be easily shaken off in the bright light of day. This is a luxury that most of our ancestors would envy, living in constant terror of the forces of darkness as they did. But the twentieth century threw up some surprising examples of how easily the fears embodied in the various aspects of the vampire can still make themselves be taken very seriously.

One of the more bizarre manias of the 1990s was the goatsucker scare that hit Latin America. It eventually subsided to the level of occasional spasmodic recurrences, but has never fully been explained away. On the 5 May 1996 the London *Observer* reported of the phenomenon: 'A giant bat-like creature is terrorising the village of Calderon in the northern Mexican state of Sinaloa, where dozens of goats have been found dead with their blood sucked dry, witnesses told national television network Televisa. Calderon goat farmers have cobbled together a rough 'wanted' sketch of the bat.'

The fuss had begun early the previous year out in the Caribbean on the island of Puerto Rico when farmers in the mountainous interior began finding their goats dead and completely drained of blood through a single small puncture, usually in the chest. As the death toll of animals rose into the hundreds, real panic spread through the island. Speedily dubbed el Chupacabras (goatsucker in Spanish), the perpetrator was first described by Canovanas housewife Madelyne Tolentino as a curious blend of alien and kangaroo, four or five feet tall and with slanting red eyes, vampire-like fangs, long talons and a spiky crest running down its back.

A drawing based on her testimony was published by radio journalist and UFO investigator Jorge Martin and suddenly the Chupacabras became famous throughout Central and South America. The media leaped on the story and soon the beast was being spotted all over Puerto Rico, with many descriptions that seemed to have leaped straight from medieval demonology, even down to the sulphurous stench that was said to accompany the beast. Although the government stolidly refused to admit that anything untoward was happening, other groups organised search parties to hunt the marauder down. In vain, as it happened, and people came to believe it was hiding out in the endless labyrinths of the island's cave system between kills.

Then in early 1996 the attacks dwindled and ceased altogether for a month or so, only to be resumed with chickens as the main item on the menu. Chicken farmers now found their livestock drained of blood from small puncture wounds, then many other kinds of small animal were killed including rabbits and geese, gradually working up to sheep, goats again and even cows. A theory spread that Chupacabras had been laying low after an injury. If so he soon got his strength back and became wilder than ever. Reports now came in of it smashing fences and cages with unnatural strength. Theories about

the beast's origin ranged from satanic ritual to the idea of it having escaped from a UFO, of which there had lately been a spate of claimed sightings in Puerto Rico. Many assumed it was an escaped alien pet or some genetic experiment gone wrong.

A tailing off of attacks in Puerto Rico coincided with a rash of them in neighbouring Spanish-speaking mainland regions like Florida, Texas and particularly Mexico. It seemed as if the Chupacabras, or what now seemed several of the creatures, had somehow taken to the sea and dispersed. In May 1996 Mexican television news announced a spate of animal, and particularly goat, mutilations in rural areas which sparked a major scare, with villagers barricading themselves and their animals indoors at night.

Although the Mexican government denied there was any real cause for alarm, reports began to come in of humans being attacked. One of the first was Teodora Reyes, a villager from the state of Sinaloa who displayed on television the wounds she had sustained in a brush with the creature. Then, in a metamorphosis that Dracula would have applauded, there came a flood of sightings in which Chupacabras seemed to have taken on the form of a giant bat with a reported wingspan of up to five feet. This is when the London *Observer* picked up the tale. Farmer Angel Pulido from Jalisco state held up to the public gaze on television twin puncture marks on his arm received, he said from 'a giant bat which looked like a witch.'

Suddenly all over Mexico people reported waking in a depleted condition with puncture wounds somewhere on their person and the furore began to spread up the West Coast through the United States. It is perhaps no coincidence that alongside its goatsucker scare, Mexico was also flooded with reports of UFO sightings, including mass sightings over Mexico City itself.

So just on the threshold of the third millennium a kind of vampire proved itself still quite capable of becoming a perceived reality and although the fuss has died away, reports still occasionally come in from as far north as Maine and as far south as Chile and Argentina.

* * *

African legend still has its share of blood-sucking demons like the Asasabonsam that the Ashanti people of Ghana tell of. This is vaguely human in appearance but equipped with sharp iron fangs and clawed feet at the end of long thin legs. Its custom is to sit on branches over paths, dangling its legs like innocent vines till some luckless traveller passes below like a walking dinner. Incidentally, the only obvious indigenous Australian vampire on record is the Yaramayahoo, which is very similar. It is said to be a small red creature with tentacled hands and an enormous mouth. It lives in fig trees and drops down on passers-by, wraps itself around them and drinks their blood. The victims usually survive but find themselves a little smaller than before. If attacked often enough they turn into Yaramayahoos themselves.

However, in Africa, more lethal in practice than such demons have been the secret societies based on blood rituals which have periodically led to extremely violent outbreaks. In West Africa this is best demonstrated by the secret cults of leopard men that prospered in the first half of the twentieth century (though probably based on much older traditions) across Liberia, Sierra Leone, Ivory Coast and Nigeria. Members wore leopard masks and skins and used steel claws or knives when out on the hunt to mimic the slashing of a leopard's claws when attacking their victims, who were usually women and children. The bodies were then carried off to secret dens or shrines in the jungle where their blood would be drunk and the body portioned out for a cannibalistic feast. A magical potion called borfima was brewed from the victim's intestines, along with other exotic ingredients, which the leopard men believed gave them superhuman powers and allowed them to shapeshift into true leopards.

Applicants to join one of these groups had to go out at night and kill someone, then return with a bottle of their blood and drink it in front of the others. Group killings were not entirely random or carried out purely for sadistic pleasure. Usually there was some reason, such as that one member of the group fell ill or his crops failed. This would be blamed on witchcraft of some kind, to banish which a human sacrifice was needed. Such excuses were easily invented though, as shown by the periodic killing sprees of some groups.

Once the need for human sacrifice was agreed, a victim was chosen and a date set, then a member of the group was chosen as the executioner or Bati Yeli. He would don a mask and leopard skin and work himself into a bloodthirsty trance before going out hunting. Ideally the leopard men liked to catch their victims alive to be finished off in their jungle hideouts; they were killed on the spot only if they put up too much of a fight.

There are earlier records but the first serious outbreaks of leopard men activity in Nigeria and Sierra Leone came around the end of the First World War. The colonial authorities cracked down hard and after many hangings the movement was driven underground again, but continued to erupt occasionally over the next two or three decades. Typical of the colonial perception of the problem is this extract from an article headed THE HUMAN LEOPARDS OF SIERRA LEONE by A Gray C.B. K.C. in the *Journal of the Society of Comparative Legislation* (1916, Vol. 16, No. 2 pp. 195-198) concerning the many recent laws against secret societies in general and leopard men in particular: 'They take their names from the animals whose skins are used to disguise the murderers, the most notorious being the Human Leopard Society, of which the Alligator and Baboon societies are either branches or imitators. All of them are offshoots of the ancient Poro confederacy which has for centuries wielded secret and mysterious authority over the Sierra Leone tribes; every member of the Human Leopard Society is also a member of the Poro. This high tribunal holds its court in a secret enclosure in the bush, where no profane foot may enter . . . The history of the Human Leopard Society is interesting from the point of view of anthropology. The murders have their origin in cannibalism and fetish.'

In Liberia there was a burst of leopard men activity in the 1930s vividly described by Dr Werner Junge in *African Jungle Doctor* (1952) in which he describes his experiences in the country from 1930. In this decade during which he ran hospitals at Bolahun in the heart of the jungle and at Cape Mount on the coast, he had many encounters with the work of both the Crocodile and Leopard Societies, six cases of which he described in detail. For example, on page 176: 'There, on a mat in a house, I found the horribly mutilated body of a fifteen-year-old girl. The neck was torn to ribbons by the teeth and claws of the animal, the intestines were torn out, the pelvis shattered, and one thigh was missing. A part of the thigh, gnawed to the bone, and a piece of the shin-bone lay near the body. It seemed at first glance that only a beast of prey could have treated the girl's body in this way, but closer investigation brought certain particularities to light which did not fit in with the picture. I observed, for example, that the skin at the edge of the undamaged part of the chest was torn by strangely regular gashes about an inch long. Also the liver had been removed from the body with a clean cut no beast could make. I was struck, too, by a piece of intestine the ends of which appeared to have been smoothly cut off, and, lastly, there was the fracture of the thigh – a classic example of fracture by bending.'

Junge appealed to various government departments in vain for action, and the matter was only cleared up when a Gola paramount chief responded to the popular appeals for help. One of the ringleaders turned out to be an old missionary from

Bassaland, the head of a mission school. According to Junge: 'It was he who had brought this ancient and blood-thirsty religious order of the leopards from his native Bassaland, south of Monrovia, and revived it in Cape Mount, where this kind of human sacrifice had for long been extinct.' Despite being found guilty by a court, the only punishment the old missionary received was to be banished back to his homeland where he died two years later.

In Nigeria there was upsurge of activity just after the Second World War. In 1946 forty-eight cases of attempted and actual murder were attributed to leopard men and in the first seven months of the following year there were forty-three. What is more, the attacks were noticeably aimed at scaring white people. One of the colonial heroes of the hour was Terry Wilson, a newly appointed District Officer in the eastern Old Calabar Province among the Annang and Ibibio tribes. After a spate of characteristic murders in his area, mostly of young women, he and his police raided the house of a local chieftain named Nagogo acting on a tip-off. There indeed they found a leopard-skin cloak and a mask and steel claw; not only that but digging nearby uncovered the bodies of thirteen victims. This seemed a victory but leopard men activity only increased. Many more ritual murders happened in the following weeks, including a wife and daughter of the now imprisoned chief Nagogo. Thinking this atrocity might move his prisoner to betray the cult, Wilson showed Nagogo their mutilated corpses, but his heart just gave way and he died of grief.

Despite 200 police reinforcements being called in, the conflict only escalated until the whole country was in terror of the marauding leopard men, who seemed immune to capture or harm. Wilson and his officers narrowly escaped personal assassinations, murders were committed in broad daylight rather than the usual dusk, and one female victim was even sacrificed within the police compound.

Finally the District Officer set an ambush on a stretch of path where there had been several murders, using as bait a village woman and one of his officers posing as her son. While they ambled temptingly along the track, Wilson and twelve officers hid in the bush nearby. Right on cue there came the sudden howl of a leopard and a tall man in a leopard-skin and mask leaped out on the pair, swinging a club. Before help could arrive, the young officer lay dead with a smashed skull and the apparition had fled. They were about to carry the body home when Wilson had an inspiration. Telling his men to leave it where it was, he sent them all off to question people in the neighbourhood while he hid himself in some bushes overlooking the body. Finally around midnight his patience was rewarded when a large creature crawled from the jungle and pounced on the corpse, slashing at it like a leopard. When Wilson challenged the leopard man, it snarled like a true big cat, turned and attacked, receiving a bullet in the chest for his pains.

This turned the tide of events. With proof that leopard men were not superhuman and immune to normal weapons, witnesses and informants came forward, leading to the arrest of seventy-three suspects, of whom thirty-nine were found guilty of murder and hanged at Abak prison. The cult's bloody and well hidden temple in the jungle was also found, with a flat, bloodstained slab of rock for an altar. A large effigy of a human leopard towered over it and human bones were scattered around.

In this case there proved no doubt about the existence of the cult and breaking it ended a spate of murders, but the outcome was not always so happy. Some of the apparent epidemics of leopard men activity were shown to be the work of real man-eating leopards and many simple murders were disguised to look like the work of the cult. It's now impossible to say for certain what the balance was, beyond that there was and remains a sporadic leopard men cult among the Bantu, particularly in West Africa but all across the continent, but that its significance has often been exaggerated both hysterically and as political propaganda. This was especially the case with the Mau Mau rebellion in Kenya during the 1950s. Some rebels are known to have embraced the practices of the leopard men and other secret societies, but their atrocities were also wildly exaggerated to demonise all the rebels.

More recently there has been evidence, from Italy of all places, of another resurgence this type of cult applied to criminal ends. On 18 October 2007 the story spread around the world of a Nigerian mafia-type gang that was broken up in Italy. Five members were arrested in Brescia, Lombardy and the southern town of Aversa near Naples. Another was already in prison in Italy. These six were said by Carmine Grassi, the Brescia police officer in charge of the investigation, to be the ringleaders of the 'eiye' mob group involved in prostitution, extortion and credit card scams in northern Italy. Like the mafia they used extreme violence to keep other Nigerian gangs off their territory, often amputating body parts. Initiation rites when joining the gang included drinking human blood as part of a blood pact. The accused were said to have met up at a Nigerian university.

Leopard men, crocodile men and the like are perhaps closer to werewolves than vampires as we usually think of them, but as we have seen elsewhere, vampires and werewolves have been considered close relations in Eastern Europe and many of their hungers and habits overlap.

* * *

For most of us of course vampires are simply a cultural fiction far removed from the gory reality of secret societies like the leopard men. They are just part of the symbolic language of our lives, though an enormously pervasive one. Open any newspaper and you are almost sure to find a mention of vampires before long. Enter 'vampires' into a search engine on the internet and you will be deluged with responses. For instance, while writing this paragraph I did just that and Google produced an estimated 19,500,000 responses in 0.06 seconds. Top of the list was an Associated Press article about an energy measure which had been passed in California. Speedily dubbed the Vampire Slayer Act, its aim was to abolish the energy drain caused by the standby function of so many electronic and charging devices, estimated by the US Department of Energy at about five per cent of the country's total energy use – or enough to power the whole of Italy.

The United States is home to some thriving vampire cults which blossomed especially in the 1990s but still seem to be going strong. The main centres seem, unsurprisingly, to be in New York and San Francisco; but all other large cities have thriving if often underground communities. Through the internet many other virtual communities also exist, not just across America and Europe but drawing members from around the world.

In 1989 Stephen Martin, editor of the journal Quadrant for the C.G. Jung Foundation of New York, gave the popularity of vampires a psychological twist in an article in the November issue of *Psychology Today*: "Vampires are living parts of our humanity that people in a technological age have ignored. They have to do with the darkness and magic that is not given its due. If we ignore the unconscious, it becomes avaricious, voracious … the vampire is another side of our culture that needs a voice."

The lines are blurred across the spectrum of vampire enthusiasts between, at the one extreme, participants who are merely dressing the part because they like the Goth look or are off to a fancy dress party, to those who regularly take part in blood-drinking rituals and claim to have an overwhelming desire or real need to consume human blood. In between is a hazy group with which it is impossible for an outsider to tell if they are blood-drinkers or not. The likely guess is that some are but prefer to keep it quiet, while others aren't but like to tease with the possibility that they are.

Among the blood drinkers there are two more or less distinct groups – the feeders and the donors, who are a much prized minority. Some are both but on the whole enthusiasts seem to prefer being either one or the other. It's a risky business of course, in these days of blood-borne diseases like AIDS and Hepatitis, but mostly the participants are careful about health checks and hygienic in their feeding. Vegetarians are said to have the sweetest blood and few of the self-proclaimed 'real' vampires claim immortality or any other supernatural powers; they just say that drinking human blood gives them an energy rush.

Of course such decorous behaviour, while probably being the norm in these circles, does not always apply. Most fetishistic blood drinkers and donors pose no threat to anyone besides themselves, but it can all go horribly wrong. To quote just one example from the London *Daily Telegraph* on 18 January 2002 (among other sources), a German couple were on trial for killing a friend with sixty-six stab wounds after first assaulting him with a hammer, and then celebrating the deed by drinking his blood. Daniel and Manuela Ruda claimed to have developed a taste for vampirism while visiting London and Scotland, where they used to frequent ruins and cemeteries at night, often sleeping on graves. Manuela claimed she had even allowed herself to be buried once to see what it felt like. While in Britain they had also developed a taste for drinking human blood which they continued after returning home, often obtaining it from willing volunteers over the internet.

Thus far thus normal in the twilight world of quasi-vampires but the pair went further than most. A couple of years before the trial they had apparently signed their souls over to Satan and on the night in question he appears to have called in the debt. Manuela Ruda, dressed in full Goth regalia and with an inverted crucifix and target standing out from the shaven side of her skull, told the regional court in Bochum that on the night they lured Frank Haagen (or Hackert) to their flat they had felt the presence of a 'strange force' and 'other beings'. After a while her husband had stood up with 'terrible glowing eyes' and had hit their friend with a hammer. Haagen had stood up and tried to say something but then Manuela, holding a knife that seemed to be glowing, had heard a voice commanding her to stab him in the heart, which she did. Haagen then 'sank down. I saw a light flickering around him. That was the sign that his soul was going down. We said a satanic prayer. We were then exhausted, and alone, wanted to die ourselves. But the visitation was too short. We could no longer kill ourselves.'

The couple then carved a pentacle on their victim's chest, drank his blood and then had sex in the oak coffin where Manuela usually slept. They then drove around armed with a chainsaw awaiting Satan's next command, later admitting disappointment that they had not immediately turned into vampires able to dispense with motor vehicles. The alarm was raised by Manuela's mother who received a worrying letter from her shortly afterwards in which she declared: 'I am not of this world, I must liberate my soul from the mortal flesh.' When the mother and police entered the flat they found not only Frank Haagen's mutilated and partly decomposed body beside Manuela's coffin in the living room, but a list of fifteen probable intended victims. They were soon arrested at a petrol station.

The Rudas freely admitted to the killing but denied responsibility, Manuela claiming: 'It was not murder. We are not murderers. It was the execution of an order. Satan ordered us to [do it]. We had to comply. It was not something bad. It simply had to be. We wanted to make sure that the victim suffered well.' Her husband compared themselves to a vehicle involved in a fatal accident. 'The car would not be charged,' he said. 'The driver is the bad guy. I have nothing to regret because I haven't done anything.' They said they had chosen 'Hacki', as they nicknamed him, for sacrifice because he was 'so funny and would be the perfect court jester for Satan'.

Several witnesses testified that the couple suffered from personality disorders and their defence argued for leniency on the grounds of diminished responsibility, but Judge Arno Kersting-Tombroke sentenced Daniel and Manuela to fifteen and thirteen years respectively in a secure psychiatric hospital, adding that because they could kill again they might never be released.

Many of Germany's leading psychologists have examined the Ruda case, which fed alarm at the growth of Satanism, especially in the depressed regions of the former East Germany. Official guestimates at the time put the number of dedicated followers at 6,000, though it probably was and is much greater, given the difficulty of measuring such an amorphous phenomenon.

* * *

Blood drinking was also a major feature in the celebrated case of the so-called 'Acid Bath Vampire' John George Haigh in the 1940s. In his *Confession* in 1949, written just before he was hanged he claimed that all his murders were preceded by a particular dream in which: 'I saw a forest of crucifixes which gradually turned into trees. At first I seemed to see dew or rain running from the branches. But when I came nearer I knew it was blood. All of a sudden the whole forest began to twist about and the trees streamed with blood. Blood ran from the trunks. Blood ran from the branches, all red and shiny. I felt weak and seemed to faint. I saw a man going round the trees gathering blood. When the cup he was holding in his hand was full he came up to me and said "drink". But I was paralysed. The dream vanished. But I still felt faint and stretched out with all my strength towards the cup . . . For three or four days I always had the same dream, and each time I woke up, my horrible desire always became stronger. You will now understand what happened to young Swan [Donald McSwann, his first victim] when he found himself alone with me that autumn evening. I knocked him out with the leg of a table, or a piece of tubing: I don't remember exactly now. Then, I slit his throat open with a penknife. I tried to drink his blood but it wasn't easy. I didn't know yet which was the best way to go about it. I held him over the kitchen sink and tried somehow to gather the red liquid. In the end, I managed to drink directly from the wound, with a sense of deep satisfaction.'

There have been suggestions that Haigh exaggerated his blood drinking in the hope of escaping the noose, by being committed instead to Broadmoor, the hospital for the criminally insane, but he did not retract any of it after he had been sentenced to death. He blamed his perverse thirst on a road crash during the War, when he had been a fire-watcher in London during the Blitz. His car had overturned after colliding with a lorry. When he regained consciousness, blood was pouring down his face into his mouth. That was when his bloody dreams had begun, though it was a few years before he acted on them. Besides the six murders for which he was convicted, in all of which there was a large financial motive, Haigh claimed to have committed three other murders purely for the sake of drinking his victims' blood.

Other famous twentieth century 'vampires' include Fritz Haarmann who stunned Depression hit Germany in the 1920s when it emerged that for years he had been killing and butchering young boys and making a comfortable living by selling off their meat and clothes. He was dubbed the 'Vampire of Hanover' because of his alleged habit of killing his victims by gouging out their throats with his teeth. Also in Depression Germany there was the Dusseldorf Vampire Peter Kürten who murdered children, women and men indiscriminately and in the most sadistic, sexually driven ways, and who famously asked the prison psychiatrist on his way to the guillotine: "Tell me, after my head has been chopped off, will I still be able to hear, at least for a moment, the sound of my own blood gushing from the stump of my neck? That would be the pleasure to end all pleasures."

In Poland in 1969 Stanislav Modzieliewski of Lodz was convicted of seven murders and six attempted murders. One witness against him was a young woman he attacked and who had survived by pretending to be dead while he drank her blood, which he declared to have been 'delicious'. Also in Poland in 1982, Juan Koltrun was nicknamed 'the Podlaski Vampire' after killing two of his seven rape victims and drinking their blood. In Italy Rantao Antonio Cirillo of Milan attacked more than forty women over a seven year period from the late 1970s. After raping them he would drink blood from their throats. Meanwhile in Russia Andrei Chikatilo, the 'Forest Strip Vampire' was convicted for over fifty savage murders of mostly women and children between 1978 and 1990. He confessed freely to often having eaten their body parts and drunk their blood.

The list could go on – John Crutchley, Marcello de Andrade, Richard Trenton Chase – but the point is made: the twentieth century was as full of ferocious and literally bloodthirsty killers as seventeenth century France was of werewolves. But these were mostly solitary killers, or ones who at most worked in pairs. While 'harmless' blood-drinking vampire groups abound in North America and Europe, it is very rare for them to develop into predatory groups feeding off the innocent public and leaving a trail of corpses in their wake. No-one should be too complacent though. It could probably happen anywhere given the right anarchic conditions and suitably charismatic leaders. The power of belief and ancient, ingrained predilections is nowhere better illustrated than in the case of the sex and blood-fuelled cult of Magdalena Solis in Mexico.

In 1963 the crafty and promiscuous Santos and Cayetano Hernandez managed to convince the villagers of remote Yerba Buena, in Taumaulipas state, that the Inca gods would shower wealth on them in return for complete loyalty to the Hernandez brothers. This included satisfying their every sexual whim. To cement their hold over the villagers they were made to clear out caves in the mountain overlooking the village to be used as temples; and they were made to take part in elaborate rituals devised by the brothers, who lived as priestly kings. However, after several months of this, when the villagers began to notice that for all their sacrifices there had been no visible improvement in their conditions, the brothers realised they had to raise the level of drama.

From Monterey in the neighbouring state of Nuevo Leon, they recruited Magdalena Solis, a blonde lesbian hooker, and her brother Eleazor who was also her pimp. Back at the village and with appropriate theatrical staging, this pair was introduced to the villagers as their mountain gods made flesh and the orgies continued on a redoubled scale. As three of the ruling quartet were homosexual most villagers must have experienced varieties of sex that would not otherwise have crossed their imaginations, though what they made of it is not on record.

Eventually, of course, the villagers grew restless again as there was still no sign of heavenly reward. This time the stakes were raised by the introduction of human sacrifice. Magdalena Solis, as High Priestess, named some of the troublemakers as

sacrifices to turn aside the wrath of the gods. Over six weeks eight victims were ritually clubbed to death in increasingly elaborate ceremonies in which the high point, in echo of the Catholic Mass, was the drinking of the victim's blood in elaborate chalices.

Again, this state of affairs could not last. Trouble began with jealousy over a peasant girl between Magdalena and Santos Hernandez. This girl, Celina Salvana, had been Santos's favoured mistress till Magdalena had taken a fancy to her and Santos had passed her over. However, young Celina had soon tired of being a lesbian and had begun meeting Santos again in secret. When she found out, Magdalena was furious and named Celina as a human sacrifice. On the night of 28 May 1963 she was bound to a sacrificial wooden cross and beaten senseless by Magdalena before being finished off by the congregation. When her body was thrown onto a funeral pyre the night was far from over. Still in a maddened frenzy, Magdalena pointed out yet another apostate in the crowd and the farmer was hacked and beaten to death also.

All this happened to have been witnessed by a terrified schoolboy who was not part of the cult. Fourteen year old Sebastian Guerrero ran almost twenty miles to the nearest police station in Villa Gran. His hysterical story was not at first taken seriously but eventually the police were convinced enough to send an officer in a jeep back to the village with the boy. That was the last they were seen alive. After several days of no news an armed patrol of police and soldiers went to Yerba Buena to see what had happened. They found the hacked corpses of the boy and policemen, Luis Martinez, whose heart had been torn out.

After a battle in which Santos Hernandez was killed, Magdalena and her brother were found in a marijuana fuelled haze in a nearby house, apparently oblivious to what had been going on. Ceyetano Hernandez turned out also to be dead from a separate dispute with a villager. The Solis siblings and twelve of their immediate followers were sentenced in June 1963 to thirty years in prison.

* * *

What we have just considered are extreme examples of where an interest in vampires and blood rituals can lead, reminding us that the theme still has a genuine potency for evil. By contrast, most of the vampire enthusiasts I came to know during the writing of this book have been the most charming people you could hope to encounter. There is, or can be, something terribly healthy about allowing oneself to be fascinated by all that vampires represent, though I still can't quite put into words what it is. That others share the feeling is demonstrated by the success of Tim Burton's 2007 film version of

Stephen Sondheim's musical *Sweeny Todd: The Demon Barber of Fleet Street* starring Helena Bonham Carter and Johnny Depp. This explores similar territory and has reached a far wider audience than might be expected of an old fashioned horror story. And no doubt there will be more films in the vein of Coppola's *Dracula* and *Interview With the Vampire* that will again tease the wider public with the dark mysteries surrounding vampirism. In literature vampire stories continue to stream off the presses on all levels from pulp fiction to Elizabeth Kostova's subtle 2005 Dracula novel *The Historian* for which the movie rights were bought by Sony.

As I said at the beginning, my main motivation for writing this book was simple curiosity about vampires and it has been a long, strange and wonderful, if often chilling, odyssey getting from there to this last paragraph. Along the way I seem to have become a bit of an authority after all, at least on those aspects of vampires that caught my interest. I hope if you have read this far (and not just skipped to the end to see what the conclusion is) that you've enjoyed the ride as much as I have. Perhaps now I can take down that rosary hanging over my desk . . . ?

APPENDIX ONE

POLIDORI'S *THE VAMPYRE*

Polidori's *The Vampyre* opens with the appearance in London high society of a mysterious Lord Ruthven. This gloomy soul succeeds in being invited to all the most fashionable gatherings despite appearing to take no pleasure at all in them: 'the light laughter of the fair only attracted his attention that he might by a look quell it, and throw fear into those breasts where thoughtlessness reigned.'

In the course of his morose socialising, Lord Ruthven makes the acquaintance of the story's hero, young Aubrey, who is fascinated by the enigmatic stranger and flattered by an invitation to accompany him on a tour of Europe. On the way to Rome Aubrey is often puzzled by Ruthven's behaviour. He seems indifferent to any suffering they encounter and everyone he does befriend seems to come to a sticky end soon afterwards. In Rome Aubrey receives letters telling him of the most dreadful scandals that have come to light in London since their departure. It appears that Ruthven, despite his dourness, had managed to seduce just about every female who had crossed his path, leaving a trail of ruined lives in London that might have impressed even Byron.

Armed with this knowledge, Aubrey manages to prevent a similar fate befalling a girl in Rome, then he breaks with Ruthven and heads off alone for Greece. In Athens he meets a beautiful peasant girl, Ianthe, daughter of the house where he lodges. She accompanies him on his sketching trips and entertains him with tales of her native land. Among them are stories of vampires that at first Aubrey dismisses as morbid fantasy; but when she describes them he is struck by their remarkable likeness to his erstwhile friend, Lord Ruthven. Gradually Aubrey finds himself falling in love with the fey and innocent Ianthe, but against his better judgement, as he can see no future in a match between himself, an English gentleman, and an unlettered Greek peasant.

To distract himself from her charms he goes on longer and longer excursions. But when he mentions one particular place he intends to visit, his hosts beg him not to. Or at least, if he must, to be sure to leave before nightfall because it was said to be a haunt of vampires. To humour them, Aubrey agrees but in the event he forgets and then is overtaken by a furious thunderstorm. His horse bolts in terror, ending up in a dark forest and finally coming to a standstill by a lonely hovel. During a lull in the storm Aubrey hears terrified screams from within, accompanied by mocking, manic laughter. He breaks down the door and rushes to the rescue, only to be pounced on in the dark by someone with superhuman strength who throws him to the floor and is about to strangle him when there is a commotion outside.

His attacker flees and Aubrey is rescued by torch-bearing peasants who have arrived in the nick of time looking for Ianthe, who herself had followed Aubrey to see he came to no harm. Ianthe herself is found dead nearby in the hut: 'There was no colour upon her cheek, not even upon her lip; yet there was a stillness about her face that seemed almost as attaching as the life that once dwelt there:- upon her neck and breast was blood, and upon her throat were the marks of teeth having opened the vein:- to this the men pointed, crying, simultaneously struck with horror, "a Vampyre, a Vampyre!"'

Aubrey is carried in a fever back to Athens where Ianthe's parents die broken-hearted by the news of her savage death. Lord Ruthven meanwhile shows up and nurses Aubrey with such care that despite initial misgivings their friendship is renewed. They travel on together and in the wild Greek mountains are attacked by bandits. Ruthven is wounded by a bullet. It seems no great injury but he weakens rapidly and soon lies at the point of death. Now Ruthven exacts from Aubrey an oath by all he holds most sacred that for a year and a day he will say nothing about either him or his death. And when the oath is given he expires.

When Aubrey tries to bury his friend, however, he finds the body missing. With the spell of Ruthven's living presence removed, Aubrey begins to remember unsettling things about him. Among his effects is found a sheath that matches an unusual dagger found at the scene of Ianthe's murder. Then, passing through Rome on his way home, Aubrey finds that the mischief he thought he had prevented on their last visit has in fact happened. The maiden in question has gone missing and her family is distraught.

Arriving in London, Aubrey is reunited with his beloved sister who has delayed her entry into society till his return, so that he can be her chaperon. On their first outing, however, Aubrey is stunned by a familiar voice whispering in his ear: 'Remember your oath!' It is none other than his old friend and enemy Lord Ruthven. Unknown to Aubrey he had upon his deathbed in Greece bribed the robbers to lay his body high on a mountain, exposed to 'the first cold ray of the moon that rose after his death.' By this time-honoured means he had been re-animated. Aubrey now knows without doubt he is dealing with a vampire, but is honour-bound to say nothing till the year is up. To his further alarm, Ruthven begins to court his sister.

Aubrey's fears and enforced silence lead to a nervous breakdown and he becomes an invalid whose only hope of deliverance is the approaching day when he will be freed from his oath. He loses touch with everything going on around him until by chance he learns that his sister is to be married on the very eve of the day his oath expires. The bridegroom is a certain Earl of Marsden whose portrait, which she carries in a locket, is of course that of Lord Ruthven. Aubrey begs her to postpone the wedding till he can reveal what he knows, but as everyone thinks he has gone mad this is out of the question. And when he then throws a fit of frustrated fury their suspicions are only confirmed.

On the wedding day Aubrey escapes the servants guarding him and goes to disrupt the proceedings, but is spotted by Lord Ruthven who drags him away and returns him to custody. Upon which poor Aubrey has another fit, bursts a blood vessel and falls terminally ill. News of this is kept from his sister so the marriage can go ahead and the happy couple set off on honeymoon.

Feeling death approaching, Aubrey summons his sister's guardians and when the midnight bells free him from his oath he tells them all he knows about his new brother-in-law, then dies: 'The Guardians hastened to protect Miss Aubrey; but when they arrived, it was too late. Lord Ruthven had disappeared, and Aubrey's sister had glutted the thirst of a VAMPYRE!'

Appendix Two

Varney The Vampyre

The story of *Varney the Vampire* opens with a virginal victim, Flora Bannerworth, lying vulnerably in an ancient bedchamber during a violent storm. Her charms are dwelt on in lingering, if not drooling detail: 'A creature formed in all fashions of loveliness lies in a half sleep upon that ancient couch – a girl young and beautiful as a spring morning. Her long hair has escaped from its confinement and streams over the coverings of the bedstead; she has been restless in her sleep, for the clothing of the bed is in much confusion. One arm is over her head, the other hangs nearly off the side of the bed near to which she lies. A neck and bosom that would have formed a study for the rarest sculptor that ever Providence gave genius to, were half disclosed. . . . Oh, what a world of witchery was in that mouth, slightly parted, and exhibiting within the pearly teeth that glistened even in the faint light that came from that bay window. How sweetly the long silken eyelashes lay upon the cheek. Now she moves, and one shoulder is entirely visible – whiter, fairer than the spotless clothing of the bed on which she lies, is the smooth skin of that fair creature, just budding into womanhood, and in that transition state which presents to us all the charms of the girl – almost of the child, with the more matured beauty and gentleness of advancing years.'

She is half-woken by the hailstorm and in a flash of lightning is alarmed by the glimpse of a tall figure at her window trying to break in. In the next flash she sees it again and shrieks, seeing that: 'A tall figure is standing on the ledge immediately outside the long window. It is its finger-nails upon the glass that produces the sound so like the hail, now that the hail has ceased. Intense fear paralysed the limbs of the beautiful girl. That one shriek is all she can utter – with hand clasped, a face of marble, a heart beating so wildly in her bosom, that each moment it seems as if it would break its confines, eyes distended and fixed upon the window, she waits, frozen with horror. The pattering and clattering of the nails continue. No word is spoken, and now she fancies she can trace the darker form of that figure against the window, and she can see the long arms moving to and fro, feeling for some mode of entrance.'

Then by the glow of a nearby mill set ablaze by the lightning all doubt at what she has seen is dispelled: 'There can be no mistake. The figure is there, still feeling for an entrance, and clattering against the glass with its long nails, that appear as if the growth of many years had been untouched. She tries to scream again but a choking sensation comes over her, and she cannot.' Paralysed by fear, Flora can only watch as her unearthly visitor finally breaks one of the small panes of glass, unlatches the window with a skeletal hand and enters the room: 'The light falls upon the face. It is perfectly white – perfectly bloodless. The eyes look like polished tin; the lips are drawn back and the principal feature next to those dreadful eyes is the teeth – the fearful looking teeth – projecting like those of some wild animal, hideously, glaringly white and fanglike. It approaches the bed with a strange gliding movement. It clashes together the long nails that literally appear to hang from the finger ends.'

Flora finally manages to scream and edge away from her dreadful visitor but he catches her by her long hair streaming over the bedclothes: 'The glassy horrible eyes of the figure run over that angelic form with hideous satisfaction – horrible profanation. He drags her head to the bed's edge. He forces it back by the long hair still entwined in his grasp. With a plunge he seizes her neck in his fang-like teeth – a gush of blood and a hideous sucking noise follows. The girl has swooned and the vampyre is at his hideous repast!'

Attracted by her scream, others in the household come running and after an agonising delay succeed in breaking down the door and during a confused scuffle, during which the vampire is shot, Flora's rescuers catch a brief clear glimpse of her attacker: 'That face was one never to be forgotten. It was hideously flushed with colour – the colour of fresh blood; the eyes had a savage and remarkable lustre whereas, before, they had looked like polished tin – they now wore a ten times brighter aspect, and flashes of light seemed to dart from them. The mouth was open, as if, from the natural formation of the countenance, the lips receded much from the large canine looking teeth.

'A strange howling noise came from the throat of this monstrous figure, and it seemed upon the point of rushing upon Mr. Marchdale. Suddenly, then, as if some impulse had seized upon it, it uttered a wild and terrible shrieking kind of laugh; and then turning, dashed through the window, and in one instant disappeared from before the eyes of those who felt nearly annihilated by its fearful presence.'

The vampire bears a remarkable likeness (allowing for his monstrous condition) to one of Flora's ancestors whose portrait hangs on her bedroom wall. A visit to the family tomb confirms suspicions because that character's coffin is empty. Then to everyone's alarm it turns out that a new neighbour, Sir Francis Varney, who wishes to buy the Bannerworth's property is himself the spitting image of that portrait, and the maddening conviction grows that he is the vampire . . .

Varney's protagonist for much of the book is Admiral Bell who is the uncle of Flora Bannerworth's fiancé. The Admiral succeeds in thwarting the vampire for a time but never quite pins Varney down long enough to destroy him. Eventually the vampire outlives all the characters at the beginning to molest fresh generations till remorse finally gets the better of him and he throws himself into the sulphurous crater of Mount Vesuvius.

SELECT BIBLIOGRAPHY

Baring-Gould, Sabine.
THE BOOK OF WEREWOLVES Senate Books, London 1995
Online copy: www.unicorngarden.com/bov/sabine.htm

Belford, Barbara.
BRAM STOKER: A BIOGRAPHY OF THE AUTHOR OF DRACULA
Weidenfield & Nicolson, London 1996

Copper, Basil.
THE VAMPIRE IN LEGEND, FACT AND ART
Robert Hale, London 1973, 1990

Farson, Daniel.
THE MAN WHO WROTE DRACULA
A biography of Bram Stoker; Michael Joseph, London 1975

Frazer, Sir James George.
THE FEAR OF THE DEAD IN PRIMITIVE RELIGION
Macmillan and Co, London 1936

Haining and Tremayne.
THE UN-DEAD
Constable, London 1997

Hoyt, Olga.
LUST FOR BLOOD
Stein & Day 1984

Kimber.
THE ORIGINS OF DRACULA
1987

Ludlam, Harry.
A BIOGRAPHY OF DRACULA
The Life Story of Bram Stoker
The Fireside Press 1962

McNally and Florescu.
IN SEARCH OF DRACULA
A TRUE HISTORY OF DRACULA & VAMPIRE LEGENDS
New English Library, London 1973

Ronay, Gabriel.
THE DRACULA MYTH
W.H.Allen & Co., London 1972

Russell, RV.
THE TRIBES AND CASTES OF THE CENTRAL
PROVINCES OF INDIA 1916

Summers, Montague.
THE VAMPIRE: HIS KITH AND KIN
Kegan Paul, Trench, Trubner & Co. London 1928
Reprinted as THE VAMPIRE; Senate Books. London 1995

Summers, Montague.
THE VAMPIRE IN EUROPE
Kegan Paul, Trench, Trubner & Co. London 1929
Reprinted by Bracken Books. London 1996

Thorne, Tony.
COUNTESS DRACULA
Bloomsbury. London 1998??

Volta, Ornella.
THE VAMPIRE;
Tandem Books 1965

Wright, Dudley.
VAMPIRES AND VAMPIRISM
William Rider & Son. London 1914, 1924 (revised)
Reprinted as THE BOOK OF VAMPIRES
Causeway Books. New York 1973